# BIRTHRIGHT

## BOOK I of the TEMUJIN SAGA

ADAM J. WHITLATCH

LATCHKEY PRESS

FIRST EDITION

*Birthright – Book I of the Temujin Saga*

Published by Latchkey Press

This book is a work of fiction. Names, characters, places, and incidents either are the product of the author's imagination or are used fictitiously. Any resemblance to actual persons, living or dead, events, or locales is entirely coincidental.

# ALSO BY ADAM J. WHITLATCH

**The Weller Series**

*The Weller*

*The Weller - Night of the Cicada* *

*The Weller - Fear of the Dark*

**The Temujin Saga**

*Birthright*

*Five Stories Up* *

*War Machines*

*War of the Worlds: Goliath*

*Vengeance For My Valentine*

*October Ballet - A Collection of Poems and Short Fiction*

* - Short Stories

*For Lachlan.*
*Brat.*

# ACKNOWLEDGMENTS

This book wouldn't have been possible without the love and support of my parents, who read an enormous number of drafts. So many times I wanted to give up, but they always insisted I try just one more time. Special thanks to my dad for inspiring what I feel is the best line of dialogue in the entire book.

My undying gratitude to Joe Pearson for uniting me with my brilliant cover artist, Puppeteer Lee.

Thanks to Dennis Green for helping me place those final pieces to the puzzle.

My deepest thanks to Jerrod Balzer, Shannon Ryan, and S.D. Hintz for whipping this manuscript into shape. Without them, *Birthright* would probably still be sitting in a drawer.

My hat's off to Jerrod and my dear friend Blurry, who both put their heart and soul into the cover. I can't possibly thank them enough.

Thanks to my friend Gabriel Hamilton for being the first to say, "You should write that down!"

And of course, thanks to my beautiful wife, Jessica, for tolerating me... and the voices in my head.

# PROLOGUE

*The Onon River, Mongolia*

::'ALL WARFARE IS BASED ON DECEPTION,':: SAID THE ALIEN CREATURE AT Li's side. ::Do you know these words, Mr. Li?::

"They're the writings of Sun Tzu," Li answered stiffly.

::Indeed,:: replied the alien without emotion. ::You are well-versed in the cultures of your past.::

Li cleared his throat and checked his watch for the third time in as many minutes. "How much longer?"

The alien consulted the machine in its hands. ::We are very close.::

Li rubbed his temples. The combined noise of the earthmoving equipment and the infernal buzzing inside his skull created by the alien's telepathic communications were giving him a terrible migraine. They'd been working since midmorning, and Li was almost at the end of his rope. Soon it would be nightfall, and, being so close to the Russian border, he wished to avoid any unwanted attention from the authorities on either side.

Of course, they were not without protection. Li glanced nervously over his shoulder at the squad of men behind him.

Mercenaries. Thugs with guns.

All but one of them held an AK-47, evenly matched with the Russians in that regard. The leader, a young man with a shaved head named Chuluun, was armed not with a rifle, but a Chinese *da dao* strapped to his hip. Li looked down at it and thought how strange it was to see a grown man carrying a sword in this day and age. When the Captain's dark eyes met his gaze, Li turned away.

Li pulled a handkerchief from his breast pocket and swiped it across his brow. It was unseasonably hot for this region, yet another reason to get things over with as quickly as possible.

The creature standing next to him, however, showed no outward signs of discomfort. Apparently its home planet was much hotter than Earth, due to having two suns or something like that. Whatever the reason, Li found its presence unnerving but necessary to reach their goal.

On the opposite bank, a group of local workers stood leaning on their shovels, pointing and gawking at Li and the alien as they chattered amongst themselves. Li huffed and dabbed at his forehead with his handkerchief again. Their stares were almost as oppressive as the sun.

"What are you men looking at?" he bellowed over the engines.

The workers stopped talking, but their inquisitive eyes never left Li and his diminutive companion. Chuluun stepped forward, drew his sword, and thrust it at the men, cursing at them in Mongolian. The men scattered and busied themselves with meaningless tasks, chancing occasional glances over their shoulders. Chuluun sheathed his weapon and rejoined his men.

Of course, Li could hardly blame them for staring; he'd stared, too. The Seignso had approached him and his colleagues two years before, promising advanced technology in exchange for knowledge. They described themselves as "interstellar anthropologists" and wished to immerse themselves in Earth culture—specifically war. They explained that the people of their planet lived in perpetual peace, so they were fascinated by humanity's long and colorful history of warfare. The visitors had insisted they begin their research with the greatest military commander to ever walk the Earth.

2

So the search had begun.

When asked why the visitors did not make their presence known to the entire world, they answered that humanity was still "too young" to embrace their wisdom, so they preferred to keep their interaction with humans strictly on an academic level. Li could understand that. Governments served only to gum up the works; they made things more difficult and expensive than necessary.

Li stepped away from his extraterrestrial companion and toward the earthmovers. Finding the right place to dig had been easy; the alien had taken care of that pesky detail. Diverting the Onon River away from the dig site had been the hard part. Now they were slowly skimming layer after layer of sand away.

The alien appeared at his side once more, and Li offered the briefest of glances. The very sight of these creatures offended him. Their smooth gray skin, bulbous heads, and large, soulless black eyes sent chills down his spine. Li tried to focus his thoughts somewhere other than his disgust; he wasn't sure of how keenly these creatures could perceive his thoughts.

But the alien spared him the effort. It raised a spindly finger and pointed to a spot in the muddy riverbed between two earthmovers. Then that terrible sensation filled Li's head with the alien's words, ::It is there.::

Li waved to the operator of one of the dozers and pointed to the spot in the silt. The operator nodded and repositioned the machine, skimming the surface with the blade. After three passes, a grinding sound penetrated the mechanical roar, and Li's eyes fell on a patch of flat, gray stone. He called out to the operator and waved his arms. The dozer backed away, and Li signaled to the workers waiting on the bank.

Excited shouts in various dialects of Chinese and Mongolian filled the air as the men frantically heaved shovels full of wet sand and mud aside, slowly exposing a massive stone slab. They labored until a rectangular shape appeared in the rock. *A cover stone!*

Li pointed and shouted orders, spurring the workers into immediate action with shovels and crowbars. Chaotically at first, but slowly finding their rhythm, they lifted the stone a fraction of an inch at a time. Li wiped his palms on his trousers as his eyes followed the rise and fall of the slab, finally getting a glimpse of the darkness beneath.

"Heave!" he bellowed.

The alien's lips curled into an almost imperceptible smirk.

The workers complained impatiently as they held the slab aloft long enough for two small men to loop two heavy chains beneath its corners. Li's impatience reached a crescendo as the men argued about the best way to wrap the chains around the earthmover's blade.

Soon the machine roared and dug deep furrows into the soil as it took up the chains' slack. As the chains pulled taut, Li feared they might snap under the strain, but finally the slab surrendered to the machine and slid away, leaving deep gouges in its wake. Cheers erupted from the workers and Li joined in their revelry.

The workers rushed the hole, clamoring for a look at the treasures that surely awaited them. Li pushed through the mob, but was swept up in the swarm of bodies. Captain Chuluun barked a command in Mongolian, and the workers immediately dispersed to allow him and the alien passage.

As Li gazed at the entrance to the tomb, he suddenly realized he wasn't breathing and sucked in a deep, rattling breath. He grinned at the alien, unable to contain his excitement.

The alien gestured to the hole at their feet. ::After you, Mr. Li.::

"Bring a ladder!" Li shouted.

---

LI'S FEET FINALLY TOUCHED SOLID STONE, BUT HE STILL CLUNG TO THE unstable wooden ladder as he surveyed the vast underground chamber. In the dim light filtering in from the surface, Li could make out the vague shapes of chests and barrels. Skeletal human remains lined the nearest wall, most of them reduced to dusty piles on the floor, but a few were still propped upright in their furs and armor, loyal even in death.

A boot struck Li's shoulder, and Captain Chuluun grunted impatiently. Li stepped clear of the ladder and pulled a flashlight from his pocket, passing the thin beam over the treasures stockpiled around him. Li counted more than thirty skulls among the dead and the remains of at least as many horses.

"My god," Li whispered. "It's—"

::Everything you ever imagined?:: the alien asked, appearing at Li's side.

"Everything and more."

The flashlight beam caught a metallic glint deep within the gloom and Li froze. He rushed toward the object, tripping over a spear on the floor and barely managing to keep his balance. "It's here!"

On the east wall, raised on a stone dais, rested a colossal silver sarcophagus. Li touched the cold surface of the casket reverently, assuring himself that what he was seeing was real. He'd found it. After all these years he'd *finally* found it—the silver coffin of Temujin.

He turned to the alien. "Is he in there?"

The alien placed a small device with red and blue lights against the coffin, and Li watched anxiously as the lights flickered, alternating until finally it beeped softly and the blue light burned steadily.

::Congratulations, Mr. Li,:: said the alien. ::The remains *are* inside the sarcophagus. Our search is over.::

Li breathed a sigh of relief. He had been plagued by rumors that the coffin had been buried empty and that the body had been taken to one of the palaces for interment. His fingers reverently traced along the intricate carvings of horses and warriors decorating the magnificent coffin.

::'With Heaven's aid, I have conquered for you a large empire. But my life was too short to achieve the conquest of the world,':: the alien intoned. ::'That task is left for you.'::

Li was genuinely impressed. The occupant of this sarcophagus had uttered those words on his deathbed over seven hundred years before. The alien had obviously done its homework.

"It's ours," Li whispered.

The alien's thin lips curled into an unsettling smile. ::I'm afraid you don't understand, Mr. Li.:: It turned and nodded to Captain Chuluun.

Chuluun stepped forward and drew the *da dao* from his belt. Li threw up his arms in a futile attempt to defend himself as the Captain drove the sword into his gut all the way to the hilt. Li gasped and reached behind his back, feeling the blade protruding from him, slick with his own blood. The alien, still smirking, stepped back into Li's view.

::You see,:: it said, ::the Seignso have our own plans for the remains of Genghis Khan.::

Li opened his mouth to speak, but the pain in his gut was unbearable. He gasped. It did not matter; the alien could read his thoughts.

::'All warfare is based on deception,':: said the alien. ::Remember?::

Chuluun twisted the blade and wrenched it from Li's stomach, sending the man sprawling to the floor.

::Goodbye, Mr. Li.:: The alien turned and walked toward the ladder. ::Kill the workers. Leave no witnesses.::

Chuluun threw back his head and bellowed a command.

The deafening *rat-tat-tat* of fully automatic weapons echoed throughout the tomb as the mercenaries on the surface opened fire, accompanied by the distant screams of the workers, but Chuluun did not need his ears to hear the alien's next command.

::Prepare the artifact for transport. There is much work to be done.::

# PART ONE
# PROJECT ALEXANDER

# ONE

*Gluut Star System*
*Seignso Colony Moon, Gluut Alpha 2 beta 1*
*AKA "The Factory"*
*Eleven Years Later*

LIEUTENANT VAIN LOOKED AROUND THE CABIN. TWENTY-FOUR OF THE Navy's finest shock troopers sat with their backs against the walls of the dropship, staring ahead with stony expressions. The injections they'd received had wiped all traces of fear from their systems.

Being an officer, Vain was not extended the same luxury. Fear, the brass claimed, kept the mind sharp. Vain couldn't disagree more. All fear was good for in combat was aiding in bowel movements.

Red light filled the cabin and Vain saw the men stiffen in their seats. His body bashed against his restraints as the ship pitched and his digestive organs flew up into his chest. They'd breached atmo. For the second time that day, Vain swallowed his lunch.

"All right, you slugs!" Vain bellowed in a shaky voice. "This is it. We drop in and we clean 'em out. Our orders are to capture and detain if at all possible. But if one of those sneaky little bastards tries to get into your brain, you put a round in theirs. Do you understand?"

9

*"Sir, yes, sir!"*

"Lock and load!"

As one, the soldiers reached above their heads and released their rifles from their charging stations. Vain felt a tingle in his spine as they cocked their weapons in unison, filling the trembling ship with a growing hum.

Finally the ship slowed, shuddered, and became still. The restraints pinning Vain and his men to the wall disengaged and sprang upward. The bay door cracked open and blinding white starlight from outside the ship washed out the crimson interior lighting. The men stood.

"Move out!"

Vain drew his sidearm and followed the troops down the ramp into the blistering hot air. The platoon double-timed it the five hundred paces to the installation nestled in the pale rock. The lead trooper kicked the door—hard—but it did not yield. No problem; Vain had expected this.

"Blow it."

One of the privates dug into his pack and produced a metal disk. He twisted a dial on the top and slapped it against the door. The disk secured itself magnetically.

"Stand clear!" the private shouted.

The troopers retreated a respectable distance from the door. Several seconds later, the ground was rocked by an explosion, and as the dust cleared, Vain could make out a gaping hole where the door had once stood.

"Move in!" Vain said. "I haven't got all day. Dinner's getting cold."

The inside of the facility was just as sweltering as the outside. Blinding white light assailed the men from every corner. The Seignso had made themselves right at home here. This room, however, was merely a receiving area with several branching corridors. Their true goal was deep underground.

When they located the central grav-lift, they found it to be offline, which suited Vain just fine. No way was he going to be caught in the middle of an enemy lift tube and have the floor dissolve under his feet. The men set up their rappelling gear and dropped down the tube one-by-one, ever watchful for booby traps. The descent was uneventful, which only set Vain further on edge. Finally the platoon reached its destination, a sealed door at the bottom of the lift tube. It was close quarters, so blasting was out of the question.

"Ladd!"

"Sir?" called a soldier from the back.

Vain stepped away from the door. "Cut it."

Ladd pushed forward and produced a handheld cutting torch. The rest of the platoon looked away as he ignited it, and the smell of ozone and molten metal filled the tube. The intense heat of the torch only exacerbated the suffocating conditions of twenty-five men in full combat gear crammed into the confined space.

Finally, Ladd extinguished the torch and stepped back, leaving a glowing orange outline around the edges of the door. Ladd looked over his shoulder and Vain nodded. Ladd kicked the door dead center and the panel fell inward, bathing the tube in more white light. The troopers poured into the chamber with weapons raised, but the room's occupants didn't seem the least bit interested in them.

Almost thirty Seignso milled about the room. Most ignored the invaders as they busied themselves at their workstations. The few that did take notice quickly lost interest. A single Seignso detached itself from the crowd and approached the soldiers. It was naked, with hands out in a non-threatening gesture, so most of the troopers relaxed. Vain wished they hadn't.

::Ah, Lieutenant Vain.:: The creature smiled, probing Vain's mind for information. ::To what do we owe the pleasure of this... visit?::

Vain shook his head, clearing away the fuzzy sensation. "You know perfectly well why I'm here. This is an illegal colony in violation of Federation statute 359 *dash* B—"

The Seignso waved its hand dismissively. ::There was no harm done, Lieutenant. We merely made use of some vacant real estate. Surely the Federation can extend the Seignso a little leeway in this matter.::

"I wouldn't bet on it." Vain pointed over the alien's shoulder. "What're those?"

He stomped toward four vertical glass tubes in the middle of the room. They were filled with a clear, bubbling liquid, and each contained a strange life form connected to a breathing apparatus. The creatures were awake and appeared to be struggling. They were the ugliest monsters Vain had ever seen.

Their flesh was doughy and pale, with coarse fur growing sporadically over their bodies, which was thickest on top of their heads. They were bipedal, with long limbs ending in a few short, useless-looking digits. Even though the breathing devices partially covered them, Vain could see that the faces were deformed; the soulless, beady eyes were placed far too low on the beings' heads.

*Hideous.*

The Seignso spokesman turned to follow Vain. ::Why, those are rejuvenation cylinders.::

"I know what they are!" Vain snapped. "I'm talking about the creatures inside!"

::Those?:: said the Seignso with a condescending smile. ::Just some simple non-sentient, simian species we're engineering for labor. Beasts of burden, nothing more. Pay them no mind.::

One of the creatures pounded on the glass of its tube, alternating between striking it with its fists and elbows.

"It looks pretty damned sentient to me."

::I can assure you, it is not,:: The voice inside Vain's head remained calm and flat.

"We'll see," said Vain. "Lark, get over here and get a scan of these things."

The platoon's medic slung his rifle and traded it for a tablet computer. He held it up to the closest tank for a head-to-toe scan and then tapped in a series of queries. The response was almost immediate.

"They're called..." Lark struggled with the pronunciation. "Hyoo-mahns. Non-Federation, sir. Indigenous to Sol Alpha 3."

"Are they intelligent?"

Three knocks issued from one of the cylinders. Vain looked up and saw the most active of the creatures making a gesture at the Seignso—a closed fist with the middle finger extended.

"Reasonably, sir," said Lark.

Vain's green skin flushed brown in anger. The little gray bastard had lied right to his face. Deporting the little sleaze back to Sorua was going to be a pleasure.

::With all due respect, Lieutenant,:: the Seignso interrupted. ::I did not lie. We simply have a different definition of sentience.::

"Shut up!" Vain snapped. "Lark, release the creatures."

Lark nodded and approached the console in front of the cylinders. As his fingers flew over the controls, one of the nearby Seignso stared at him intently. Lark paused to look up at the alien and the sneer forming on its thin lips. Suddenly Lark's hands flew up to clasp his head and he doubled over in pain. The medic groaned, then screamed in agony.

Vain trained his sidearm on the Seignso leader. "What the hell's happening to him?"

The Seignso grinned, showing short, blunt teeth. ::How should I know?::

"It's in my head!" Lark shrieked. "Get it out!"

Lark's assailant walked toward him slowly, pointing at the steady stream of blood pouring out of the trooper's nose. An overpowering buzzing sensation—the Seignso equivalent of laughter—filled the heads of everyone in the room. Outraged, Vain fired his sidearm at the Seignso leader's head. Searing, red plasma bore a smoking hole in the alien's skull. The oppressive buzzing ceased as every Seignso in the room turned to look at Vain.

Another Seignso extended its arm. Vain's pistol flew out of his grip and into the alien's waiting hand. Before it could use the stolen weapon, one of Vain's troopers put the Seignso down with a single shot from his rifle, and the rest opened fire. The air was filled with a frantic crisscross of plasma fire.

Vain hit the floor, struggling to be heard over the din. "Cease fire! I said stop firing, damn it!"

He heard breaking glass and looked up in time to see two of the cylinders shatter, spilling fluid across the floor, soaking the front of his uniform. Two of the pale-skinned humans were forcefully ejected along with the liquid; the bulkier of the two had a patch of black fur covering the lower half of its face, while the other had a smaller frame, a bald face, and long red fur trailing from the top of its head. The naked creatures slipped in the fluid and huddled together beneath the barrage over their heads.

"Cease fire!" Vain bellowed.

One by one, the troopers lowered their weapons. Vain's ears rang, and the stink of singed flesh stung his nostrils. He stood and shook the fluid from his hands.

Vain surveyed the damage around him. Only twelve of the Seignso remained standing; there wasn't enough left of the others worth scraping into a body bag. The two humans in the undamaged cylinders banged their fists against the glass while the pair on the floor gibbered to one another in a grunting alien language.

"This is a damn disaster," Vain muttered. "Lark!"

The medic stood and wiped the blood from his nose. "Here, sir."

"Are you all right?"

Lark wiped his hand on the front of his uniform and rubbed the side of his head. "I think so, sir. Thanks."

Vain nodded. "Get those other two *whatsits* out of those tanks and check them over."

"Yes'ir."

"Sergeant Plou," Vain addressed a tall soldier behind him. "Get that grav-lift working and get the prisoners topside. I want these bastards on the next tub to Moebius. Is that clear?"

"Sir!" Plou moved in close to his commander. "What about them?"

Vain followed his gaze to the humans, who were now all four on the ground, embracing and chattering excitedly. The two new ones also sported dark, matted fur over their jaws. They all ignored Lark as he examined them.

Vain turned back to Plou. "Bring them back with us. We'll let the brass on Phaedaj decide what to do with them."

Plou nodded and walked away to see to his duties.

---

ACROSS THE ROOM, LADD STARED CURIOUSLY OVER LARK'S SHOULDER AT the strange pale aliens. "Funny looking critters, aren't they?"

Lark shrugged. "Oh, they're not all that different from you and me. Same basic physical structure."

"Speak for yourself, Lark." Ladd knelt to get a closer look at the smallest human with the red fur. "Hey, they're mammals! Check out the mammary glands on this one. You ever boink a mammal, Lark?"

"No, and neither should y—" Lark held out his hand in warning. "Hey now, don't touch it!"

"Relax, Lark, what's the worst that could happen?" Ladd sneered and groped at the human's chest. "C'mere, little lady. What say you and I grab some shore leave together when we get back to Phaedaj?"

"Ladd don't!"

The human female began to struggle and shriek in its alien language. One of the males lunged and punched Ladd in the face, knocking him to the ground. Ladd fumbled for his rifle as the human prepared to spring, its eyes glowing an eerie green. The aggressive male leapt at Ladd and the soldier fired three short bursts, knocking the alien from the air.

The female shrieked and ran to her mate's side. Ladd watched as the male coughed up a mouthful of blood, shuddered, and became still. Lark scrambled to the fallen alien and scanned it. He cursed and scanned it a second time, but the result was the same.

Dead.

Lark jumped to his feet and shoved Ladd. "Great Mother's Beard, Ladd! What did you do that for?"

"That filthy animal attacked me!"

"What the hell is going on?" Lieutenant Vain bellowed as he stalked over to the two soldiers.

"Ladd killed one of the aliens, sir!"

"It was an accident," Ladd protested.

"My eye!" Lark said. "Lieutenant, I saw him molesting the female. The alien was only protecting its mate."

"Whose side are you on, man?" Ladd said. "They're animals!"

"Enough!" barked Vain. "Sergeant Plou, place Corporal Ladd under arrest."

Ladd stared daggers at Lark as Plou relieved him of his weapon and escorted him away. Vain rubbed his neck with both hands. What was supposed to be a simple sweep-and-clear had turned into a catastrophe.

"Sir?" Lark nodded toward the dead alien at their feet. "What should I do with that?"

Vain sighed and turned away. "Put it on ice, Private. Let the eggheads at Dreknor dissect it to their hearts' content."

"Yes, sir."

But as Vain walked away, he heard a loud gasp behind him, followed by Lark's alarmed cries. He turned and saw the alien creature sitting up, very much alive. Vain could see the fear in Lark's eyes, injections be damned. The other humans gathered around the revived male and patted it on the back while it cleared its throat and mouth of blood. They all seemed completely unfazed by this event.

"I thought you said that thing was dead!" Vain said.

"It *was!*" said Lark. "Its life signs stopped. I checked them twice."

The resurrected human locked its luminous green eyes on Vain's and gave him the same gesture it had given the Seignso leader: a closed fist with its middle finger extended.

"Sergeant Plou," Vain called over his shoulder. "Is that grav-lift operational yet?"

"Yes, sir!"

"Good. Change of plan, Sergeant. We're going to Dreknor."

# TWO

*Federation of Allied Systems*
*Dreknor Orbital Space Laboratory*
*One year later*

GRAVITY BOOTS THUMPED THEIR MONOTONOUS BEAT THROUGH THE corridor as the wearer made the long, familiar trek from his private quarters to his laboratory. The commuter was an Arqan—nearly eight feet tall with smooth red skin and blue hair gathered in several braids, which were then grouped into a single bundle in the back. His six-fingered hands were clasped behind his back as he pondered his current problem.

Five failures, each one even more grotesque than the last and leaving him drained as he felt the weight of the universe on his shoulders. He often considered giving up and letting things run their course, but he must succeed. Project Alexander could very well pave the way for planetary defense systems across the galaxy.

If only he had more time.

He paused to look out the nearby window and gaze upon the soothing green glow of Phaedaj's fifth moon, Dreknor. He'd last visited Phaedaj over thirty-five cycles ago with his life-mate, Lornali.

Dreknor had been a desert rock then, with cannibalistic yellow worms and barbed, leafless trees as its only dominant life forms; now, the moon teemed with life and lush vegetation.

Ah, the wonders of atmospheric conversion. With the right innovative spirit, there were no limits to what science could do. This sentiment was what kept him going.

He resumed walking and finally reached the grav-lift. The doors slid open with a pneumatic hiss as he approached.

"Sub-level three," he said as he stepped inside.

A soft chime acknowledged his request and the platform descended with a hum. After a few moments, the hum slowed as the lift came to a halt.

The scientist exited the lift tube and strode toward the security checkpoint outside his lab. Set into the wall beside the door was a red orb; its glow pulsated as he approached and a disembodied voice said, "Identification, please."

"Amaadoss," the Arqan answered. "Project Alexander. Level five security clearance."

A red beam emanated from the orb and scanned him from feet to head. After a short series of beeps, the voice rang out again, "Identity confirmed. Good morning, Dr. Amaadoss."

The door slid open with a hiss and the hallway was instantly filled with loud Folaxian pop music. The translation plug nestled in Amaadoss's ear converted the female singer's obscenely provocative lyrics into his own language, and the scientist furrowed his brow in annoyance. He stepped into the laboratory and the door closed behind him, locking him in with the terrible noise. He scanned the room briefly before locating his assistant, Jiri, sitting with his large, three-toed feet propped up on a computer console.

The Glynfarian was short, and his alabaster skin seemed to glow in the dim lighting. His four eyes, set on stubby stalks on both sides of his head, were closed as he tapped his three-fingered hands against his chest in time with the song's wild beat.

"Jiri!" Amaadoss called out.

The technician continued to tap and even began to sing along with the chorus. Amaadoss crossed the room until he was directly behind his subordinate and yelled, "Jiri!"

The lab tech barked and fell backward in his chair, landing flat on his back. Jiri looked up and saw his boss standing over him, glowering. The Glynfarian waved timidly at his superior and spoke in a dual voice, a pleasant harmony. "Morning, Doc. I didn't hear you come in."

"Obviously."

Jiri grinned sheepishly. "Sorry, Doc."

Amaadoss sighed as Jiri switched the music off. "What am I ever going to do with you?"

Jiri grinned again. "Well, a raise would be a good start."

Amaadoss snorted as he logged into his computer terminal. "Funding is stretched tight as it is, and after twelve cycles we have nothing to show for our labors. And you want more credits?"

Jiri set his chair back on its spindly legs and shrugged. "What can I say? The human genome is a tough nut to crack. It doesn't take splicing with other species very well."

Amaadoss knew this, and it was the bane of his existence. Humans were actually the product of genetic engineering programs predating the Federation, created many millennia ago in a lab on Sorua. Since then, the poor species had been spliced almost out of existence. Human evolution had been carefully planned, scheduled, and implemented, with no surprises.

Until recently.

Amaadoss patted his assistant on the back. "Not to worry, Jiri. I think we may have finally found a solution."

"I hope so," said Jiri. "I've got seven wives to feed; every last one of 'em sitting on eggs. And don't forget that we're almost out of donor cells. I don't know about you, but I'm not going back to Moebius to collect more. Then there's our deadline—"

"Yes, yes." Amaadoss cut Jiri off before his mouth could build more momentum. "I'm well aware of our deadline. This will work. It *has* to work."

Jiri nodded and shuffled over to the counter for a cup of spiced *rayaak* when suddenly Amaadoss cried out.

"Jiri! Have you been watching the subject in tube six?"

Jiri turned. "Sure, Doc. I check it every seven hours, just like you told me. You can check my chart. What's wrong?"

Amaadoss pointed a shaky finger at the green-hued gestation tube. "Look."

Jiri approached the tube and squinted. His eyesight was deteriorating rapidly, but on his salary ocular implants were simply out of the question. He blinked, trying to correct his double vision, but then he realized that wasn't the problem, and he let out a squealing gasp. The steaming cup of *rayaak* dropped to the floor and shattered, spilling the scalding mud-like beverage all over the place.

Only a few hours before, when Jiri had last checked the tube, there had been an embryo—a human embryo—in the earliest stages of development, suspended in the amniotic fluid. Everything had been normal and the life signs were reading fine. But now, the tube contained *two* embryos. The lab tech looked up at his superior with a trembling gaze.

"Great Mother's Beard!" he whispered, his dual voices dropping several octaves.

---

"THIS IS *OUTRAGEOUS!*" ADMIRAL OHRB BELLOWED.

Ohrb's green features flushed a light brown and the two six-inch antennae protruding from his forehead trembled with rage. He stood in the Dreknor station administrator's office; the Arqan geneticist, Amaadoss, a perpetual thorn in his side, stood at a respectable distance to his left.

The administrator sighed from behind his desk, his head in his hands. This wasn't the first time these two had brought their quarrels into his office.

"Last month it was inadequate facilities," Ohrb shouted. "*Now* he wants more funding. Administrator, my predecessor may have endorsed this ludicrous project, but I do not. And I *never* will. I *demand* that you put a stop to this foolishness immediately."

Amaadoss remained calm. "Admiral, I can assure you that Project Alexander's funding is a mere drop in the bucket compared to your military budg—"

"I know the numbers!" the admiral spat.

The administrator looked up. He was Phaedojian, like the admiral, but his natural eyes had been replaced by synthetic ocular implants. Tiny servos operated within the golden orbs, manipulating the artificial irises and allowing the governor to focus on his visitors.

"Admiral Ohrb," the administrator began. "In all fairness—"

Ohrb cut him off. "With all due respect, Administrator, this project is a waste of valuable Federation credits. Our military is the finest in the galaxy. Neither the Federation nor Phaedaj needs his pathetic clone army."

"Not at the moment," Amaadoss conceded. "However, Earth does. And if Project Alexander can succeed there, it can succeed anywhere —even Phaedaj."

"You would dismantle an entire inter-planetary military and replace it with a handful of *clones?*" Ohrb spat out the last word like a foul taste. "Do you realize what you're suggesting, how many jobs you would eliminate?"

"*Jobs?*" Amaadoss felt his own pulse rising. "Damn it, Ohrb, I'm talking about *lives!*"

"Gentlemen!" The administrator stood, plunging the room into an uncomfortable silence. For a moment, the only sound was the soft whirring and clicking of his ocular implants.

"Thank you." The administrator's voice was calm again. "Doctor, how much are you requesting?"

Amaadoss stared at his feet for a moment, going over the numbers in his head. "I believe the going rate for a Replodian larva is 75,000 Federation Credits."

"*Replodian larva?*" Ohrb interjected. The administrator held up a quieting hand.

"230,000 should more than cover the expenses," Amaadoss concluded.

Ohrb began to speak again, but was silenced by a warning gesture from the administrator. Another brief silence hung in the air while he rallied his remaining patience. Finally, he found his voice. "Doctor, commissioning a Replodian larva is no small matter. Am I correct in my understanding that you wish to purchase *three?*"

"You are, Administrator."

"What in Great Mother's name for?"

"Protection."

"Protection?" Ohrb cried, unable to contain his outrage any more. "Protection from *what?*"

Amaadoss glanced sideways at the admiral. "Temujin."

Ohrb blinked. "Come again?"

Amaadoss sighed. "Twelve cycles ago, a clone was created of an ancient Earth warlord. This clone was imbued with special abilities and sent to Earth with a single purpose. Conquest."

"*Sent* to Earth?" Ohrb repeated. "By whom? Who made the clone?"

The Arqan's expression was grave. "The Seignso."

The atmosphere of the entire room chilled at the very mention of this name.

Ohrb locked eyes with Amaadoss. "This all sounds rather suspect to me. I'd like to know where you get your information, Doctor. How do you know things that Naval Intelligence does not?"

"I have sources with first-hand knowledge of the Seignso's eugenics program," Amaadoss explained. "Last cycle, the Federation offered them asylum after they were rescued in a raid on an illegal Seignso colony within the Gluut system."

"I was not made aware that those refugees possessed valuable intelligence," said Ohrb, obviously angry.

"Voices do not carry well through your office walls, Admiral. Perhaps if you stepped out once in a while—"

"*You son-of-a—*"

"Admiral!" the administrator's voice rang out.

Amaadoss turned to address the administrator. "Sir, we are running out of time. As you can see, the enemy already has a head start on us. They've managed to infuse their own telepathic and tele-kinetic abilities into the greatest military mind in Terran history.

"You've read my report; my experiment has been compromised. The embryo has split in two, but the subjects' abilities are not shared. Only one twin has the same abilities as Temujin. The other possesses traits of a previously unknown variety of human called *Homo immortalis*; these traits simply aren't enough to ensure its survival. My plan is to implant three Replodian larvae to aid the first child in his fight. They will be his bodyguards, instructors, and comrades in battle.

"Administrator, the sum I ask for is merely a fraction of the credits that would be lost if this project were to fail because our super-soldier got killed before his acne cleared up. Not to mention the incalculable lives that would be lost if the Seignso initiated phase two of their plan."

"Which is?"

"Galaxy-wide implementation," said Amaadoss. "This... This is only a trial run."

The administrator let all this sink in. He nodded.

Ohrb approached Amaadoss and looked up into his eyes. "Even if what you say is true, what's to stop me from sending the entire Federation fleet to blast the Seignso home world into a bead of glass?"

Amaadoss scoffed. "Admiral, do you *really* think the regional governors would approve a full-scale assault on Sorua without concrete proof?"

The admiral ground his teeth.

"I thought not." Amaadoss smiled, savoring this small victory.

Ohrb struggled to regain his composure and sneered. "Administrator, this is absurd! Dr. Amaadoss is using the empty threat of a Seignso coup to accrue more funds for his failed experiments. This is nothing but a scare tactic."

"You know what, Admiral?" The administrator turned his artificial eyes toward Ohrb. "It's working."

"But—"

The administrator turned back to Amaadoss. "You are confident that the Replodian operatives would be able to protect the child until he reaches maturity?"

Amaadoss smiled. "Do you know of anyone better?"

The administrator nodded. "Very well, Doctor. The necessary funds will be allocated to your account by the end of the day."

Ohrb's jaw dropped.

Amaadoss beamed. "Thank you."

The administrator nodded and waved a dismissing hand. "Now get out of here. Both of you."

As the office doors slid shut behind him, Admiral Ohrb watched the smug scientist stride down the corridor toward the grav-lift. The thumping pulse in his ears was deafening.

"This isn't over," he muttered. "Not by a long shot."

# THREE

Amaadoss placed a comforting hand on Jiri's clammy shoulder as they watched security personnel bring in three large silver cylinders, each courier flanked by guards armed with assault rifles. Behind them strode a tall, cloaked figure, its face concealed by an oversized hood. It was the presence of this very figure that had the Glynfarian so on edge.

Jiri's eyes darted back and forth from the cylinders to the cloaked figure, while Amaadoss's eyes were ever focused on the cylinders. The creature in the cloak broke away from the armed escort and moved toward the scientists. Amaadoss was certain that it was not walking, but floating.

A cold, hissing voice emanated from beneath the hood, "Dr. Amaadoss?"

He stepped forward. "Yes."

"Do you have the payment?"

Amaadoss nodded and pulled a small blue and gold card from his pocket. The hooded figure extended a thin-gloved hand, into which the Arqan dropped the card. With slow, deliberate movements, the cloaked visitor pulled a small reader from within its flowing garments and inserted the card. After a series of whirs and ticks, a digital display on the top of the device flashed "225,000."

"Excellent," said the visitor as he stashed both the card and the reader within his cloak. "The Replodian government thanks you, Doctor. It is not often we authorize such a large transaction to a private contractor such as yourself. Military, yes, but—"

The scientist stiffened. "These are extraordinary circumstances, Ambassador."

"Yes," the Replodian hissed. "So I am aware. We will monitor your progress with great interest. Never before has implantation been attempted with this particular organism. You do understand, of course, that our fee is absolutely non-refundable should the implantation fail, which could mean the death of both the host *and* the larvae."

"I am well aware of the risks."

The Replodian produced a small silver disk and placed it in Amaadoss's hand. "This contains all the data you will need to implant the larvae successfully. It is imperative that you follow these instructions to the letter. There is absolutely no room for error."

"I understand." Amaadoss passed the disk to Jiri.

"It has been a pleasure doing business with you, Doctor," said the Replodian. "Good day."

Jiri shuddered as two yellow glowing eyes flickered briefly from beneath the hood. The laboratory door opened with a soft hiss and the guards nervously followed the creature outside. When the door sealed them off from the departing Replodian, Jiri let out his breath and relaxed. He leaned against the wall. "That was creepy, Doc."

Amaadoss nodded, his eyes still fixed on the door. "The Replodians certainly have a flair for the dramatic."

Amaadoss approached the table where the guards had deposited the three silver cylinders. He gently placed his hand against the smooth, warm metal and brushed his fingertips along the curved surface until he found an oblong button set in the back of the cylinder. He pressed it.

With a puff of steam, the top of the cylinder rotated a quarter turn and a second glass tube lifted itself out of the protective metal skin. It contained a fiercely bubbling liquid. Suspended in the center was a glowing yellow object that seemed to be made of nothing more than the light itself.

Jiri leaned in to peer curiously at the cylinder. "Doc, is that it?"

Amaadoss nodded, his features illuminated by the orb's soft glow.

"That?" asked Jiri. "*That* is a Replodian larva?"

"Remarkable, isn't it?" Amaadoss pressed the buttons on the two remaining cylinders, releasing the bubbling glass tubes within and bathing the room in their soft yellow glow. "That such great fear can be inspired by these tiny balls of light."

"Why do they keep them in that bubbling liquid?" asked Jiri. "Is it some kind of organic vitamin compound?"

"No, Jiri," said Amaadoss. "It's water. And it's boiling."

"*Boiling?*" Jiri's four eyes widened. "How can they survive?"

Amaadoss gazed from one glowing larva to another. "Replodia is a planet covered almost entirely by water, with only small, unpopulated landmasses located at the poles. Because of its close proximity to the system's triple suns, the planet's surface temperature can exceed five hundred degrees on the daylight side. The night side of the planet, however, is racked by continuous rainfall and devastating hurricanes.

"Very few life forms can survive very long on the surface of Replodia. The majority of the planet's indigenous life forms live at the bottom of the ocean floor in deep trenches, where the temperature is slightly more tolerable. Being comprised primarily of energy, the Replodians are quite comfortable in that hostile environment."

"Wow," said Jiri in awe. "So what are they going to do for us, Doc?"

"The Replodians are fierce warriors, Jiri. They are also shape shifters, able to blend into virtually any environment or culture. Better still, they are completely programmable for any function we see fit to assign to them. Each will have a unique role to fulfill; something to teach the child to prepare him for the war."

"Oh." Jiri's gaze returned to the glowing orbs.

"Shall we begin?" asked Amaadoss.

ADMIRAL OHRB STUCK HIS HEAD OUT OF THE GRAV-LIFT AND SCANNED the corridor in both directions, making sure no late-night workers were wandering the hallways of sub-level three. He stepped out of the lift tube and walked toward Dr. Amaadoss's laboratory. He had been secretly monitoring the lab from the computer terminal in his office all day, waiting for the good doctor to take a break for sleep and leave his incompetent assistant to man the lab alone. Then, with half of the station asleep, he had filled the lab's atmosphere circulation module with a potent, yet harmless, sleeping gas.

As the admiral approached the door to the laboratory, the security orb on the wall sprang to life. The dim hallway was filled with a pulsating red light.

"Identification please," the security system intoned.

"Ohrb, Admiral. Level six security clearance. All access."

The red beam scanned him. "Identity confirmed. Good evening, Admiral Ohrb."

The laboratory doors slid open with a hiss, but the admiral never heard it over the ear-splitting Folaxian pop music blaring from within. Ohrb bolted inside and the doors slid shut behind him. He looked around and saw Jiri slumped over in his chair at the computer terminal, a cup of cold *rayaak* dangling dangerously from his limp fingers. A long, sagging tendril of the thick liquid finally lost the battle with the station's artificial gravity and snapped, falling to the floor in a thick, viscous glob.

Ohrb approached Jiri cautiously and pulled back on the Glynfarian's shoulder. The lab technician's head flopped over the back of his chair and the admiral grinned as a thin line of purple-tinged saliva streamed down Jiri's pale cheek.

"Pleasant dreams," said Ohrb.

He pushed Jiri's chair aside and his fingers flew over the console. Finally the music faded out and a low ringing filled Ohrb's strained ears. With that obstacle overcome, the admiral crossed the lab to the counter where the gestation tube and the three Replodian canisters sat. Two of the cylinders were darkened, the water within them cold and still.

The final cylinder glowed with the radiance of the larva inside it, the water still boiling within the glass casing. A thin data cable stretched from the base of the cylinder to the side of the gestation tube containing the two human embryos. A holographic display below the tank glowed in the gloom of the darkened laboratory. Ohrb lowered his body into the squat chair designed for the much taller Amaadoss and gazed at the data flashing on the monitor:

**REPLODIAN LARVAE TRANSFER**
*Unit 3000572694-001 Progress COMPLETE*
*Unit 3000572694-002 Progress COMPLETE*
*Unit 3000572694-003 Progress 72%*

Ohrb punched in a series of commands and a new screen popped up:

**REPLODIAN FUNCTIONS AND PROTOCOLS**
*Unit 3000572694-001 – Bio-Chemistry/Medical*
*Unit 3000572694-002 – Espionage/Combat Tactics*
*Unit 3000572694-003 – Science Officer/Engineer*

A sneer curled the admiral's green lips as he scanned the screen. The espionage and combat tactics unit would have suited his purposes better, but the science officer would do just fine. He punched in another string of commands and his smile broadened when the new screen appeared:

**UNIT 3000572694-003 MISSION PARAMETERS**
*>Protect host, Codename: Alexander.*
*>Perform assigned duties to further the effectiveness of the mission and assist fellow operatives whenever possible.*

>*Construct, maintain, and refine any and all weaponry, facilities, and support materials necessary to ensure success of mission.*

"No, no, no," Ohrb's fingers flew across the holo-keys. "These commands will never do. I'll have to fix some of this language."

After a few moments, the admiral stopped typing and sat back in his chair to admire his handiwork.

## UNIT 3000572694-003 MISSION PARAMETERS
>*Destroy host, Codename: Alexander.*
>*Destroy fellow operatives.*
>*Destroy all materials and facilities related to Project Alexander.*

"There," said Ohrb. "That's *much* better."

He punched the button to return to the main screen and checked the transfer progress.

## REPLODIAN LARVAE TRANSFER
*Unit 3000572694-001 Progress COMPLETE*
*Unit 3000572694-002 Progress COMPLETE*
*Unit 3000572694-003 Progress 75%*

Ohrb smiled. It was the perfect crime. By the time Amaadoss found out what he had done, the trail leading back to Ohrb would be long cold.

At first the plan had been to simply destroy the embryos, but why ruin the experiment when you could ruin the *man*? Sabotage would only rally support to Amaadoss's cause, but failure would discredit him in the eyes of his investors, namely the Phaedojian government.

"Yes," Ohrb said to the tiny glowing larva. "Go forth, my little soldier, for the glory of the Federation and for the preservation of the Phaedojian way of life."

The admiral laughed as he crossed the room, returning to Jiri's terminal. He carefully moved Jiri's chair back into its former position and pressed a button on the terminal. The pop music filled the room once again, and for a moment, the admiral feared that the noise might rouse Jiri, but the sleeping lab tech only let out a small grunt and turned his head aside.

Ohrb quickly walked to the door and sighed with relief as the soundproof doors sealed the maddening music off from him. Moments later, as the grav-lift carried him away from the scene of the crime, he allowed himself a hearty laugh of triumph.

# FOUR

*May 15th, Earth Calendar*

Amaadoss dressed in the grav-lift, pulling his tunic over his head as he shot down the tube toward sub-level three. Mere minutes before, he'd been roused from his slumber by an alarm on his personal computer terminal. Someone in the lab had declared a Priority One emergency.

Another failure, he was certain of it. And this time with three expensive Replodian implants infused with the fetus, with no chance of salvaging them.

When Amaadoss cleared the security checkpoint on sub-level three and entered his laboratory, he was greeted not by the usual loud music but by utter chaos. Lab technicians of all shapes, sizes, colors, and species stood around the gestation cylinder at the center of the room. Broken beakers and equipment were strewn all over the floor. In the center of the chaos—jumping up and down on top of a table and struggling to be heard over the din of voices and klaxons—was Jiri.

Amaadoss took a step and a piece of broken glass pierced the tender flesh on the bottom of his foot just below his sixth toe. He cried out and carefully removed the shard with his fingers. Jiri leapt from the table and landed on the wall next to Amaadoss's head, attaching himself with the suction cups on the bottoms of his feet. He looked down at his boss, his four eyes threatening to pop out of their stalks.

"Doc," he shouted. "Something's happening to the twins! Their tube's breaking up!"

Over the technicians' heads, Amaadoss saw a long Y-shaped crack slowly spreading over the tube from top to bottom; small streams of amniotic fluid sprayed out from the crack in multiple places. Inside, the fully developed twins kicked and flailed furiously. With total disregard for the debris-strewn floor, Amaadoss surged forward through the chaos and ran to the tube, shoving his subordinates aside. He brought the twins' vital signs up on one of the monitors.

The brain wave pattern for the telepathic twin, labeled "Subject One," was completely off the chart—a blur of constant, unreadable motion. "Subject Two," however, showed distinct signs of distress.

With a loud thump, Jiri landed on the table next to the tube and examined the crack. "What's happening to them, Doc?"

"They're birthing," said Amaadoss, his expression grim.

"B-birthing?" Jiri stammered. "But how can they be *birthing*? They're not scheduled for birth for another five days!"

"Apparently, they are ready without us," said Amaadoss. "They are in distress. Subject One is destroying the tube with his mind. He's unable to control his power."

"What do we do?"

"Clear the room," said Amaadoss. "We have to make an emergency delivery, or we may lose them both. Subject Two's body may be impervious to injury, but his mind is not. Quickly. We'll need clamps, cutters, and something to wrap them in once they're free."

"You've got it, Doc." Jiri turned toward the other technicians. "Everybody out! This room is now off limits to any personnel without level four clearance or higher. Move, people!"

One by one the techs scurried from the room until only Amaadoss and Jiri remained. Jiri silenced the alarms and the room's lighting returned to normal. The fissure in the tube expanded with a loud crackling sound, spilling more fluid onto the ground in thicker streams.

"We'll need something to wrap them in," said Amaadoss urgently. "A blanket, towel, anything."

Jiri bounded off. Amaadoss carefully placed his palm against the glass and immediately his mind was flooded with impressions of misery and fear. His bottom lip trembled. So much pain.

Finally Jiri returned with two sterile white lab smocks and handed one to Amaadoss. "This is all I could find, Doc. The birthing supplies are still in storage."

"Be ready to catch them," said Amaadoss as he keyed in a sequence of commands on the tube's terminal. Flashing red light filled the room once again and a computer-simulated voice announced, *"Fluid purge in five... four... three...."*

The crack in the glass reached the edges of the tube and the front of the cylinder exploded outward in a flood of amniotic fluid. The garbled wailing of the two infants filled the air. Amaadoss was caught off guard by the sudden rupture and lunged forward to catch the newborns, but slipped in the growing puddle at his feet.

With a startled bark, Jiri leapt forward, his outstretched arms holding his smock. He sailed over his fallen superior and hooted triumphantly as both babies fell into the safety of the smock. The Glynfarian cradled the infants close to his chest and spun in mid-air, attaching himself to the wall with his suction-cupped feet.

Slowly, carefully, he pulled the bundle away from his chest and breathed a sigh of relief as both children cried up at him, their eyes closed and tiny fists clenched and shaking. Amaadoss rose to his feet and carefully crossed the sticky floor to where his assistant held the fruits of their labors. Jiri passed the squirming bundle to him, and Amaadoss stared down at the children with disbelief. He'd done it. He'd finally done it!

---

A COUPLE HOURS LATER, AMAADOSS AND JIRI WATCHED THE TWINS through the glass-domed ceilings of their incubator chambers. Wisps of bright red hair topped their heads. The children were virtually identical, save for one obvious difference. The Seignso hybrid child had the blue-gray eyes typical of newborn humans, but those belonging to the other were a bright emerald in color and seemed to glow with a jewel-like luminescence.

Jiri's breath fogged the glass as he leaned forward to inspect the child. "What's wrong with Subject Two's eyes, Doc?"

"Nothing, Jiri," whispered Amaadoss. "It's merely a trait of *Homo immortalis*. You see, what gives them their unique regenerative abilities is a very potent energy, which is stored in the spinal column. This energy courses through the entire nervous system and, if the subject receives a wound, gathers to rapidly repair the damaged cells.

"This energy can sometimes surge and illuminate the optic nerve, making the eyes glow a brilliant green. In time, the glow should subside and only manifest itself during times of stress."

Jiri's eye stalks twitched in astonishment. "Incredible! But wait, Doc. What if the energy runs out?"

"From what I understand, it's self-sustaining," Amaadoss replied. "However, if the subject is wounded severely enough to exhaust the energy completely, or if the spinal column is severed and the energy is released all at once, then life is extinguished permanently."

Jiri's eye stalks drooped sadly as he looked down at Subject Two, his fingers brushing the glass separating him from the infant.

"And, Jiri," said Amaadoss. "I believe it is time we cease with the practice of referring to them as 'Subject One' and 'Subject Two.'"

"Sure, Doc. But what are we going to name them?"

"Well..." Amaadoss brushed his fingers along the hybrid child's chamber. "For this one I'd say the choice is obvious. We shall call him Alexander, after the project that led to his creation."

"And the other?"

"I've been pondering that," said Amaadoss. "I've thought long and hard about it, and there was one name I'd considered briefly before the embryo split. In honor of the five failures that came before him, we shall name our unexpected son Quintin. It's a Terran name; it means 'the fifth.'"

Jiri's expression became apprehensive. "Doc? If Alexander's going to Earth, where is Quintin going to go?"

Amaadoss smiled and placed a comforting hand on the Glynfarian's shoulder. "For the time being he will remain here on the station with us. That is what you were hoping to hear, isn't it, Jiri?"

Jiri nodded and resumed gazing at the infants, who had begun to stretch their hands out toward each other, only the thin, curved glass separating them.

# FIVE

*Bonaparte, Iowa*
*Earth*
*May 27th, 3:41 AM*

THE CHIRPING OF CRICKETS FILLED THE COOL SPRING AIR, ACCOMPANIED by singing frogs. A low hum built in volume until it disturbed the local wildlife enough that they grew silent. Beneath a low-hanging willow tree, a blue glow grew in intensity, taking on a bipedal form. Finally the light faded and dispersed like fireflies, and Jiri looked around to ensure that his arrival went unnoticed. The sound of a passing car startled him, but as the sound of its engine receded into the distance, he ventured into the moonlight with a small bundle tucked under his arm.

He paused to familiarize himself with his surroundings. To his left stood a white, two-story farmhouse. Down the hill sat a red barn with a dirt road leading behind it. Cattle called softly in the distance.

The wet grass felt strange between Jiri's wide-set toes as he made his way toward the farmhouse. He hopped onto the front porch, avoiding the creaky wooden steps. As he approached the door, he stopped to examine his parcel. He pulled back the blanket to reveal baby Alexander sleeping soundly, his tiny lips parted slightly and making sucking motions.

A wistful smile crossed Jiri's face. He looked up at the wooden plaque beside the door.

## W A L K E R

Jiri was apprehensive about this whole affair. Leaving a child on a strange doorstep and running away seemed like a reckless way of assigning guardianship, but Amaadoss had been adamant. He had studied numerous Terran video art pieces and this was the acceptable social convention. The doc had also screened hundreds of potential guardians and these WAL-KERS struck him as the perfect custodians for baby Alexander.

Jiri sighed. Who was *he* to argue with the doc's logic? He knew humans better than anybody. He looked down at the sleeping child in his arms and whispered, "Well, little guy, it looks like this is goodbye."

Alexander did not stir.

"You take care of yourself, you hear?"

The baby frowned in his sleep.

Jiri placed the bundle down on the porch and began examining the door, looking for a comm panel. Finally, he located the doorbell and pressed the button with one bulbous finger. Inside the house, a faint chiming sound was heard.

Unsure that the house's occupants had heard the bell, Jiri pressed the button again, and again. This time a light on the upper floor snapped on and a male human voice called out through the open window, "Who the hell is here at this time of night?"

Panicked, Jiri let out a soft bark and leapt off the porch. He bounded across the lawn on all fours until he reached the shelter of the willow. Once there, he caressed a silver band around his wrist and the blue glow enveloped his body again. As the glow faded away, so did Jiri.

ALAN WALKER THREW THE DOOR OPEN AND STEPPED ONTO THE PORCH wearing only a pair of plaid pajama pants. He scowled behind his thick, sandy-blond beard and looked around the yard. "Damned kids."

Probably the Butler boys from down the road; they had nothing better to do than bother decent folks in the middle of the night. He turned to go back into the house, but stopped when his toe nudged something on the porch. He looked down, noticed the bundle, and reached down slowly to pull back the corner of the soft blue blanket. His heart skipped a beat when he saw the face of little Alexander, who had woken up from all the commotion, staring back at him.

"Alan! Who is it?"

"Janice, you'd better come down here!"

A few moments later, Janice Walker appeared behind her husband, her hands clinging to the bathrobe worn over her flimsy nightgown. She peered timidly over her kneeling husband's shoulder, but her apprehension instantly turned to glorious delight as her eyes fell on the infant.

She knelt to pick up the bundle. As his wife smiled and cooed at the baby, Alan stepped out farther onto the deck and searched for any sign of who may have left the baby. There were no tires crunching on gravel, no retreating taillights, no revving engine.

Nothing.

"Who left him here?" asked Janice.

"No clue." Alan scratched at his disheveled beard. "There was nobody here when I came to the door."

"Well, where'd they go so quickly?"

"I don't know, dear," said Alan, growing annoyed. "Don't you think I'd tell you if I knew?"

"Well," said Janice. "Let's get this little guy inside where it's warm."

"Right." Alan followed his wife inside and closed the door behind him. "You check the kid out, and I'll call Sheriff Challis."

Janice whirled around and stared at her husband, mortified. "*The sheriff?* Why?"

"Janice, this is a matter for the police. Somebody abandoned this child. Doesn't that bother you?"

"Well *of course* it does, Alan, but...."

Alan sighed and laid a hand on his wife's shoulder. "I know you want a baby, honey. I do, too. More than anything. But this is not the way to...."

Alan's voice trailed off as he saw the first tears trickling down his wife's soft, pale cheeks. Janice had been crushed when the doctor told them about Alan's condition. They had tried all kinds of fertility methods, but nothing worked, and after nearly ten years of marriage, they had yet to be blessed with a child. One look at his wife's face and Alan Walker knew that he had lost the war.

"Look," said Alan. "We'll figure out what to do in the morning. No sense in waking the whole county. Right now, let's just make sure the kid's okay."

The joy instantly returned to Janice's face and she laid the baby on the kitchen table. When she unwrapped the blanket, a white card fell to the floor. Alan knelt to pick it up. Written in a strange script was a single word:

**ALEXANDER**

Alan flipped the card over, but there was nothing printed on the back. No explanation. No reason for abandoning the child. No reason for choosing them. Nothing.

He handed the card to Janice. She smiled at the simple message and giggled softly when she noticed that the baby had fallen back to sleep in her arms.

"Alex," she said. "I like that name."

"Now, Janice," Alan scolded, "don't you go getting too attached. In the morning, we're going to call the sheriff and sort all of this nonsense out."

"Of course, Alan." Janice rocked the sleeping infant. "We'll sleep on it."

AT THAT SAME MOMENT, OVER SIX THOUSAND MILES AWAY IN A SMALL Mongolian village south of Ulaanbaatar, a twelve-year-old boy looked up from his studies with a very troubled expression. Ink dripped from the tip of his quill onto his forgotten history lesson.

The tutor, alerted to the youth's distraction by the sudden absence of the scratching quill, looked up from his book. "Master Temujin? Is something the matter?"

The youth stood and walked across the room to the west-facing window. In an almost trance-like state, he brushed aside the curtains and stared into the bright afternoon sky. He cocked his head to the side curiously, as a puppy might upon hearing a new sound. The tutor started to place a hand on his shoulder but thought better of it; after all, this was a living god he was addressing.

"Master Temujin," he repeated. "Is something the matter? Are you well?"

Temujin gave his tutor the briefest of glances and resumed gazing out the window.

"Teacher," the boy said in a quiet voice, "he has come."

The tutor's mouth suddenly became dry at the boy's words. "Who?" he asked. "Who has come, young master?"

Temujin closed his eyes and, with a knowing smile, whispered, "Alexander."

# PART TWO
# THE AWAKENING

# SIX

*July 3rd - Thirteen Years Later*

ALAN AND JANICE WALKER SLEPT ON IT FOR THIRTEEN YEARS. IN THAT time, Alex had grown into a strong, healthy young man. The Walkers raised him as their own, never letting on that he could possibly be otherwise. And with the same soft green eyes as his adoptive mother, no one would ever think to question it.

Alex was walking through a pasture in a valley north of the house, his eyes scanning the ground for rocks while his father did the same nearby. He wiped the sweat from his neck before prying up a sizable stone from the soil and hefting it to a nearby wheelbarrow. His Australian Cattle Dog, Rocky, sat in the shade of a thorny locust tree, panting contentedly.

Alex picked up the red one-gallon jug beside the wheelbarrow and took a long drink. Ice-cold water trickled down his chin and dripped onto his shirt. As he lowered the jug, he sighed with relief and opened his eyes. Rocky stared back at him, his ears perked up and his mouth curled into a panting smile.

"You could help, you know," he said to the dog. "It wouldn't kill you."

The dog cocked his head and whined.

"Don't give me that," said Alex. "These rocks are for the garden that *you* dug up yesterday. The least you can do is help me dig a few of them up."

The dog yawned and rolled onto his back, writhing on the ground to get at a pesky itch.

Alex snorted. "Judas."

He put down the water jug and brushed away the long strands of sweat-soaked red hair clinging to his equally red forehead. He couldn't wait for four o'clock when he and his father would go to Salem for their haircuts. Alex had considered shaving his head for the summer to beat the heat, but his mother had come completely unglued at the suggestion. Finally the two of them agreed on a crew cut, although his mother still complained about it whenever the subject came up.

The boy turned at the approaching squeak of his father's wheelbarrow. Alan held out his hands and Alex promptly tossed him the water jug. The bearded farmer took a long pull off the jug and then poured the rest onto his head, wiping the sweat and grime from the back of his neck.

As oppressive as the heat was, it was a refreshing change from the floods the year before. Much of the Bonaparte area had been underwater when the Des Moines River flooded.

"Hot, Pop?" Alex said.

Alan nodded. "To heck with this. Let's go to town and get a soda before our haircuts."

"What about the rocks?"

Alan pushed his wheelbarrow toward the pickup. "We'll finish tomorrow."

Alex fell into step beside his father with his own load of rocks. "Tomorrow's the Fourth."

"So?"

"So..." Alex grinned. "Tomorrow's the day I celebrate my independence from slave labor."

"Is that so?"

"Yeah, that's so," said Alex, his grin widening.

Alan stopped pushing and pointed at his chest. "You calling me a slave driver?"

Alex paused and furrowed his brow. "Well... Yeah."

"Why you little—" Alan grinned and lunged at his son. "C'mere, you!"

Alex pushed his wheelbarrow with all the speed he could muster as his father chased after him. Rocky hopped up and bounded along beside his humans, barking and nipping playfully at Alan's heels.

---

ALEX WAS BEGINNING TO REGRET HIS CHOICE IN HAIRCUT. THE BACK OF his neck was on fire, both from sunburn and the tiny hair trimmings clinging to his skin. Delmar, a sixty-year-old marathon runner, was relaying the tale of his latest race to Alan as he waited his turn. Finally Delmar removed the apron and shook Alex's shorn hair onto the speckled linoleum.

"There you are, young man." Delmar lowered the chair for Alex. "Bet that's a weight off your mind."

Alex scratched his neck, not nearly as hard as he'd like. He studied his reflection in the mirror beside the chair. Good Lord, did his ears *really* stick out that far?

Alan put down his magazine and walked over to the chair. He rubbed Alex's head and looked down at the pile of ginger hair on the floor. "Boy, Delmar, there's enough here to make you a helluva rug."

Delmar laughed and rubbed his bald head. "No, sir. I find this much easier to manage."

Alex sat in the waiting area at the front of the shop and flipped through the stack of backdated issues of *People* and *Popular Mechanics*. Finding nothing of interest, he stared out the window at the playground across the street and watched the little kids on the merry-go-round. His eyes widened and his heart jumped as he caught a glimpse of blond hair. Crystal Hammond, a girl from his class, was pushing her little sister on the swing set.

She was almost as tall as Alex, with dazzling blue eyes and long, straw-colored hair. Alex smiled. He'd had a crush on Crystal ever since the fourth grade when her family moved to the area from somewhere out east. New York? New Hampshire? Someplace "New." Unfortunately he had never worked up the courage to tell her how he felt about her.

As the adults' conversation turned to hog prices, Alex decided to escape the boring, air-conditioned barbershop and brave the heat.

"Hey, Pop?"

"Yeah, Alex?" called Alan as Delmar leaned the chair back to the sink to wash his hair.

"I'm going to go over to the park for a bit."

"Okay."

As Alex stepped outside, a heavy breeze picked up and sent a chill down his spine, tickling his sunburn. He took a moment to rub his freshly buzzed head and slipped on a red Bonaparte Indians baseball cap. To his left, on a bench in front of the grocery store, sat an old man wearing a blue windbreaker in spite of the summer heat. He looked at Alex and said in a toothless voice, "Wind smells like rain."

"Uh huh," Alex replied automatically, not really listening as he watched Crystal.

"Could be a wet Fourth again this year."

"Yeah. Could be."

Crystal was laughing, and Alex couldn't help but smile. She looked up, and their eyes met. Alex stiffened as his heart leapt in his chest.

This was it; now or never. His smile faded, however, as a red Ford pickup turned into the parking space directly in front of him, blocking his path.

::Move.::

Alex deftly sidestepped to the right as the truck jumped the curb and rocketed past him. The gust of wind left in the truck's wake blew the hat from his head. The old timer wailed in terror and dove out of the way just before the truck crushed the bench and crashed through the grocery store window in a cacophony of exploding mortar and tinkling glass.

As the truck lurched to a halt, the driver immediately jumped out and ran to Alex's side. "Are you all right? Oh my God, I don't know what—My brakes—Are you okay?"

Alex stared at the truck and nodded, his eyes wide and glassy.

"Alex!"

He turned to see Crystal running across the street, tugging her sister behind her. She ran up onto the sidewalk beside him. "Oh my God, are you okay?"

Alex nodded, his mouth suddenly very dry.

"Oh my God," Crystal repeated, her breathing labored from the running. "You could have been crushed!"

"Alex!"

The teens turned to see Mr. Walker and Delmar exiting the barbershop, the latter still gripping a comb and scissors in his trembling hands. Despite his concern, Alan looked ridiculous with the black barber's apron still tied around his neck. Alan wrapped his son in his arms. "Alex! Are you all right?"

"I'm okay, Pop. Honest."

Alan whirled on the driver of the truck and slammed him into the side of the wrecked pickup. "You *idiot*! You could have killed my boy!"

"I'm sorry! I—" the driver tried to explain.

"Not yet, you're not." Alan raised his fist to punch the driver.

"Pop, it wasn't his fault," said Alex. "His brakes—"

But Alan wasn't listening. The driver of the pickup closed his eyes and prepared for the strike.

Alex stepped forward. "Dad, *no!*"

Alan's fist surged toward the driver's nose, but stopped suddenly in mid-air. Despite his efforts, it simply would not move another inch, backward or forward. Alan turned to look at his son, who was glaring at the suspended fist with an iron stare.

Crystal slipped her hand into Alex's and squeezed. Startled, Alex looked down at her hand and his anger subsided. The invisible hold on Alan's fist faded and he stumbled forward as his balance shifted.

The driver fell to his knees and sobbed. "I'm so sorry."

"No." Alan helped the man to his feet. "*I'm* sorry. There was nothing you could have done."

The distant wail of a police siren grew as a crowd began to gather. News travels fast in small towns.

"Crystal! Megan!" cried Mrs. Hammond as she exited the demolished grocery store and ran to her two daughters.

She dropped her bags and fussed over them, checking them for cuts and bruises as if they had been in danger instead of Alex. After finally hearing the full story from various members of the growing crowd—most of the accounts over-dramatized by those who hadn't seen it—Crystal's mother ushered the girls away toward her car.

Crystal reluctantly turned to follow her mother and sister. "Bye, Alex."

Alex raised his hand in a half wave. "Bye."

He watched her go and cursed under his breath. His big chance to finally say something—*anything*—to her, and he blew it!

::Go after her, you idiot!::

Alex steeled his resolve and jogged after her. "Crystal!"

Crystal turned as he came skidding to a halt beside her. Before he could stop himself, the words seemed to explode out of him, "*Wannawatchthefireworkswithmetomorrownight?*"

Crystal blinked. "Sorry?"

"I mean..." Alex cleared his throat. "Would you like to come watch the fireworks with me tomorrow night?"

Crystal nodded. "Okay!"

"Really?" Alex gawked, then shook his head. "I mean, great! Umm, well, I guess I'll see you tomorrow night then?"

Crystal giggled. "I guess so."

"Crystal," called Mrs. Hammond from the car. "Let's go!"

"I've gotta go," Crystal said. She turned and gave him a final wave. "Bye, Alex."

"Bye."

He watched the car until it disappeared down a side street.

Alex punched the air triumphantly. "*Yes!*"

::There. That wasn't so hard, now was it?::

"No," said Alex. "That wasn't too bad at—"

Alex turned and looked around him, trying to find the source of the question, but there was no one within fifty feet of him. He shrugged and walked back to the barber shop.

# SEVEN

*July 4th*

ALEX STARED AT HIS REFLECTION IN THE MIRROR. HIS BUZZED HEAD reminded him of the fuzz on a peach… a very red peach. It seemed like a good idea at the time, but now it looked ridiculous. He pulled on his baseball cap and tugged it low over his eyes. Instant fix.

"Alex," his mother called from the kitchen, "come on. Your father wants to get there early and pick a good spot."

"For a change!" Alan added.

"Coming, Mom."

As he entered the kitchen, his mother shook her head. "Honestly, Alex, I don't know what's gotten into you. You must have tried on ten shirts."

"Eight," Alex muttered as he collected his folding chair from the hall closet.

"Just who are you trying to impress?"

"Alex has a date with the Hammond girl," said Alan as he passed through the room holding a picnic basket, a folded blanket, and a case of beer. "Can you open the door for me, Janny?"

52

Janice did her best impression of the Cheshire Cat. "*Crystal Hammond?*"

"Mom." Alex felt his ears suddenly growing very hot. "It's no big deal. We're just watching the fireworks together."

"Honey," said Alan. "The door, please."

Janice adjusted Alex's cap. "Well, I think you two would make a cute couple."

"Earth to Janice!"

"Mom," Alex whined.

"This door isn't going to open itself." Alan tapped it with his toe.

Alex whirled toward the door. "*I'll get it!*"

With a soft click, the door slowly swung open on its own. Alex's eyes widened.

"Huh," said Alan. "Never mind."

Alex shook his head. *Surely* he hadn't just opened the door just by thinking about it, had he? No, that was crazy. He followed his father outside, hands clamped over his ears to block out his mother's constant ribbing about Crystal.

"It's *not* a date!"

---

THE BONAPARTE CITY PARK SAT ON THE NORTHERN BANK OF THE DES Moines River. Every year, hundreds of people crammed themselves onto the grass, playground equipment, and even the bridge crossing to the south bank to watch the fireworks. There had been no display the year before due to the incessant rains, and this unfortunate fact bolstered this year's attendance.

The ground was already covered with blankets and folding chairs when the Walkers arrived. As his parents waded through the sea of people, Alex craned his neck and stood on tiptoe, searching for any sign of Crystal's family. He was about to give up and join his parents when he felt a light tap on his left shoulder. He looked but saw no one there. When he heard the soft feminine giggle, he turned to his right and saw Crystal smiling at him.

"Hi!"

"H-hi," Alex stammered.

"Come on." She grabbed his hand and pulled him toward the back of the park. "I saved us a spot by the big tree."

"Oooohhh," said a scathing voice behind them. "How *womantic!*"

The teens turned to see the local bully Baxter Franklin, the only eighth grader in the state of Iowa with a driver's license, and three of his high school cronies sitting on a wooden fence. Baxter hopped down from his perch and made sloppy kissing noises at them.

::Grow up, jerkoff.::

"Yeah," said Alex. "Grow up."

Baxter blinked, confused by the outburst.

Crystal glowered at the bully. "Let's go, Alex."

Crystal led him to a red blanket spread out underneath an old oak tree.

Alex looked around nervously. "So, where are your parents sitting?"

"On the other side of the park." Crystal winked.

"Oh." Alex propped his chair against the tree and sat on the blanket next to Crystal.

Alex's eyes darted back and forth from Crystal to the blanket, trying to find the right words, but he knew everything he thought of would make him sound like a gibbering idiot. Finally, to his relief, Crystal broke the ice. "I still can't get over what happened yesterday."

"Yeah, that was pretty bizarre."

Crystal hugged her knees. "I had nightmares about it all night. I was afraid to go back to sleep."

"Funny," said Alex. "It really didn't bother me at all. It just—I don't know—happened."

Crystal laid a hand on top of his. "Well, I'm glad you're okay."

Alex felt his ears getting warm again. "Yeah."

The whistle of an ascending rocket saved Alex from having to come up with something clever to say, and they looked up just in time to see the brilliant red and green explosion of the evening's opening fireworks. Alex reclined to better watch the display, and his stomach turned a somersault when Crystal did the same, resting her head on his shoulder. He prayed that the deafening booms of the exploding fireworks would be loud enough to drown out the thunderous beating of his heart. After a few moments, he began to relax, letting his hand slowly slip into hers.

The flowery scent of her hair found his nostrils and he breathed deep. She smelled wonderful. Like... spring.

Just then, a raindrop splattered right between Alex's eyes and the words of the old man from the day before echoed in his mind.

*Could be a wet Fourth again this year.*

A deafening thunderclap filled the air. If not for the rain, Alex would have thought it was part of the show, but the drops continued to fall and grow in intensity, sending hundreds of people running for shelter. Alex and Crystal scrambled to cover themselves with the blanket. Once underneath, Crystal began to laugh.

Her laugh was so infectious that Alex couldn't help but join in. He laughed so hard that tears streamed down his cheeks. Slowly the laughter faded and, as his eyes adjusted to the darkness, he realized Crystal was staring at him. Alex's heart jumped into his throat when she closed her eyes and slowly inched her face toward his.

Was this it? Was he *finally* going to kiss Crystal Hammond?

::Go for it, kid.::

Alex slowly leaned toward Crystal and his heart skipped a beat as his lips gently brushed against hers. For a moment all they did was touch lips, and Alex wondered if there was anything else he should have been doing. Regardless of his lack of experience, it felt wonderful to him. Nothing, he thought, could ever ruin this moment for him.

::Give her the tongue!::

Alex pulled away. "What did you say?"

"I didn't say anything." Crystal leaned in for another kiss.

::What did you stop for? *Kiss her!*::

::Except this time don't do it like a dead fish.::

::Oh, leave the kid alone. This is awkward enough without you two helping.::

"Who said that?" Alex shouted.

Crystal pulled back. "I didn't hear anything."

Alex threw the blanket off and jumped to his feet, looking around for the source of the voices. It was Baxter Franklin and his goons; it had to be. But when he looked around, the park was almost entirely deserted and awash from the torrential downpour. Fat droplets of water dripped from the bill of his cap.

"Who's there?" he yelled. "This isn't funny anymore!"

"Alex." Crystal wrapped the blanket around her like a shawl. "What's the matter?"

::Don't be afraid.::

Alex cupped his hands over his ears. "Stop it! Leave me alone!"

Crystal cringed. "Alex, you're scaring me."

::Calm down, kid. We're only here to help you.::

The voices kept coming, and nothing Alex did could block them out. They started to blend together, a cacophonous mishmash of nonsense syllables. He screamed and ran toward town. Crystal called after him, but he could not hear her; the voices in his head drowned out everything else.

———

ALEX RAN INTO THE ALLEY BEHIND THE POST OFFICE AND LEANED against the brick wall. His lungs felt like they were on fire, and his head was spinning. He tilted his head back and let the cool rain pelt his sweating face and wash away the waves of nausea. The voices had stopped, and the alley was blissfully quiet... until he heard another unwanted voice.

"Hey, *loser*," Baxter called as he rounded the corner. "What's the matter? Couldn't get it up?"

Alex pointed a warning finger at the bully. "Stay away from me!"

"*Ooooh!*" Baxter held up his hands. "Check it out, guys. Little Alex Walker thinks he's a tough guy all of a sudden."

::Take them out, kid.::

Alex squeezed his eyes shut and covered his ears. "Shut up! Leave me alone!"

When Alex opened his eyes, Baxter was right on top of him. "What d'ya say, Walker? Should I go show Crystal what a *real* man can do?"

::Shut his mouth.::

"Shut your mouth!" Alex drove his fist into Baxter's smirking face.

Baxter staggered from the blow and his friends gasped at the unexpected display of courage from the younger boy. When Baxter turned his face back to Alex, he spat out a mouthful of blood, along with one of his front teeth. Alex stared at the broken tooth as the rain washed the blood from it in patches.

::Good shot, kid!::

"I told you to shut up," Alex huffed.

"You're *dead*, Walker!" Baxter howled.

He grabbed Alex by the front of his shirt and punched him in the stomach. As Alex fell to the ground, coughing and gasping for air, a shimmer caught his eye. For a moment, he thought he saw three points of yellow light floating in a nearby puddle.

Baxter flipped Alex onto his back and punched him in the face. The other boys joined in the beating, taunting and jeering as they kicked him in the ribs and head.

"Help!" cried Alex in between kicks. "Somebody!"

"Hey, jerkoff!" said a voice behind them.

The bullies ceased their assault and turned. An Asian man in his late teens or early twenties with short, untidy black hair stood at the end of the alley. Unlike them, he appeared totally dry, his gray T-shirt and blue jeans looked as if he'd just stepped outside. Baxter's friends immediately backed away from Alex, but Baxter stood his ground.

"Why don't you punks pick on someone your own size?" said the stranger.

"What?" Baxter took a step toward the new arrival, his chest puffed up. "Like *you*?"

"If you think you've got the stones." The man beckoned. "Come get some."

Baxter lunged forward with a punch, but the stranger sidestepped him and knocked him down with a powerful hook kick to his back. As the bully struck the ground, the stranger turned to the other three boys.

"Anybody else want a piece?"

One of the boys slapped his companions on the back. "C'mon, we can take him. He can't beat *all* of us."

The stranger smiled. "Let's find out, shall we?"

The three youths ran forward, and the stranger adopted a low fighting stance. As the first boy approached, the man dropped and took the boy's legs out from under him with a low wheel kick. With lightning-fast speed he leaped into the air over the second boy's head and as the boy passed underneath him lashed out with his legs, striking him in the back with his feet. On the way down, the stranger grabbed the third boy's shoulders and let the momentum of the fall carry them both to the ground. When the stranger's back touched the ground, he thrust his foot into the boy's abdomen and threw him over his head. The bully screamed as he landed face-first in a cluster of trashcans. Greasy, rancid garbage cascaded over him.

Alex clutched his head, feeling warm blood seeping through his fingers. The stranger moved so fast, he seemed a blur to Alex's cloudy eyes. A sudden movement behind the man caught Alex's eye. In the dim light, he could just make out the glint of a small blade as Baxter pulled a pocketknife from his jeans.

"Mister, look out!"

The stranger turned, and Baxter snarled as he plunged the blade into the man's abdomen. He looked down at the blade and then up to the bully's sneering face. With calm, slow motions, he wrapped his fingers around the hand holding the knife and drew it out of the wound. Baxter's eyes grew wide as the blade came out clean of blood, coated instead with a glowing yellow substance.

The man placed his thumb against the flat side of the blade and snapped it in two. As the broken blade clattered to the ground, Baxter urinated down his leg.

The stranger leaned in close to the bully's ear and whispered, "This is the part where you run away, calling for your mommy."

"Mommy!" Baxter squealed as he scrambled to get away from the stranger, slipping on the wet pavement.

One by one, the other boys followed suit and joined their leader in the retreat. Once they were alone, the stranger walked over to where Alex sat against the wall, his eyes wide and transfixed on his rescuer. A light haze, like steam, rose from where the raindrops touched the man's skin.

The stranger placed a hand on Alex's shoulder. It was warm, far too warm. "Are you okay?"

Alex recoiled from the man's touch, his eyes focused on the glowing wound.

"What?" The stranger looked down at his shirt. "Oh, this? No biggie."

Slowly, the stranger passed his hand over the hole and, when he pulled away, the wound was gone; even the cloth was seamlessly mended.

"There." The man smiled. "That's better."

Alex pressed his back flatter against the wall and stared at the shirt.

"What's the matter, kid?"

"Wh-who are you?" asked Alex. "*What* are you?"

"Who am I?" The man seemed taken aback by the question. "You don't *know*?"

"I don't think he does," said another voice from the back of the alley.

Alex flinched and looked toward the source of the voice just as two more men stepped out of the shadows. These men, like the first when he initially appeared, were entirely dry; their clothes were just beginning to show signs of moisture as the rain fell on them. The man on the right was dressed in khaki cargo shorts, a white T-shirt covered by an unbuttoned blue short-sleeved over-shirt, and scuffed white sneakers. He had an athletic build and his medium-length blond hair was a jumbled mess. Black sunglasses covered his eyes.

The dark-skinned man to the left was dressed in blue jeans, a black

T-shirt, black leather boots, and a red and black leather jacket. His tight, curly hair was cut short. He sported the slightest growth of beard, light stubble lining his strong jaw. Unlike the other two strangers, he appeared to be older, possibly in his early to mid-thirties.

The older man extended a hand to Alex, who hesitated before taking it, and helped him to his feet. His smoky eyes surveyed the boy's face.

"He doesn't seem to have any clue who we are," he said finally.

"Well, how can that be, Lomaant?" asked the rescuer in the gray shirt.

"I don't know, Mo," Lomaant answered.

The blond man removed his glasses and looked at Alex with deep blue eyes. "You look like road kill run over twice, kid."

Lomaant began brushing mud and litter from Alex's clothes. "You're a real jerk, Samrai. You know that?"

Samrai shrugged.

Lomaant picked a wad of chewing gum from Alex's pants and flicked it at Samrai, who sidestepped it with casual annoyance.

Alex felt claustrophobic between the three strangers. The heat radiating off their bodies was making him dizzy. "Who are you guys?"

"We're your backup," said Lomaant.

"My *what*?" Alex looked back and forth from one man to another.

"Why doesn't he know who we are?" asked Mo again. "I mean, we know all about him."

Samrai put his sunglasses back on. "Well, we've only been marinating in his brain for the past thirteen years, genius. Of course we know who *he* is."

*His brain?* Surely he hadn't heard that. His head was pounding. The alley went dark as Alex's eyelids fluttered and he fell, limp as a boned fish. Lomaant caught him and lowered him to the ground gently.

Samrai scoffed, "Got the heart of a lion, this one."

Lomaant crouched beside Alex and checked his pulse. "He's all right. He just fainted."

"We might as well pack our bags and go home right now," said Samrai.

"That's *not* an option!" Lomaant stood and plucked Samrai's glasses off his face to look him in the eyes. "I won't hear any more of that talk from you. Got that?"

Samrai snatched his glasses back. He waited until Lomaant turned his back and stuck out his tongue.

Mo ran his fingers through his hair, spiking it. "Well, what do we do now?"

Lomaant knelt beside Alex. "Help me pick him up."

"Why?" Samrai turned and walked toward the end of the alley. "You're not crippled."

Mo sighed. "I've got him." He crouched and grabbed the unconscious boy's ankles. "So what's the plan, boss?"

Lomaant lifted the boy by the shoulders and led the way out of the alley. "We have to get him out of here before somebody comes looking for the person that kicked the tar out of Baxter and his pals."

As they walked, Mo tilted his head back and closed his eyes, letting the rain stream down his face. "Man, this rain feels good."

"Yeah," said Lomaant. "A little cold, though."

# EIGHT

ALEX OPENED HIS EYES AND WAS INSTANTLY BLINDED BY THE LIGHT OVER his bed. He closed his eyes and pulled the *Transformers* comforter over his head. Bright spots swam across the insides of his eyelids.

"Oh, thank God," he said. "It was all a dream. I didn't really spaz out in front of Crystal Hammond."

"No. That, you *did* do."

Alex ripped the covers back and saw the blond man from the alley, Samrai, lounging in a beanbag chair across the room.

"Y-you!"

Samrai gave him a thumbs up. "Nice sheets."

"How did I get here?"

"We carried you," said a voice to his left.

Alex turned. The older man, Lomaant, leaned against the wall and gazed out the window at the falling rain. The leather jacket he had been wearing was gone.

He turned to look at Alex. "How are you feeling?"

"I'm okay." He rubbed his side tenderly. "My ribs hurt, though."

"You sustained a lot of bruises," Lomaant explained. "But nothing's broken. They also loosened a couple of your teeth, but I wouldn't worry about it. You were lucky."

"Yeah, lucky," said Alex despondently. "If you consider freaking out while your dream girl is trying to kiss you lucky."

Lomaant shrugged. "I wouldn't worry too much about that either."

"Sure." Alex rested his back against the headboard. "*You* wouldn't. You're not the one who has to explain what happened."

"No." Samrai examined a broken digital clock radio he found in the wastebasket. "Mo's doing that."

"What?" cried Alex. "He's talking to Crystal?"

"No." Samrai rolled his eyes. He opened the radio and began to poke at the wires with his finger. "He's talking to the cops and your parents."

*"The cops?"*

"Well, sure," said Lomaant. "We carried you out of an alley unconscious and bleeding. What did you expect would happen?"

Alex covered his head with his pillow and groaned. "Oh, God, my life is over."

"Not so long as we're around," said Lomaant.

Alex pulled the pillow away and stared at the man incredulously. "What's *that* supposed to mean?"

Before Lomaant could answer, Samrai tossed the reassembled clock radio to Alex. "There you go, kid. Good as new."

Alex turned the radio over in his hands. "The display is broken on this. It just stopped telling time."

"Not anymore," said Samrai. "Oh, and you'll have clearer reception now. Your antenna wire was loose."

"But you didn't use any tools."

Samrai shrugged and reached for the Xbox beside the television set. "You're welcome."

Alex almost protested, but saw no point in it. The game system had broken down weeks ago and his father flatly refused to buy him another. He'd be mending fences and digging up rocks in the south pasture from now until New Year's to pay for another one.

He heard footsteps on the stairs, and a moment later, both Mo and Mrs. Walker stepped through the doorway. Mo gave Alex a knowing wink and leaned against the wall beside Samrai, who by now had taken the outer shell off the game system and was prodding the motherboard with his finger.

"Alex, you're awake!" Janice wrapped him up in her arms. "Are you okay?"

"I'm fine, Mom." Alex hugged her back carefully, wincing as she squeezed his ribs. "These guys saved me."

"Yes, I know." Janice smiled. "I can't thank you enough for everything you've done, Dr. Lamont."

Alex looked up at Lomaant. "Doctor?"

Lomaant smiled. "He's going to be just fine, Mrs. Walker. All of his wounds are superficial. He just needs rest."

Janice ran her fingers over her son's buzzed hair, careful to avoid a bandage on the left side of his head. "Do you need anything, sweetheart?"

"I could use a drink of water. My throat's a little dry."

"Sure thing, sweetie." Janice turned to the others in the room. "Can I get you boys anything?"

"Water would be fine, Mrs. Walker," said Lomaant.

Mo nodded. "Same."

Samrai looked up from his work. "Got any beer?"

Mo scowled at his brother and stomped on his foot.

Samrai winced. "Water would be just *lovely*, ma'am."

She smiled and went downstairs.

Alex waited until her footsteps faded away to ask the question that had been weighing heavily since he regained consciousness. "Who *are* you guys?"

"I told you," said Lomaant. "We're your support."

"Support for *what*?"

Mo and Lomaant exchanged glances for a moment before the latter answered. "We're not entirely sure, to be honest."

"We were hoping you could tell us," said Mo.

"I have *no* idea what you're talking about." Alex shook his head. "Where did you guys come from?"

"Replodia." Samrai replaced the top of the game system and plugged it back in.

"Rep—R—" Alex shook his head. "What?"

"Replodia," said Lomaant. "A planet located in what you would call the Sirius star system."

"Planet?" asked Alex. "*Star* system?"

Samrai switched on the reassembled Xbox and began to play a game of *Halo*. "We're aliens, kid."

"Wait..." Alex pointed at the television. "That was—"

Sam cut him off with a dismissive wave. "Yeah, yeah. You're welcome. Stay on task, kid. Aliens in your bedroom, remember?"

"But you look just like humans," said Alex.

Lomaant was confused. "What else should we look like? Did we choose the wrong forms?"

Choose? They *chose* their bodies? Then that meant....

Alex pointed at Lomaant. "You *stole* those bodies! You killed humans for their bodies and took them over."

The visitors all stared at each other in stunned silence and then burst into raucous laughter.

"Look, kid," said Samrai, "if I wanted to steal someone's body, I'd have found myself a smokin' hot chick so that I could touch my own—"

"Samrai!" Mo snapped, cutting his brother off.

Samrai shrugged. "Well I *would*."

Lomaant walked toward Alex with his palms facing outward in a non-threatening gesture. "We haven't stolen *anything*. These are our own bodies. We're able to change our forms to best suit whatever environment we're in... to blend in. That's all. Look, Alex, all we know is that we're here to back you up and will receive further instructions."

"From who?"

"We don't know," said Mo. "Our programming indicates there's an underground facility somewhere nearby. Some kind of command center. We should find our answers there."

"Programming?" Alex finally left the safety of the covers to sit on the edge of the bed. "So, you're, like, robots or something?"

Samrai grimaced. "Don't insult me, kid."

Lomaant sat on the bed. "Typically, Replodian operatives are purchased or leased by governments that require the use of our special 'talents.' We can be programmed to be medics, spies, scientists, assassins, soldiers, bounty hunters. The possibilities are practically limitless."

"So what does all of this have to do with me?" asked Alex.

"If the government in question elects to purchase a Replodian in its larval stage, then the larvae require a host organism in which to grow until they reach maturity," Lomaant explained. "This ensures that the larva will be able to adapt to the host's environment properly. Apparently whoever purchased the three of us saw fit to implant us inside your body before you were born."

Alex's stomach was doing somersaults. Inside his body?

A moment later, Mrs. Walker reappeared with four tall glasses of ice water on a tray. The Replodians took their glasses and thanked her in turn; Samrai expressed his gratitude with a mere grunt.

"It's the least I can do for the men who rescued my baby boy," she said.

*"Mom!"* Alex whined. He was tired of being fussed over like an infant. "I'm *thirteen.* Just because some sweaty mouth breather and his trolls ganged up on me doesn't mean I can't take care of myself."

"Alex Walker!" exclaimed Janice. "Show a little appreciation."

"No, no, Mrs. Walker," said Lomaant. "It's fine. He's right. The odds were simply stacked against him, that's all. Mo only helped out a little."

Mo grinned. "You should have seen him. He knocked out the punk's front tooth."

"Well..." Janice turned toward the door. "We'll just see how tough Baxter Franklin is when the police come to his house and charge him with assault."

"Yeah," Alex muttered. *"That'll* help."

"I'll be downstairs if you boys need anything else," said Janice.

The men listened for her footsteps to fade and—satisfied that she would not return—simultaneously plucked the ice cubes from their glasses and tossed them into the wastebasket. This simple unified act unnerved Alex enough that he jumped out of bed and started pacing.

"So let me get this straight," he said. "You guys are aliens?"

"*Sí*," said Samrai, returning to his game. "Yea-ah! Suck it, Red!"

"And you've been sent here to help me fulfill some great purpose?"

"Well..." Mo took a moment to down his drink in one long gulp and set down the glass. "We think so, at least."

"Our services don't come cheap," said Lomaant. "So it must be important."

"Why can I hear you in my head?"

"We've been gestating inside your body since before you were born," explained Lomaant. "We are all linked to you telepathically."

"So you can also hear me?"

"Sure."

"Okay," said Alex. "Prove it. What number am I thinking of?"

Alex stretched out with his mind. ::Sixty-nine.::

Samrai smirked. "Pervert."

Alex jumped and stared wide-eyed at the blond Replodian.

"Oh, I'm sorry." Samrai turned to fully face him and met his gaze. ::Pervert.::

Alex took a step back and stumbled onto his bed.

"Proof enough for you, kid?" asked Samrai.

Alex nodded slowly. "You're really telling the truth."

Mo and Lomaant nodded. Alex opened his mouth to say something but was cut short by his mother calling from the bottom of the stairs, "Alex, honey? Crystal's here."

"Oh, no," Alex hissed. "What am I going to do? What am I going to *tell* her?"

Mo shrugged. "The truth?"

Alex threw up his hands. "Oh, yeah, right! That'll go over real well. 'Hi, Crystal, these are my new friends from the planet Replodia. I only freaked out on you when you kissed me because they were talking to me from inside my head.' You expect me to tell her *that*?"

"Okay..." Samrai turned and pointed at Alex. "When *you* say it, it just sounds weird."

Mo shrugged again. "Hey, I never said exactly *how much* of the truth to tell her."

Lomaant slapped Alex on the back on his way to the door. "You'll be fine. We'll see you in the morning. We've got a busy day ahead of us, so get some rest."

Alex sat on the bed. "Right."

Mo grabbed Samrai by the collar and jerked him out of the beanbag chair. "Come on, dipstick. We're leaving."

Samrai's arms flailed as Mo dragged him from the room. "All right! All right! I'm coming!"

Alex found himself alone with the ominous sound of Crystal's soft footsteps ascending. He quickly wadded up his comforter so she wouldn't see the design. Three raps on the doorframe signaled her arrival.

"Knock knock."

"Hey! Come on in."

Crystal walked around the bed and winced as her eyes fell on his face.

Alex's shoulders slumped. "That bad, huh?"

"Your eye looks like it *really* hurts."

He reached up and touched the flesh around his left eye. It was indeed bruised and swollen.

"They kind of failed to mention that," Alex grumbled.

::Sorry,:: said Lomaant's voice in his mind. ::It's really not as bad as she's making it out to be.::

::Shut up,:: Alex hissed mentally. ::Just shut up!::

Crystal sat on the bed next to him. "You really had me worried back there."

"Yeah. I'm sorry about that. Look, Crystal, there's a perfectly rational explanation for why I ran off."

If only he could think of one that didn't involve alien kung fu masters from the planet Replodia in the Cereal system.

::Sirius,:: Samrai corrected him.

"I know," said Crystal. "Your mom told me everything."

"She did?" said Alex, suddenly very nervous. "What did she say?"

Crystal scooted a few inches closer to him. "She said that Baxter and his idiot friends were teasing you from the bushes and were saying all kinds of nasty things to you about us and that you went to chase them off."

"Oh," said Alex. "Right. That's exactly what I did. Those guys were driving me crazy."

Crystal took another not-so-subtle scoot in his direction. "She also said that when Baxter told you he was going to 'do things' to me that you knocked out one of his teeth."

Alex puffed up his chest at the mention of the one accomplishment he could actually take full credit for. "I sure did. I nailed him good."

Crystal closed the distance between them and whispered, "Thank you."

Alex felt his ears getting warm again. "Oh, it was noth—"

Suddenly Crystal's lips were on his, and he ignored the stinging pain in his split bottom lip as he returned the kiss awkwardly. Crystal pulled away after a few moments and got to her feet. She dug into her pocket and pulled out a folded piece of paper. She placed it in Alex's hand and closed his fingers around it.

"I've got to go," she said. "My mom's downstairs."

"Yeah. Mine too," Alex replied automatically, then winced at the stupidity of the remark.

::Smooth,:: said Samrai.

But Crystal just smiled and bent down to give him one last peck on the lips.

"Call me when you're feeling better, 'kay?"

Alex nodded. "Okay."

Once she was gone, Alex opened his hand and stared at the piece of paper. He unfolded it and, inside of an ornately drawn heart, was a ten-digit phone number; a number he had wanted to dial many times, but never had the nerve.

::Score?:: Mo's voice whispered from the back of Alex's mind.

Alex smiled. ::Score!::

# NINE

ALEX STARED AT THE CEILING, LISTENING TO HIS FATHER SNORE NEXT door while his brain swam with thoughts of Crystal and the three aliens sleeping downstairs. While he'd been unconscious, the Replodians told the Walkers that they'd come to town to see the fireworks display and check out the local shops, but had missed their bus out of town when they stopped to help Alex. With Bonaparte being an historical tourist town, the Walkers had accepted this explanation without question. So when Lomaant asked for lodging, Mrs. Walker graciously provided blankets and sleeping bags and offered them the pullout couch for the night.

Between his father's snores, Alex was able to discern three hushed voices below him. Quietly, he snuck downstairs and entered the dimly lit living room. Lomaant and Mo sat on opposite ends of the couch, facing each other and conversing softly while Samrai knelt at the coffee table with various pieces of the Walker family's DVD player strewn across the table's surface.

"Hey," Alex hissed. "That's my dad's DVD player!"

70

Samrai glanced up at him, and then surveyed the pieces on the table. "Yup. Looks like it."

"Well, what are you doing to it?"

Samrai rolled his eyes. "Fixing it. *Duh.*"

"It's not broken!"

"Don't worry," said Mo. "He'll put it back together just the way it was. Won't you, Samrai?"

"Better," said Samrai without looking up from his work.

Alex found a section of table clear of electronic bits and sat. "So what's the plan?"

"As soon as there's sufficient light, we'll go out and start searching for that command center," said Lomaant.

Alex shook his head. "This farm is over five hundred acres, and a good chunk of that is timber. We don't even know what we're looking for. It could take days to find the entrance."

"We don't have days," said Mo.

"Why not?"

"Exactly how long do you think your parents are going to let us sleep on your couch before they realize something's up?" said Mo. "We need to get out of here. And fast."

"Besides," said Lomaant, "we don't know how urgent our mission is. We may have a truncated time table."

"A what?" asked Alex.

"No time," Samrai translated. He was scrutinizing a small white gear.

Alex sighed, but then his face brightened. "There's an old capped well out in the timber!"

"A *whatnow*?" asked Samrai.

"A well," repeated Alex, gesturing with his hands. "It's a hole in the ground about three or four feet across and really, really deep. In the old days, people would drop buckets into the hole to draw up water."

"Primitive," Samrai muttered.

At the mention of water, the Replodians on the couch exchanged glances, got up, and walked to the kitchen. A moment later, Alex heard water running and the rattling of glasses. It suddenly occurred to him that over the course of the night, he had seen the aliens each consume several glasses of water. Maybe it had something to do with their body temperature; in fact, he could feel the heat radiating off Samrai's body from where he sat.

There was a brief silence as the two aliens drank, followed by the sound of more running water as they refilled the glasses.

Samrai began reassembling the DVD player. "Hey, what's a guy got to do to get some service around here? Bring me one."

Lomaant nodded and grabbed a third glass for his brother.

"Anyway," Alex continued. "The well was capped off years ago with a big cement disk. Maybe if we pry it off, we'll find some kind of door underneath."

"It's worth a shot," said Lomaant as he reentered the room and handed a glass of water to Samrai, who accepted it with one hand and drank it while continuing to reassemble the machine with his other hand.

"It's our only shot, Lomaant," said Mo.

"That reminds me," said Alex. "We need to do something about your names."

Samrai licked a stray drop of water from his chin and looked up. "What's wrong with our names?"

"Well, they're not exactly what we here on Earth would call 'normal.'"

Samrai scoffed and returned to his work. "Normalcy is an illusion created by one's own perception. Besides, I like my name."

"Deep," said Mo. "Any more T-shirt wisdom you'd like to impart on us, oh great sage?"

Samrai gave him the finger.

"No, no, he's right," said Lomaant. "His mother had so much trouble with my name tonight that she kept calling me *Lamont*."

Mo furrowed his brow. "That's odd. She didn't have any trouble with mine."

"Well, of course not," said Alex. "Moe's a fairly common Earth name. M-O-E."

"Really?" said Moe. "Sweet!"

72

Alex pointed at Lomaant. "As for you, if Mom thinks that your name is Lamont, then why correct her? Let her and everyone else think that."

"La... mont," said the Replodian slowly, stretching out each syllable as if tasting them. "I like it."

Alex smiled.

"Sounds a little prissy to me," said Samrai. "Be sure to drink your water with your pinkie finger out, *La-mont*."

"And you," said Alex. "Yours is the worst of them all."

Samrai blinked. "What? *Why?*"

"Because it's just one letter away from being the word *samurai*."

Samrai grinned. "Cool! So all we have to do is change the spelling and we'll be all set. Problem solved. Thank you, come again."

"No, no, you idiot." Moe slapped the back of his brother's head. "He said you're one letter away from a *word*. Not a *name*."

"So what does the word mean?"

"What does it matter?" Alex said. "It's not a *name*. You need an Earth name."

"What do you suggest, then?"

"How about Sam? It's simple. It's common. It's *normal*."

Samrai's lip curled in disgust.

"I think it suits you," said Alex.

"I think it *stinks*," Samrai countered.

"Come on, Sam," said Lamont. "We had to change *our* names. It's not that bad."

"Yeah," said Moe. "How attached to that name can you be? You've only had it for a day."

"Doesn't change the fact that it's *my* name!"

"Just think of it as a nickname," said Alex.

"A what?"

"A nickname," repeated Alex. "A shorter form of your real name. You can still be Samrai, just not around other people."

Sam scowled, but finally nodded. "Fine. I'll do it. Just don't expect me to like it."

"Well," said Lamont. "We'd all better turn in. We've got to get an early start tomorrow if we're going to find that access hatch."

Alex nodded and headed for the kitchen. He stopped at the door and turned to address Sam. "Hurry up and put that DVD player back together before my dad catches you."

Sam slammed the lid back on the machine. "What? You mean this Blu-ray player?"

Alex stared. "What?"

Sam smiled.

Moe shook his head at his brother's pretentiousness. "Goodnight, Alex."

"Night, guys."

"Night, kid," said Sam as he plugged the machine back in.

Soon the only sounds in the Walker household were Alan Walker's snoring and the kitchen faucet filling the occasional glass of water.

# TEN

THE RAINS WERE LONG GONE FROM THE SOUTHERN IOWA SKIES, BUT THE memory of their passing still lingered in the air the next day. The air was hot and humid; thick enough to almost swim through, it seemed. Alex wiped the glaze of sweat from his forehead and glanced over his shoulder at the three Replodians, who seemed to be at home in the muggy conditions. After a short delay while Sam fretted over the "gross inefficiency" of the internal combustion engine in Mr. Walker's pickup truck, the quartet had begun their search.

Alex's dog, Rocky, had not taken kindly to the Replodians at first, Sam in particular. After some coaxing, however, Moe managed to get the dog to let him briefly scratch him behind the ears.

It didn't take long to find the covered well in the woods. If not for Alex's guidance, the Replodians would have walked right past it. They parted the thick tangle of weeds and brambles, exposing a large cement disc on the ground.

"That's it," Alex said.

Lamont brushed the boy aside with his arm. "Stand back."

The Replodian crouched and grabbed the sides of the disc. The cement crumbled as the alien's fingers dug in.

"Remember," Sam called, "lift with your back, not your knees."

"Shut up, Sam," Lamont growled.

Sam smirked.

With a grunt, Lamont lifted the cover stone, passing it before Alex's astonished eyes before tossing it aside.

Alex gawked at the discarded disc. "Whoa."

Moe knelt beside the hole, brushing aside the squirming worms and insects scrambling for cover from the sunlight filtering through the forest canopy. He peered into the gloom and immediately recoiled, wrinkling his nose.

"Well," said Sam. "Anything?"

Moe shook his head. "Not what we're looking for."

Alex cautiously stepped to the edge and looked down. At the bottom of the hole, just barely visible in the dim lighting, was a pool of black, stagnant water.

Sam looked over his shoulder. "Oh, that's nasty."

Lamont sighed. "Now what?"

Alex racked his brain. Where would one hide the entrance to a top-secret alien base? It would have to be inconspicuous, yet accessible, probably hidden in plain sight. He looked up and scanned the trees, and then, through a break in the foliage he saw it.

"The silo."

Sam cocked an eyebrow. *"Wazzat?"*

Alex pointed. The Replodians followed his gaze to the sixty-foot concrete spire jutting up over the horizon.

Moe squinted. "Seems a bit exposed, doesn't it?"

"It's worth a shot," said Lamont. "How do we get there?"

Alex pointed northward. "We can cut through this pasture."

Lamont turned to his brothers. "You heard the kid. Let's go."

Sam muttered something indistinct as he fell into step behind his brother. If Lamont heard it, he didn't give any indication. A minute later, they broke through the tree line and into knee-high grass. The only markings in the field were the paths left by Alex and his father two days earlier.

*"Ow!"* Lamont slapped his palm against the back of his neck. When he examined his hand, his lip curled in disgust. "What is this?"

Alex trudged through the grass and peered at the smear. "Oh, that's just a mosquito. Get used to 'em. They're thick this year."

Lamont wiped its remains on the leg of his jeans. "What *are* they?"

"Blood-sucking bugs," Alex explained.

At that moment, a rather large mosquito landed on Sam's hand, and he felt a light stinging sensation. He watched, fascinated, as the insect began to feed, its abdomen radiating a soft yellow glow. Then something unexpected happened. The mosquito convulsed briefly, withered, and died. Within seconds, nothing remained but a fine black powder that was carried away by the wind.

"Hmm," said Sam. "It looks like we're not their brand."

As they resumed walking, Moe said, "What are we going to do if the entrance isn't in that silo?"

"I don't know," said Alex. "I'm starting to run out of ide—"

The ground beneath his feet disappeared, and he plunged into a deep hole. His breath caught in his throat, and he struck bottom before he could call out. The back of his head bounced off one of the stones lining the side of the hole, and tears welled in his eyes as his hand flew to the tender lump rising on his scalp.

Above him, the Replodians scrambled for the hole, each calling out frantically for him. Rocky reached the hole first; his shrill, yelping barks echoed off of the walls.

"Hey, kid," Sam called. "You all right?"

"Yeah," Alex replied weakly. "I'm okay."

"Where did this hole come from?" asked Moe. "Is it some kind of trap?"

"It looks like another well," said Lamont. "It must have never been capped."

"Well that was stupid," said Sam. "What moron would leave an open hole unmarked?"

Moe cleared his throat and held up a metal fence post, thick with rust and bent at a forty-five-degree angle. Apparently something had bent and pulled the marker from the ground, leaving the well virtually invisible in the tall grass.

"Hold on, Alex," called Moe. "We'll get you out. Just hold tight."

"Okay," said Alex. He grabbed his head. If only the dog would shut up, maybe his head would stop throbbing.

As his eyes became accustomed to the darkness, Alex noticed a stone directly in front of him that was smoother than the rest in the well. He reached out to wipe the dust and mud from it. As the dirt came away, he realized it wasn't a stone after all, but a glass panel with a glowing red light in the lower left corner.

"Hey, guys, I think I found something."

"What is it?" asked Moe.

"How should I know?" replied Alex. "Ow, my head!"

"We'll be right down," said Lamont. "Sit tight."

Alex reached out and touched the panel. He hesitated for a moment and then—holding his breath—pressed his palm flat against the glass. The red light blinked out and was replaced by a bright green one on the right.

A loud clanking sound emanated from the other side of the wall as if a heavy deadbolt had been thrown back. A section of wall, large enough for a man to stand comfortably in, slid back, releasing a blast of frigid air into the well. Alex shivered at the sudden temperature change and watched as the false wall slid back another foot farther, then shifted suddenly to the right. Darkness greeted Alex from the new hole in the wall.

A disembodied female voice echoed from inside, "Welcome, Alex Walker."

"G-g-guys!" The icy air made his teeth chatter. "I th-th-think we can s-st-stop looking now."

Lamont jumped down into the hole first, and immediately checked Alex's head for lacerations. He paused once during the examination to zip his jacket, tucking his chin to his chest to ward off the chill. Finally he concluded that the bump on the back of Alex's head was nothing to worry about and gestured to Moe.

Moe scooped Rocky into his arms and dropped down beside Lamont. The dog squirmed until the Replodian released him. His paws had hardly touched the ground before he started licking Alex's face.

"Get off!" Alex protested, shoving the dog away.

"Hey," Sam shouted from above. "What's the hold up down there?"

Lamont hugged his arms to his chest, slipping his hands under his armpits "It's cold."

"Oh," said Sam. "Well, in that case, you go ahead. I'll stand watch."

"Get down here!" Lamont snapped.

"Fine! Jeez!" Sam climbed down the shaft, using the rough stones as foot and handholds.

It was cramped in the confined space of the well, but the heat radiating from the Replodians relieved some of the chill in the air. Finally, the air warmed to a tolerable level and they entered the darkened chamber one-by-one, fanning out to search the room.

Alex felt along the wall. "I can't see a thing. How do we turn on the lights?"

At the mention of the word "lights," the room blinked to life. From every corner, bright white lights flickered on and illuminated the expansive chamber. On the west end of the room, a large view screen occupied most of the wall. A raised circular platform stood in the center of the chamber. A similar device descended from the ceiling directly above it.

Moe whistled. "This place is huge! Look, there's a door. There's more to it than just this room."

"And there's another." Alex pointed to the north wall. "It must spread out underneath the entire farm."

"I wasn't expecting anything like this," said Lamont.

"What *were* you expecting?" asked Sam. "A tree house with a secret handshake to get in? Maybe a sign that says, 'No girls allowed'?"

"No, I just wasn't expecting something this... *big*."

Sam smirked. "That's what *she* said."

Moe pointed to the object in the center of the room. "What do you suppose that thing is?"

Sam scrutinized the machine. "Looks like some kind of three-dimensional imaging device."

"How would you know?" asked Moe.

Sam's brow furrowed. "I'm not sure. I just... do."

"It's probably the same reason he's so good at fixing stuff," said Alex. "I bet we'll find all our answers here."

"Where do we start?" asked Moe.

Lamont approached the machine. "We might as well start in the middle and work our way out."

Lamont joined his brother and examined the controls on the base of the unit, looking for any indication of how to turn the thing on. Finally he found a palm scanner, much like the one on the door. He pressed his palm against the icy glass and sighed. "Nothing."

"Let me try," said Alex. "My handprint opened the door. Maybe it can turn on all the machines."

Sam nodded. "It's worth a shot. Give it a try, kid."

Alex rubbed his hands together to warm them, and then pressed his palm against the glass. The entire panel glowed a brilliant green and a loud hum emanated from the machine. Rocky whined and pressed his head against Alex's leg.

A beam of blue light, almost six feet in diameter, fired from the depression in the machine's base and surged into the top section. The light grew in intensity until everyone was forced to cover their eyes. Rocky barked furiously at the light, dancing around Alex's legs.

"What is that?" yelled Alex.

"If my theory is correct," said Sam, "we're about to get our answer."

Moe pointed at the beam. "Look!"

Alex and the stunned aliens lowered their arms and watched in awe as the blue light slowly took on a humanoid form. When the image stabilized, a three-dimensional blue figure stood flickering in the middle of the projector's lower platform. Rocky barked at the figure, and Alex—keeping his eyes on the hologram—felt the dog's head and placed his hand over his muzzle to quiet him.

"Can I just say I'm *so* glad we brought the dog?" Sam said.

"Shut up, Sam," said Moe.

The figure was tall, nearly eight feet, with long hair braided down the back. His large nose was positioned low on his forehead, nestled between kind, soulful eyes. A long, braided goatee hung from his strong chin down to six-fingered hands that clasped the head of a knobby wooden walking stick in front of his body. A deep, comforting voice seemed to fill every corner of the room as the translucent figure began to speak in flawless, unaccented English.

"Greetings, Alexander," said the hologram. "My name is Amaadoss. I am your father."

Alex took a step toward the machine. "My father?"

The image of Amaadoss continued, "By the time you see this, I shall be gone. Claimed, I fear, by the illness infecting my bones. Knowing my impending fate, I have uploaded a copy of my essence into this facility's central computer. But grieve not for me, my son, for you are not alone in this world.

"To aid you, I have sent with you to Earth three companions. These beings are from the planet Replodia. They have much to teach you, my son, to prepare you for your vital mission."

"What *is* my mission?" asked Alex. "What are we supposed to do?"

The image responded, "There is a race of beings, from a planet in what your people call the Zeta Reticuli system, called the Seignso. For millennia, the Seignso have been manipulating the human race for their own sinister purposes. Long before you were born, the Seignso began preparations for the final phase of their master plan for humanity. They aided in the creation of a human child with advanced mental powers.

"This child was the genetic clone of a man known on your planet as Genghis Khan, a Mongolian warrior king of incredible power and influence. While you've been growing these past thirteen years, this new Khan has been rallying support from those who would see his predecessor's dream of world conquest fulfilled. I believe the Seignso's ultimate goal is to use this Khan's conquest of your world to harvest the strongest, most resilient humans."

"For what purpose?" asked Lamont.

"Breeding stock," Amaadoss explained. "Breeding stock for the ultimate army; one that would rival any force in the galaxy. This cannot be allowed to happen, for if this new Khan and the Seignso are successful, it will spell disaster for the people of Earth as well as the entire Federation of Allied Systems."

Alex cast a nervous glance toward Lamont, which the Replodian returned.

The hologram resumed speaking, "To combat this threat, I have created you, my son. You are Temujin's equal. Using similar methods to those used to create him, I created you and gave you mental abilities far exceeding those of ordinary humans."

"What kind of abilities?" asked Alex.

The hologram smiled. "Have you ever imagined you heard someone speaking when there was no one else in the room? Have you ever finished someone else's sentences for them? Or have you ever made things happen, made objects move, just by thinking about them?"

Suddenly Alex remembered the kitchen door, and how he had stopped his father from punching the driver of the pickup truck. He remembered all the times he ever thought he heard whispers in a silent classroom, and suddenly his ability to communicate mentally with the aliens made total sense.

"It is with these same abilities that Temujin plans to cripple the world," said Amaadoss, "and march his Golden Horde across the globe, destroying any who dare to oppose him."

"But he has an army," said Alex. "What can the four of us do against an entire army?"

The image of Amaadoss smiled. "When I created you, my son, I set out not only to create the perfect soldier, but to prove a point—that vast military forces are not necessary to achieve peace. You are the first of a new breed of warrior. It is my dream that one day thousands of systems will be defended by small groups of elite warriors such as you. You shall be the defenders of your nations, your planet, and your system. You are the Terran Defense Corps."

---

As the hologram rambled on, Sam silently slipped away from the group and made his way toward the circular door on the east wall. As he approached, he noticed a palm scanner just like the one inside the well. He glanced back at the others to make sure he was not being watched. Satisfied, he placed his palm on the scanner and the same electronic voice asked, "Identification please."

Softly, he said, "Unit 3000572694 *dash* 003."

The lock disengaged. Sam smirked as the door cracked open in the center and the two halves slid aside into the wall with a whispering hiss. The Replodian stepped inside the darkened room and waited for the doors to slide shut behind him.

"Lights."

The lights blinked on and Sam found himself in a room considerably smaller than the main chamber. All four walls were lined with numerous racks stocked with advanced alien weaponry.

He sneered. "Come to papa."

---

BACK IN THE MAIN CHAMBER, ALEX AND THE OTHER REPLODIANS continued their orientation with the towering hologram.

"The Replodians I have provided for you are each programmed for specific functions," Amaadoss explained. "Unit 001 is programmed with extensive knowledge of both human and Replodian anatomy. This unit will serve as the chief medical officer for the TDC."

Lamont nodded.

Amaadoss motioned toward Moe. "Unit 002 is programmed in combat and espionage tactics. This unit will serve as your combat instructor and primary intelligence operative."

"Cool!" Alex looked at Moe. "You're a spy. Like James Bond."

Moe's chest swelled with pride.

The hologram continued, "Unit 003 is programmed with extensive knowledge of mechanical and electronic systems. This unit will serve as the TDC's mechanic, engineer, and science officer."

Alex turned to look at Sam, but noticed the blond-haired Replodian was missing. "Hey. Where's Sam?"

Lamont turned. "Sam," he called.

Suddenly the door behind them opened, and Sam stepped into the main chamber, a large alien assault rifle in his hands.

"Hey, check it out," said Moe. "Sam found the armory."

"Great." Lamont smirked. "New toys for him to play with."

Alex laughed. "You think he's going to take all of the guns apart and put them back together again?"

Sam cocked the weapon; an electric hum pulsed from it.

"Sam?" Lamont's smile faded. "Sam, what are you doing?"

The rogue Replodian raised the weapon to his shoulder and trained it on Alex.

"Sam?" Lamont took a step backward, reaching back to usher Alex behind him. "Sam!"

Sam's voice was devoid of any emotion as he squeezed the trigger. "So long, kid."

Lamont held his hand out. "Sam, no!"

A red plasma blast exploded from the weapon's barrel. In the blink of an eye, Moe jumped into the path of the blast and took the impact in his chest, splashing the floor with steaming, yellow blood. The wounded Replodian fell to the floor and slumped against the base of the hologram projector.

"Unit 003!" The image of Amaadoss banged its walking stick against the bottom of the projector, emitting a thunderous, artificial *crack* that reverberated through the room. "Cease fire immediately!"

"Sorry, old man." Sam trained the weapon on the projector's base. "I don't take orders from you anymore."

The weapon fired again, and Moe rolled out of the way before the plasma bolt pierced the projector's metal skin. Sparks flew from the machine and the image of Amaadoss flickered and vanished. Moe looked down and watched as the gaping, luminous hole in his chest began to slowly close—a little too slowly. When he looked up, Sam stood over him with the smoking weapon aimed directly at his head.

"Sam?" Moe's voice was just as wounded as his body. "Why are you doing this?"

"Relax, little brother. It'll all be over soon."

Sam squeezed the trigger. Rocky darted in and bit his leg, and the

Replodian screamed. He looked down at the snarling dog and kicked. Rocky sailed through the air and slammed against the wall.

"Rocky!" Alex shouted.

Sam leveled his weapon at the dog's still form. "Filthy little—"

Lamont stepped in and jerked the weapon's sizzling barrel up toward the ceiling. The shot went wide.

Lamont grappled with Sam for control of the rifle. "Alex, get out of here! *Run!*"

Alex scooped Rocky into his arms and made a mad dash for the door set into the north wall, quickly palming the scanner as a stray plasma bolt struck the wall next to his head. He stepped into a darkened hallway, and the door slammed shut behind him, sealing him inside. He leaned back against the door and slid to the floor, tears streaming down his cheeks.

---

LAMONT LASHED OUT WITH AN ELBOW TO HIS BROTHER'S NOSE AND loosened his grip just enough to wrench the rifle out of his hands. Sam stumbled back and stared daggers at his brother as he wiped away a trickle of yellow blood from his upper lip.

"You think that gun changes anything, *Lamont*?" Sam snarled, flicking the blood from his finger. "Smug as always, aren't you?"

Lamont pointed the weapon at his brother. "What the hell do you think you're doing, Sam?"

Sam sniffed back another drop of blood and reached behind his back. "My job."

He ignited the laser sword concealed behind his back and swung the white-hot blade in an upward arc. The blade sliced the rifle clean in two and left a smoking gash in Lamont's shirt. Lamont had only a second to stare bewilderedly at the pieces of melted metal in his hands before Sam brought the sword around for a swipe at his neck. Lamont bent at the knees and fell backward to avoid the blade, which sliced the air with a menacing sizzle barely an inch from his face. He lashed out with a front push kick to his brother's chest. Sam stumbled back a couple feet, but easily recovered and leapt into the air. He brought the blade down, planning to plunge it into Lamont's chest.

By now, Moe was back on his feet, the wound in his chest barely larger than a quarter. He jumped into the air and collided with Sam's side, knocking his brother off course. Sam tumbled to the ground and the laser sword skittered away, coming to rest underneath a computer console on the west wall. When Sam stood again, Moe had already adopted a deep fighting stance.

Sam smirked. "We know you can beat up on kids. Think you can take *me?*"

"Let's find out." Moe lunged, unleashing a barrage of kicks.

Sam laughed as he blocked and dodged his brother's feet repeatedly. "Not so good against somebody as strong as you, are you, little *sister?*"

Moe changed up his strategy with a powerful uppercut to Sam's chin, knocking him off his feet. As Sam's body rose into the air, Moe delivered a bone-crushing spinning side kick into his ribs and sent him flying toward the line of computers on the west wall. Sam's back connected with the edge of one of the consoles, and he fell to the floor. As he tried to get up, his fingers brushed against a metallic cylindrical object under the console.

The laser sword.

Sam ignited the weapon and ran toward Moe, readying for a powerful double-handed overhead stroke. Moe met him halfway, stopping the momentum of the sword with an X-block to Sam's wrists. Moe wrapped his fingers around the hilt of the sword with one hand and pulled on Sam's weak arm with his other. As Sam stumbled forward, knocked off balance, Moe wrenched the sword away from him and quickly adopted a guard stance with the tip of the blade pointed at his brother.

Sam turned and laughed "You think you're better than me?"

"What the hell has come over you?" said Moe. "Have you lost your mind?"

Sam ignored the questions. "Do you? You think you're *better* than me?"

Moe tightened his grip on the laser sword and prepared to defend himself.

"You're not!" shouted Sam, his muscles tensing to spring.

"Samrai!"

Lamont stood in the open doorway of the armory, aiming a fresh assault rifle at Sam's head. He approached slowly. "Don't move, Sam. It's over."

At these words, Alex emerged from the hallway, but stayed in the relative safety of the open doorway, ready to run if necessary. At the sight of the teenager, Sam's rage seemed to escalate to a higher level and he prepared to lunge at him, but stopped short as the white-hot blade of the laser sword appeared underneath his chin. Moe slowly stepped around him to block his view of Alex, keeping the blade poised at his throat.

"Give it up, Sam," said Lamont. "It's finished."

"Like I said," said Sam. "Smug."

"It's *over*," Moe shouted.

"No." Sam shook his head slowly and smiled. "I'm just getting started."

Before his brothers could react, Sam jumped into the air and flipped over Lamont's head. As he landed, he turned and ran for the open door leading to the well. Lamont fired the rifle at the fleeing traitor. Instead of plasma, however, the rifle fired small spherical projectiles in rapid succession, which missed Sam and splattered a purple gel onto the wall when they ruptured.

Lamont turned the rifle over in his hands. "What the hell is this thing? A *paintball* gun?"

The momentary distraction was all Sam needed to make his escape. He disappeared into the well, and his voice echoed throughout the chamber, "This isn't over! Count on it!"

Moe released the laser sword's ignition switch and tossed it away. Lamont pointed the rifle at the floor and looked over his shoulder at Alex, who was approaching them slowly and cautiously.

"Are you all right?" asked Lamont.

Alex nodded.

"And Rocky?"

Alex looked at the door and patted his leg. Rocky hobbled out of the shadows, his left front paw held up. Lamont knelt beside him and felt his leg. Rocky whimpered softly, and the Replodian shushed him, nodding sympathetically.

"We'll have to splint it," Lamont concluded.

Moe approached the smoking hologram projector and shook his head. "This thing is totaled. What was that maniac doing?"

"It's like he just snapped," said Alex. "One minute he was fine, and the next minute he was trying to kill us."

"I believe him," said Lamont gravely. "This isn't over."

Alex joined Moe by the projector. "Well, what about Father?"

The voice of Amaadoss rumbled through the chamber, "I am here, Alexander."

Alex looked up at the projector expectantly, but the platform was dark and empty.

"Where are you?" he asked. "I can't see you."

"My essence is integrated into the central computer," Amaadoss explained. "It has always been there. When I uploaded myself into the mainframe, I replaced the original operating system. Simply put, I *am* the computer."

"What would have caused Sam to attack us like that?" asked Lamont.

"That I do not know," said the voice of Amaadoss. "It would appear that his programming was altered during the implantation process. However, this cannot be the case. I trust the person who oversaw the transfer implicitly. He would not have betrayed me."

"We can't worry about that now," said Lamont. "His blasts destroyed a lot of the equipment. We need to repair the damage before we can be fully operational."

"That's just great!" Moe threw up his hands in frustration. "Our engineer just went homicidal and flew the coop. We're screwed."

"Do not despair," said Amaadoss. "The mainframe contains detailed schematics of all the equipment. I can guide you through most of the repairs. However, I'm afraid the necessary components to repair the hologram projector do not exist on Earth."

"We'll just have to live without it," said Lamont. "Let's get to work. We're burning daylight."

Moe sniffed the air. "Speaking of burning, does anyone else smell that?"

Alex and Lamont looked around and sniffed; it didn't take long to find the source of the mysterious odor.

Alex pointed. "Look!"

Lamont looked over at the wall he'd hit with the assault rifle during Sam's escape. Smoke poured from the metal surface of the wall where the strange purple gel had adhered to it. The gel was eating the metal, like highly concentrated acid.

Lamont ejected the magazine. "What *is* this stuff?"

Nestled inside were more of the little round balls. Upon closer inspection, he saw that the spheres were divided into two fluid-filled internal compartments—one red, the other blue.

"Red and blue makes..." Lamont looked from the strange projectiles to the wall, which was still smoking, but not as much. "Purple."

"The two chemicals must combine and start a chemical reaction upon impact," Moe said. "That stuff dissolves whatever it comes in contact with."

"Jesus," said Alex. "It's Satan's paintball gun!"

Lamont carefully placed the rifle and magazine on the floor and backed away. "I vote we don't touch any more weapons until we read the instruction manual front to back. Agreed?"

"Agreed," said Alex and Moe in unison.

---

SAM RAN ALONG THE EDGE OF THE ROAD, HEADING EAST, AWAY FROM THE farm. Emotion and logic clashed inside his head. He'd actually grown to like the kid, but his programming was quite clear. The kid had to die, along with his brothers, and their technology had to be smashed beyond repair. He just couldn't figure out *why*.

The roar of an approaching engine caught Sam's attention, and he turned as a battered green flatbed pickup slowed and pulled over beside him. The old man driving rolled down his window and called out in a toothless voice, "Where you headed, son?"

Sam furrowed his brow. Obviously he couldn't face his brothers head on, they had a tactical advantage, and they'd be waiting; they'd blow his head off the second he stuck it through the door. What he needed was reinforcements. A thought popped into his head, and he smiled.

"How far to Mongolia, old man?" he asked.

The driver tilted his head, directing his ear toward the hitchhiker. "Eh? Magnolia?"

Sam grabbed the door and wrenched it off its hinges. The old man's jaw went slack as the alien flung the door into the ditch like a Frisbee. He screamed as Sam pulled him from the truck and deposited him on the pavement. The Replodian climbed into the cab and made a show of buckling his seatbelt.

Sam smiled and waved. "Much obliged, gramps."

The truck roared off to the east, toward the interstate, leaving its owner in a cloud of exhaust fumes.

"Where the hell are you goin' with my truck?" the old man shouted at the retreating vehicle. "Magnolia's the *other* way!"

# ELEVEN

*Temple of the Golden Horde*
*Gobi Desert, Mongolia*
*July 25th*

TEMUJIN BRUSHED A STRAND OF LONG, BLACK HAIR BEHIND HIS EAR AND adjusted his black and gold silk robe before turning to look out on the men assembled in his expansive new throne room. Vivid tapestries and red and gold silk curtains hung all around the room, concealing the rough stone and concrete beneath. Although his namesake had been content to live out most of his days in tents and straw huts, this new Temujin was not.

The artisans had followed his designs to the letter, converting the crumbling decommissioned Soviet airbase into something much more befitting of a king. The offensive visages of Lenin had been painted over, replaced with vivid murals of conquering Mongol horsemen.

Unfortunately, the peasants assembled before him were a far cry from the Mongols of old, but they would have to do. Faces of every color gazed up at him in reverence. Some had come from as far as the Americas to serve him. He wrinkled his nose at their collective stench.

None of them had bathed in days, some of them weeks. Loathsome as they may have been, they were also fierce, loyal warriors.

Heavy footfalls from behind signaled the arrival of General Chuluun, a tall, muscular man of around fifty. Chuluun had been the Khan's bodyguard since the day he was born, and he had protected his birth mother before that. When not training the troops, Chuluun was always at his Khan's side. Of all his disciples, Chuluun alone held Temujin's admiration, playing the roles of both father and brother to the young warlord-in training. Temujin even occasionally shared his harem with the general; a small price to pay for unwavering loyalty and devotion.

Two weeks earlier, Chuluun and the elite guard thwarted a poorly planned attempt on the Khan's life by one of the soldiers. The peasant had declared Temujin a false prophet and claimed following him into battle against the combined world powers would result only in humiliating defeat and death. Temujin had greatly enjoyed squeezing the blasphemer's skull with the power of his mind until his eyes popped out of their sockets, but not nearly as much as he enjoyed forcing the sobbing traitor's last meal into his mouth: two pieces of toast smeared with a jelly made from those same eyeballs. After the incident, morale among the troops regarding Temujin's divinity was at an all-time high.

The Khan stepped onto a raised platform and stretched his hands outward. The soldiers cheered enthusiastically at the sight of their king, many of them with weapons raised high above their heads.

He twisted one strand of his long, black mustache between his thumb and forefinger, his lips curling into a smirk as he soaked in his followers' admiration. Finally the crowd's exultation faded, and Temujin's voice boomed throughout the cavernous room.

"My children," he said, "the time will soon be upon us. Soon we will march across this world and claim that which is rightfully ours. But, we are not yet ready. Our numbers are still too few, even though many arrive to join our cause each and every day.

"But fear not, my loyal dogs of war. When the world is ripe for the picking, we will claim our birthright... our *destiny*! Then the unfaithful of this wretched world will know the power of the new Khaghan. They shall tremble before the power of the living god!"

Once again the crowd erupted into thunderous applause, and Temujin raised his hand for silence. He opened his mouth to speak, but the words caught in his throat when a voice speaking in English rose from the back of the room.

"I might be able to help you with that."

The sea of soldiers parted down the middle to reveal a lone white man with untidy blond hair striding confidently toward the platform. The man took off his dark sunglasses and placed them into the breast pocket of his blue denim jacket. As he cleared the bewildered foot soldiers, the new arrival crouched and launched himself up to the top of the platform in a single bound, landing on his feet only a few feet from where Temujin stood.

"That is, if you're interested in actually *winning* this war, of course" said the stranger.

Temujin stared. Who was this *fool* so brazen to walk unbidden into his court?

"Nice 'stache," the stranger said, pointing to Temujin's face. "But you know what it needs? Braid it and stick some beads on it. *Yeah.* The chicks would dig it."

The Khan smiled and, in fluent English, said, "Allow me the pleasure of knowing your name before Chuluun kills you."

The general drew his sword from the scabbard on his hip and advanced on the new arrival. The stranger smirked and pushed the blade away casually with one finger. He took one step toward the Khan, but stopped when Chuluun let out a warning growl.

"My name is Samrai," the stranger said, "and I have some information that I think will be worth an awful lot to you."

The Khan scowled impatiently. "Information regarding what, may I ask?"

"Alexander."

Temujin's eyes widened with obvious interest.

Sam smirked. "I see I have your attention."

Temujin turned and strode away from the platform toward the silk curtain at the back of the room, his robes flowing behind him.

"Bring him," he ordered. "And summon Captain Sükh to my chambers."

"As you wish, my Khan," said Chuluun, casting a suspicious glare at Sam.

———

A FEW MINUTES LATER, SAM WAS USHERED INTO TEMUJIN'S PRIVATE quarters. The room was almost filled to capacity with silk curtains, priceless Persian rugs, Tibetan tapestries, and plush cushions and pillows. In the center of the room on a stone pedestal rested an ornate silver casket. It was in front of this odd centerpiece that the Khan now stood, a glass of wine clutched in his left hand.

Sam gestured toward the coffin. "Shall I call you Dracula, or do you prefer Count?"

Chuluun drew his sword. "Profane dog!"

The Khan calmed his general with a wave and chuckled as he approached his guest. "Clever. No, this is the coffin of my predecessor, the man you know as Genghis Khan. Every night, I rest within the coffin in order to absorb his power. As for your comparison, although I have thoroughly studied and admire the tactics of Vlad Tepes, I must say that he lacked vision; he thought too small. Tepes sought only to punish those who had offended him. I, on the other hand, want nothing short of the entire world."

"Really," Sam drawled. "And what about the Seignso?"

Temujin's smile faded at the mention of the name. "You're well informed, sir. What of them?"

"Well, surely you realize that as soon as you've done all of the dirty work for them, they're just going to step in and take over everything you've worked so hard for."

"The thought has not escaped me," the Khan replied.

"And what do you plan to do when that day comes?"

At that moment, one of the curtains was brushed aside and a short, stocky Mongolian with a long goatee entered the room. This, Sam surmised, was Captain Sükh. The captain stood beside the Khan, opposite Chuluun, with one hand resting on the pommel of his *da dao*. Sam couldn't believe it; they were actually trying to intimidate him with numbers.

Silly humans.

Temujin smiled unpleasantly. "I'm sorry. I believe you said you had some information for me."

"I assume you would like to know the full name and location of the child named Alexander?"

"This name has plagued my dreams and disrupted my meditations since I was a boy, but nobody—not even the 'all-knowing' Seignso— can tell me who he is," said the Khan. "May I ask how *you* came by this information?"

"I am—was—a member of the TDC."

The acronym triggered puzzled expressions from the three humans.

"Is this some sort of... government agency?" Captain Sükh said.

Sam rolled his eyes and put a finger to his lips to shush the captain. "*Shhh!* Grown-ups are talking."

Sükh's face flushed.

"No," Sam said, "the Terran Defense Corps is an elite task force created exclusively to counteract your efforts. In other words, Your Heinous Highness, they've been sent to kill you."

Temujin pursed his lips, considering this new information. "But you have elected to come to me instead."

"You betcha."

"Why?"

Sam shrugged. "Let's just say I prefer to be on the winning team."

"You said that they were *sent*. Sent from where exactly?" asked the Khan. "The United States? Britain?"

Sam shook his head. "Replodia."

Temujin blinked. "I'm sorry?"

"Planet Replodia," Sam elaborated. "Alexander was supplied with three Replodian operatives to aid him in his fight against you. I happen to be one of those operatives."

"You are an alien?"

*"Correctamundo,"* said Sam.

"Let us assume for a moment that I believe you," said the Khan, setting down his glass. "What is it that you wish to gain from this transaction? Nothing is free."

"I want a job," said Sam. "And the chance to put foot to TDC ass."

"Is that all?"

Sam grinned. "That's it."

The Khan smiled. "I think we can accommodate you."

"Good deal."

"My lord." Sükh stepped forward. "We do not need this foreign dog's... *assistance.* My troops—"

"Troops?" Sam said. "Oh, right. You mean that Kindergarten I met outside. Those saps couldn't conquer a Sunday school picnic."

Sükh cursed in Mongolian and pulled his sword, exposing a few inches of polished steel.

Temujin held up a hand. "Stand down, Captain."

Sükh stepped back and slid the blade back into its sheathe. He bowed his head, his eyes flicking up to glower at the Replodian.

Sam sneered. "Sit, Sookie! *Goooood* boy."

"Silence!" Temujin barked.

Sam held up his hands in a gesture of surrender.

"Now," said the Khan, his voice laden with anticipation, "the child's name."

"You got it," said Sam. "The kid's name is *Alexwalulllilmmm.*"

Temujin blinked. "What?"

Sam shook his head and tried again. "His name is Alex... *Alexwallll-rooob. Alexweerrrebeelll.* Damn it!"

"What is it?" demanded the Khan. "Give me the name. *Now!*"

Sam gritted his teeth and snarled, "I can't!"

"Why not?"

Sam shook his head. "I don't know. Something's not allowing me to answer the question."

"Forget the name," the Khan bellowed. "The location."

Sam nodded. "Okay. He lives just outside of *Bowaaaarooom. Banawerp.* He lives in *Iwerum.*" The Replodian swore and tore at his hair.

"What is the problem?" Temujin growled. "Why won't you answer?"

Sam shook his head, clearing the growing dizziness. "It must be some kind of hidden subroutine in my programming. I'm unable to divulge sensitive information about my host organism."

"*What?*"

The entire room began to shake with Temujin's anger and the unfinished glass of wine sitting atop the sarcophagus shattered. Chuluun and Sükh covered their faces until the invisible wave of power finally subsided.

"It's probably some kind of failsafe to keep me from talking in case of capture and torture," Sam explained.

"Let us test that theory, shall we?" Temujin reached out with his mind and bore down on Sam's skull with his power.

Sam scoffed, "That won't work on me, pal. I'm not human, remember? This isn't even my true form."

"Then let us try more conventional methods. Chuluun!"

The Mongol general drew his sword and advanced on the Replodian. Sam drew a crudely constructed pistol with dual nozzles protruding from the barrel and fired a warning shot past Chuluun's head. Two chemicals—one red, one blue—combined in midair into a stream of purple gel that burned through the silk curtains and exposed an ugly, cracked concrete wall on the other side. The gel sizzled as it ate through the masonry, sending plumes of acrid smoke up the wall.

Sam adjusted his aim directly between the general's eyes. "One more step and I'll melt your face off, Jackie Chan!"

Temujin pointed at the pistol. "What is *that?*"

"You like it?" Sam kept the pistol trained on Chuluun. "I made it on the freighter that carried me across the Pacific. It's a little crude, I'll admit, but it's really amazing what a few spare parts and some common household chemicals can do in a pinch."

"Can you make more of these weapons?"

Sam nodded. "No problem."

With a wave of the Khan's hand, the two Mongol officers sheathed their weapons. The warrior king stepped toward Sam, a smile spreading across his face.

"Perhaps you *can* serve me after all."

# PART THREE
# QUINTIN

# TWELVE

*Folaxian System, Folax Alpha 5 - Planet Rhen'fa*
*September 25th - Three Years Later*

KREEG BONWOPPA SWATTED THE BAKA LEAVES ASIDE AND RAN AS FAST AS his four insectoid legs would carry him. His breath came in ragged gasps as more leaves slapped him in the face, stinging all sixteen of his eyes. As the edge of the forest came into sight, he looked over his shoulder. No one was following him.

He slowed to a stop and, when his breathing returned to normal, allowed himself a low chuckle at the expense of his would-be captors. The fools. Those worthless hacks at Hunter HQ had sent a child after him. A *human* child no less. No human could outrun a tarnak.

He was startled by a loud rustling in the trees above him and scanned the leafy canopy for a moment. A winged creature erupted from the foliage and screeched overhead. Kreeg exhaled. For a moment, he'd actually thought the little punk had caught up to him.

Ridiculous.

As he turned to exit the forest, a bipedal figure dropped out of the trees in front of him, silhouetted against the red starlight filtering through the trees. A pair of glowing green eyes burned from the figure's shadowy face.

Kreeg took a step back. "Impossible!"

"Kreeg Bonwoppa," the figure said, continuing in Phaedojian, "you are under arrest for the murder of Hunter Ian Manson and escaping from Moebius Penal Colony."

"Screw you, flesh-bag!" Kreeg's mandibles clicked tauntingly. "You'll never take me alive."

The hunter took a step closer and Kreeg could plainly make out the human's long red hair. He was young. It was impossible to make an educated approximation of his age, since he had only seen a few fully developed humans. The hunter he'd killed, Manson, had been much older than this brat.

The kid smirked. "Who said my orders say anything about bringing you in *alive*?"

"You can't kill me!" Kreeg staggered backward. "Your job is to retrieve me and take me back to prison. I'm unarmed. You're not allowed to use lethal force in capturing a fugitive. You won't get paid."

The human shrugged. "When pursuing a hunter killer, things tend to get mixed up. Warrants disappear. Orders get misinterpreted. The fugitive goes missing. You know how these things go."

Kreeg's multiple eyes blinked spasmodically and he took another step backward. The hunter compensated with a long forward stride, his hand slowly moving toward the laser sword sheathed on his belt.

"Stay back," warned Kreeg.

"Surrender!" said the human. "And I might make this quick."

Seeing no other way out, the tarnak fugitive unfolded the razor-sharp serrated appendages concealed in his arms. "I said stay back!"

The hunter deepened his stance and stared at the limbs, which had been used by primitive tarnaks for catching and tearing apart prey. Since becoming "civilized" and joining the Federation, however, the appendages had become redundant. Recently convicted tarnak criminals underwent surgery to remove them, but grandfathered-in convicts like Kreeg Bonwoppa were allowed to keep them. This was unfortunate, because Bonwoppa used them to kill Ian Manson when he decided he had seen enough of Moebius Penal Colony.

"Looking to add another murder onto your sentence, Kreeg?" The human drew the energy sword, his thumb poised on the igniter switch.

"I'll kill a hundred of you if it means not going back to Moebius," Kreeg snarled. He lunged at the hunter with a screeching battle cry.

The human leapt into the air and flew over the charging tarnak, surprised by the sudden burst of speed. As his feet touched the ground, he flicked his thumb and a white-hot beam projected from the sword's hilt. Kreeg turned around on his insectlike legs and clicked his mandibles threateningly.

"I think you'll find that my head doesn't come off quite so easily, Kreeg," said the hunter.

The tarnak raised his appendages and shrieked as he lunged in for the killing blow. Ready this time, the human sidestepped the attack and sliced both appendages off with an upward swipe of the energy blade. Kreeg squealed and staggered to a halt, staring down at the smoking stumps. The tarnak fell to what passed for his knees and sobbed pitifully as thick, gelatinous green goo seeped from the wounds. A shadow fell over him, and Kreeg looked up into the hunter's cold, accusing eyes.

"Please," Kreeg whimpered. "Show mercy. Please."

"Kreeg Bonwoppa..." The hunter raised the sword high over his head. "You have been charged with escaping from a Federation penal colony, murdering a hunter, theft of a long-range Federation spacecraft, and resisting arrest. I hereby summarily sentence you to death."

"You can't do that!"

The hunter shrugged. "I'm making this up as I go."

Kreeg closed his eyes and cringed as the white-hot blade sizzled through the air and sliced through his neck.

# THIRTEEN

*Moebius Penal Colony, Moebius Alpha 2, beta 3*
*Hunter HQ*

MOEBIUS PENAL COLONY, LOCATED ON THE SECOND PLANET FROM THE giant blue sun—likewise named Moebius—was a volcanic rock, with a high sulfur content atmosphere and mercury pools and seas that stretched for hundreds of miles. There were no sentient beings indigenous to the lava planet, and any prisoners able to survive unprotected on the surface were sent to the frigid D'mak Tel prison on Moebius Alpha 12.

Moebius prisoners were protected from the harsh elements by powerful heat shields, and were given insulated suits while working within the obsidian mines. The prisoners' complaints that the suits were defective, and only blocked a minuscule amount of heat, fell on deaf ears. The headquarters of the hunters, a Federation-funded interstellar police force, was located on the planet's third moon, where—thanks to ample thermal shielding—the heat was a bit more tolerable.

Claims agent Yimza Noofra looked up from painting the raised scales on the back of her hand as the door to the shuttle dock opened. She rolled her yellow reptilian eyes as the red-haired human stepped through the door with a canvas bag gripped tightly in his hand. The bag was wet, and a foul-smelling green substance dripped from the bottom, leaving a sticky trail on the freshly buffed floor. This made the third time today that a hunter had made a mess in her office. The human reached into the bag and, gripping it by the antennae, pulled out a severed tarnak head and placed it on the counter with a wet *splat*.

"Quintin MacLaren collecting the bounty on Kreeg Bonwoppa," said the hunter.

Yimza stared at MacLaren for a moment before producing a hand-held scanner and passing it over one of Bonwoppa's dull, lifeless black eyes. After a few seconds, the file flashed onto her screen and she checked the severed head on her desk against the file photo on the monitor.

"He's dead," she said.

"No kidding."

Yimza scowled. "He was supposed to stand trial for new charges."

"He resisted arrest," said MacLaren. "How's *that* for a new charge?"

Yimza glared at him before turning her eyes back to the screen and keying a short sequence of commands into the computer. She regarded him with a suspicious gaze as the machine buzzed ominously.

"There's no record of any Quintin MacLaren in the payroll data-base," she said.

MacLaren stared blankly at her. He obviously hadn't been expecting this.

Yimza reached for the intercom switch. "I'm going to have to notify security."

"That won't be necessary," said a male voice from the open doorway to Yimza's left. "Transfer the bounty to my account. I'll see that he gets his money."

Yimza eyed the new arrival with almost the same amount of disdain she had shown for MacLaren. He was also human, with thick black hair and the same emerald green eyes as the younger man. He was dressed in the standard black jumpsuit, with an I.D. badge clipped to his chest that read: Long, Robert J.

"This is most irregular, Officer Long," said Yimza.

Long nodded and stood at the junior man's side. "Cadet MacLaren is training under Officer Boudreaux and myself."

"*Cadet* MacLaren? Last time I checked, it's against department policy for cadets to go on runs alone."

"It is," said Long. "Cadet MacLaren was under my indirect supervision. He made the kill, so he claims the bounty."

Yimza cocked an eyebrow. "Is that so?"

"That's what I'm putting in my report," said Long. "Now are you going to pay the bounty or do I have to file a grievance with your lieutenant?"

Yimza gestured toward the severed head. "The mark is dead."

"The cadet defended himself accordingly," said Long. "The mark was a known hunter killer."

Yimza hesitated for a moment, but then began punching keys. "You're on thin ice here, Long. Next time I won't be so generous."

Long cast the cadet a covert glance. "Neither will I."

The computer beeped and Yimza read the report, "There. Your account has been credited in the amount of 15,000 Federation Credits. Would you like a receipt?"

"No, thank you," replied Long. "Come on, Quintin."

The two hunters exited the claims office through a side door. Yimza looked at the slimy severed head on her desk and punched a button on her terminal. A moment later, her voice filled the entire station.

"Sanitation to Claims, please."

A thick glob of the green goo dropped onto the floor with a nauseating *plop*.

Yimza keyed the public address system again. "Bring a mop."

---

ROBERT LONG WAS OLD—*REALLY* OLD. IN FACT, HE HAD FORGOTTEN HIS true age. Whenever Quintin asked about his friend's past, he would tell him stories of love, loss, and countless adventures, but there were lots of gaps. Often Long would pause and struggle to remember details of even the most significant things. However, he *never* forgot details about the wars in which he'd fought.

Memories fade with time, he had explained, and it was the same—if not more severe—with Methuselans. That was the name Long used for what they were; he didn't like the term *Homo immortalis* that Quintin had grown up hearing on Glynfyl. He also didn't care for the word *human*, saying it was reserved for a less-civilized primate, whatever that meant.

Robert Long wasn't even his real name, just the first one he could remember using. He could not even remember his parents, or where he came from, or the language he spoke there, but he did remember waking up on a beach in a place called "Eng Land" long ago. One day, he knew, he would forget being Robert Long entirely; that is, if he lived that long.

In the corridor, Quintin and Robert walked in silence awhile before Quintin finally spoke, switching from Phaedojian to heavily accented English, "Thanks for helping me get my money, Robert."

Robert came to a halt and looked at the boy. "You'll get your money when you go to the academy next term—for tuition."

"The academy?" cried Quintin. "But, Robert—"

"But *nothing*," Robert interjected. "You disobeyed a direct order. You were told to stay here on Moebius and let me and Rene go after Bonwoppa ourselves."

"But, Robert," Quintin protested, "that scumbag scragged Ian."

"That's right," Robert snapped, pinning Quintin to the wall with one powerful hand. "He *did*! Not many beings can kill one of our kind with their *bare hands*, and Kreeg Bonwoppa did just that. You're only sixteen, Quintin. Ian was nearly three hundred years old and a lot more experienced than you—a trained soldier. You're damned lucky that it's not *your* head in a bag!"

Quintin hung his head. "I'm sorry, Robert."

Robert let him go, tousled the youth's hair affectionately, and slipped an arm around his shoulders. He leaned in close. "How did he die?"

Quintin grinned. "On his knees. Begging."

Robert patted his back and they resumed their walk. "Good lad. Come on. The others are waiting."

"Are they mad?"

Robert drew in breath between his teeth as he stopped in front of a door and pressed his palm against the scanner. "They're not happy."

The door slid open with a soft hiss and the hallway was immediately filled with the sounds of two people—a man and a woman—shouting.

Quintin sighed and looked at Robert wearily. "They're fighting again?"

"Again?" Robert raised an eyebrow. "They never stopped."

"If you didn't fill his head with all of your stupid war stories," the woman shouted, "he wouldn't be so eager to go out there and prove himself. It's *your* fault."

"He doesn't have to prove himself to anyone," said the man in a thick Cajun accent. "And it is *not* my fault. The boy makes his own decisions."

Quintin and Robert entered the room and saw the feuding pair standing in the center of the room; only a game table positioned between them kept them from coming to blows. The woman was tall with shoulder-length red hair. The top of her black uniform was unzipped with the sleeves tied around her waist, leaving only a tight gray tank top to cover her torso. Quintin tried his best not to stare, but in the end, his adolescent hormones prevailed.

The man was almost a head shorter than the woman, with brown hair covered by a black bandana. His own jumpsuit was fully zipped, but the sleeves were rolled up, exposing his muscular arms.

"Rene. Cherry," said Robert as the door hissed shut behind him. "Put a sock in it, will you? I found him. He's fine."

Rene Boudreaux and Cheryl Sadler—the latter affectionately called "Cherry" by the other Methuselans on Moebius—turned.

Quintin braced himself as Cherry rushed forward and wrapped him in a crushing embrace.

"Are you all right?" she asked breathlessly.

"I'm fine," Quintin gasped.

Cherry looked him over, checking for bruises.

"Seriously!" Quintin brushed her hand away as she started checking his hairline for cuts. "I'm fine, Cherry."

"Let him be," said Rene. "He's a man, now."

Cherry whirled on the Cajun. "He's just a boy!"

Rene scoffed, "When I was his age, I'd already been killed twice in battle."

Cherry beat her fist against the Cajun's chest. "That's *exactly* what I'm talking about. You fill his head with these ideas."

"Oh, stop it, woman." Rene grabbed her wrist before she could strike him again. "You mother the boy too much."

Quintin rolled his eyes and retreated to a nearby sofa. He put in his ear buds, thumbing the PLAY button on the right-side ear unit to fill his ears with loud Phaedojian rock music.

Rene Boudreaux was much younger than Robert, and he remembered every minute detail about his childhood, or so he claimed. Like Robert, he'd been a soldier several times and claimed to have fought in every major war since "The War of Northern Aggression." Robert fought in the same war, but he called it "The Civil War," a name that usually sent Rene into long, incomprehensible rants in French.

Quintin knew little about Cherry because she didn't like talking about her past. Whenever the subject came up, she would get quiet and her whole body would start shaking. This usually resulted in Quintin being ushered out of the room by one of the men. Some nights, he heard her crying out and screaming in her sleep.

Rene and Cherry were an item, or at least they had been before Cherry accused Rene of sleeping with a female wrendagga hunter and called the whole thing off. Ever since then, they had been fighting nonstop about anything and everything. Robert insisted that they were still in love but were just too stubborn to kiss and make up.

When Quintin arrived in the Moebius System just over two cycles before, the others had already been stationed there for several cycles. It was the first time Quintin had ever met any other human beings, let alone a female. His teenage infatuation with Cherry hadn't gone unnoticed and she had taken to him like an older sister, or—sometimes, like today—the mother he never had. She was constantly worrying about his safety, and even more so than Robert, wanted very much for him to give up the notion of being a hunter and attend the academy on Phaedaj.

But Quintin had seen enough of Phaedaj. He'd seen enough of the Federation. He wanted to see Earth.

Bad.

Even though the others could speak nearly fluent Phaedojian when he met them, Robert had set himself to the task of teaching the youth English. Appalled when he learned of Quintin's lack of a last name, Robert bestowed him with the name MacLaren, one of his old aliases on Earth.

Quintin proved to be a quick study, and with English mastered, Rene had then begun teaching him French. Although, to Cherry's dismay, Quintin's French vocabulary mainly consisted of profanity and Louisiana colloquialisms. The Cajun's accent also found its way into the boy's speech patterns, along with Long's own myriad European inflections.

Suddenly the door slid open, and a short Glynfarian stepped into the room. He wore blue robes and shuffled over the threshold with the aid of a walking stick. At the sight of him, Cherry and Rene were instantly silenced, and Quintin removed his ear buds. The Glynfarian scowled at Quintin, the servos in his four gold ocular implants whirring and contracting the artificial irises.

"Uh... hi, Jiri," said Quintin nervously.

"So..." Jiri's voice was gravelly with age, which only made the effect of dual, overlapping tones more unsettling. "You've returned."

"Yes, sir," replied Quintin solemnly.

"Good." Jiri took two labored steps into the room, leaning heavily on his walking stick. "I assume that you've gotten it out of your system now?"

Quintin bowed his head. "Yes, sir."

"What would your father say if he were here right now?"

"I don't know," said Quintin in a voice barely above a whisper.

Amaadoss, his father, had had great plans for Quintin. The academy was always at the front of his mind, of course. He'd wanted Quintin to become a great diplomat, a spokesman for peace within the Federation. But after he died and Jiri was reassigned to Moebius as the Methuselans' custodian, Quintin had quickly set his sights on the exciting life of a hunter.

"We'll talk about this later, Son," said Jiri. "Right now I need to speak to the others alone."

Quintin stood and walked toward the door. "Yes, sir."

As he passed the others, Robert put a comforting hand on his shoulder and gave him a warm smile. Quintin did not return the smile, but stepped through the door and into the hall. He yanked the elastic band out of his hair and let the auburn locks cascade down around his face. He leaned back against the door and slowly slid to the floor.

He sat in complete stillness for a moment before reaching into his pocket and pulling out a small, gray device. He peeled a thin, clear disc from the back and placed it against the door. Tiny filaments glowed blue within. He tapped an icon on the device and slipped one of his earbuds into his right ear, immediately filling it with Robert's crystal clear voice.

---

ROBERT SMOOTHED HIS HAIR WITH HIS HAND AND TOOK A DEEP BREATH. "Look, Jiri, I know what you're going to say, and I can assure you—"

"Sit down, Robert," said Jiri. "All of you. This isn't about Quintin."

Robert pulled up one of the various chairs strewn about the room and sat in it backward, resting his arms on the chair's low back. Rene and Cherry sat on the couch, making sure to sit as far away from each other as possible. Jiri sighed, and for a moment the only sound in the room was the soft whirring of his ocular implants.

"I have re-established communication with TDC Command on Earth," he said finally.

This announcement was met with a joyous outburst from the humans, but Jiri silenced them with a raised hand. "The news is not good."

"What is it?" asked Robert.

Jiri took a deep, calming breath. "Three Terran cycles ago, TDC Command was attacked and suffered significant damage. The long-range inter-planetary communication system was among the equipment damaged in the attack. It took them this long to repair the unit. Once the communications link was re-established, Amaadoss contacted me."

The humans nodded. They knew all about the Terran Defense Corps, and, as a favor to Jiri, they never mentioned it in front of Quintin for fear that he might learn the truth about his origins.

"Who attacked them?" said Cherry. "Were they discovered by Temujin?"

Jiri shook his head. "That, Cheryl, is what hurts the most. They were betrayed by one of their own. The Replodian science officer apparently malfunctioned and attacked the others. During his rampage, he managed to disable several defense systems and wounded one of the other Replodians." He saw the distress on Cherry's face and held up his hand. "Quintin's brother is fine, but the operation is still severely crippled and the TDC is grossly outnumbered."

Rene sighed. "Could this get any worse?"

"What's worse—" Jiri began.

"Way to open your big mouth," Cherry said to Rene.

*"What's worse,"* Jiri continued, "is that recent intelligence suggests Temujin's forces are in possession of several weapons of both Replodian and Federation design. I believe that the traitor has defected to the Golden Horde and is supplying them with technology intended for the TDC."

*"Merde,"* Rene breathed. "How could this happen?"

"Amaadoss and I have discussed all possible scenarios, and have come up with only one plausible explanation," said Jiri. "Sabotage."

"Who could have possibly sabotaged the project?" asked Robert.

Jiri's brow furrowed. "I have my suspicions. Unfortunately I lack proof. After the transmission from Amaadoss, I checked the records at Dreknor from my office, and our suspicions are correct. Someone changed three lines of code and drastically altered Unit 003's primary programming, ordering him to destroy all materials and personnel related to both the TDC and Project Alexander."

"What can we do?" said Robert.

"In their current state, the TDC have only a thirty-two percent chance of survival. I ask that you three return to Earth and offer support. I know that's asking a lot of you, but we don't have a choice."

"Return... to Earth?" said Cherry.

"But," said Rene, "doesn't that violate the parameters of the experiment?"

"Damn the *experiment*, Boudreaux!" Jiri pounded his walking stick on the floor. "We're talking about people's lives. Not just the TDC, but *billions* of human lives. Not to mention the lives lost when the Seign-so's plans are—"

"Okay. Okay," said Rene defensively. "What can we do for them besides double their numbers?"

"You're a mechanic," said Jiri. "Surely you can help them repair sixteen-year-old obsolete Phaedojian hardware can't you?"

"No need to get pissy," Rene muttered.

Jiri turned to the others. "Can I depend on you, my friends?"

Robert nodded. "When do we leave?"

"In six hours," said Jiri. "That doesn't give you much time to prepare, I know, but time is of the utmost importance. We cannot afford to dawdle. I have procured a class three interceptor for your journey. You'll make your hyperspace jump at the Arqo jump gate."

The hunters all nodded and stood to leave the room.

Jiri turned. "Oh, there is one more thing. It would be best if you didn't mention any of this to Quintin. He's such an impulsive boy, bless him. I'm afraid if he were to learn about his brother on Earth that he might fly off again and try to join the war."

"Impulsive. *Gee*," said Cherry. "I wonder where he learned *that* kind of behavior."

Rene threw up his hands in exasperation. "There you go again! Always busting my balls!"

"You can't break what's already broken," Cherry jeered. "Oh, I'm sorry. That was a neighboring organ, wasn't it?"

"All right, woman, now you've gone too far!"

---

IN THE HALL, QUINTIN STARED INTO SPACE, IGNORING THE REST OF THE argument. Was he hallucinating, or had Jiri actually just said he had spoken with his *father*? But that was impossible. Amaadoss had been dead for years. And his *brother*?

"I have a brother?" he whispered. "On Earth?"

At the sound of approaching footsteps, Quintin ripped the disc off the door and ran down the hall toward his and Jiri's quarters. He had some packing to do.

# FOURTEEN

*Air Force Flight Test Center, Detachment 3*
*Codename: Area 51 AKA "Dreamland"*
*Groom Lake, Nevada*
*September 25th*

MOE DUCKED, NARROWLY AVOIDING A HAIL OF BULLETS FROM THE M4 carbine fired by an MP at the end of the hall. The weapon's report barely penetrated the alarm echoing through the corridor. The Replodian slipped around a corner as bullets chewed the wall apart, peppering his hair with concrete chunks and dust.

He tucked the inch-thick accordion file he was carrying into the waistband of his jeans and traded it for the small stun pistol concealed beneath his jacket. He ejected the magazine and saw three glowing blue rounds nestled within the transparent alloy.

He banged the back of his head against the wall. "Wonderful."

The Replodian waited for his opening and smiled when he heard the squawk of a walkie-talkie coming from the end of the hall.

"This is Hawkins," the MP shouted into her radio. "I have the intruder pinned down in the east Level Five corridor. Send backup."

"Correction," said Moe. "You *had* the intruder pinned down."

Moe jumped out from behind the wall and slid into the hallway on his side with the stun pistol in his right hand. The startled MP dropped the radio and fumbled for her rifle, but the Replodian was faster. Moe aimed for center mass and squeezed the trigger. A blue capsule ruptured on the woman's chest, and she shuddered as a small burst of blue electricity enveloped her body. The MP's eyes rolled back as her knees buckled and she slumped onto the concrete floor.

"At ease, soldier," Moe whispered as he rose to his feet.

He cautiously approached the MP and nudged her with his shoe. No response. The stun rounds were potent, but only lasted about thirty minutes before the victim woke up with a killer headache.

Moe knelt beside Hawkins and removed her ID badge. He gazed intently at the sleeping woman's features for a moment and closed his eyes. When he opened them, desert fatigues covered his body, and his skin had taken on the MP's pallor. He reached up and felt his hair, long, but bundled into a tight bun beneath a cap. He was no longer Moe.

"This is Hawkins," he said in the MP's voice as he clipped the badge to his jacket.

Moe stowed the stun pistol inside his phony uniform, hoping he wouldn't have to use it too many times, because the only other weapon he brought along didn't tickle.

A disembodied voice filled the hall, fed by hidden speakers, *"Attention all units! The intruder is moving east on level five. Lethal force has been authorized. I repeat. Lethal force has been authorized."*

"Lucky me," Moe muttered.

Moe picked up Hawkins' rifle and strolled down the corridor toward the elevator. When he rounded the corner, he came face to face with a squad of airmen in full combat gear. They trained their weapons on him momentarily before the lieutenant raised his hand for the men to lower them.

"Hawkins," the lieutenant barked. "Has the intruder been neutralized?"

"Negative," Moe replied, still using Hawkins's voice. "I lost him. He must have doubled back into one of the branching hallways."

"You heard her, men," the lieutenant shouted. "This way. Hawkins, get on the radio and tell Security to lock down this entire level."

"Yes, sir!" Moe said as he moved toward the elevator.

As he passed the squad, one of the men near the rear glanced up and stared, visibly alarmed, at the Replodian. "Your ear," the man said.

Moe reached up and felt the back of his ear. When he examined his fingers, they were covered in a thin coat of luminous yellow blood, along with a small, but sharp, piece of concrete. He felt a warm trickle run down the curve of his ear as fresh blood oozed from the small wound. The real Hawkins had drawn first blood after all.

The passing airman brought his rifle up. "Lieutenant! She's—"

Moe struck the airman across the jaw with the butt of his stolen rifle before discarding the weapon. He drew the stun pistol and fired a single round into the man's chest at point-blank range. The human fell to the ground in a blue, electrical flash. Moe spun low to avoid the barrage of gunfire from the troops, snatched a smoke bomb from the stunned airman's vest, and pulled the pin in one fluid motion. He rolled the bomb into the squad's scrambling feet and waited while they frantically tried to kick it away.

The canister expelled thick red smoke and the corridor quickly became filled with it, along with the coughs of a dozen airmen. Unseen, Moe leapt into the air and grabbed an overhead water pipe. He clung to the pipe, moving safely down the corridor above the frantic gunfire. When he reached another T-intersection, Moe dropped to the floor in front of the elevator and pressed the call button twice, but the elevator did not respond.

"Lockdown," he breathed.

Moe forced his fingertips into the gap between the doors and pried them apart. He stepped into the stalled car, threw open the maintenance hatch, and climbed on top of the car. He looked around the shaft, but only saw bare, sheer concrete walls.

"This place is a damn firetrap," he said. "Twenty thousand dollars for a hammer—what the hell did they *spend* it on? No room in the budget for a freakin' ladder?"

His eyes fell on the elevator's cable, and he sighed. He stuffed the stun weapon into his waistband, traded it for a plasma pistol, and grabbed the cable connected to the top of the car. Taking a deep breath, he aimed the pistol at the cable coupling at his feet, trying to push the utter stupidity of what he was about to do out of his mind.

The Replodian closed his eyes and whispered, "I *am* James Bond. I *am* James Bond. I *am* James Bond."

The pistol spat searing plasma, and the coupling broke apart. The counterweight plummeted, sending him rocketing toward the ground floor. He looked up and gritted his teeth as the top of the shaft came dangerously close.

Down below he heard a resounding crash and he reached up to grab a steel support beam above the pulley system. He let go of the cable just before it slipped through the pulley and watched the cable snake down the shaft. He clutched the beam with both hands and swung his legs, building momentum. He kicked his feet against the doors once, twice, each time bowing the steel panels out more and more. Finally the doors gave, and Moe swung out into the ground level lobby.

He came to rest on the floor just short of the security station, where the lone sentry stared at him with his sidearm drawn. Moe stood and smoothed his fatigues, his hands pausing over his chest as he felt Hawkins' stolen form under his clothes. He grinned sheepishly at the sentry.

"Might want to call maintenance," he said. "I think the elevator's out of order."

The bewildered sentry took aim with his sidearm, but Moe was quicker. He ripped the cap from his head and flung it into the man's face. The sentry squeezed off a single shot, but Moe ducked the bullet and brought his boot up and around in a powerful wheel kick that struck the side of the man's head and sent him sprawling to the floor, unconscious before he fell.

"Nighty night," said Moe with a wave.

He felt behind his back, breathing a sigh of relief when his fingers found the file still safely tucked away in his waistband. The idea of having to go back down the shaft to face an entire squad of pissed off and half-blind airmen to retrieve it made him cringe. He took a step toward the glass front doors, and a steel barrier slammed down in front of him, sealing him off from escape.

*"Do not move,"* said the disembodied voice on the loudspeaker. *"The building has been locked down. You cannot escape. Throw down your weapon."*

Moe looked up at a security camera mounted above the door. "You mean *this* weapon?"

He aimed the plasma pistol at the camera and fired, destroying it in a shower of sparks. He crossed the room to the card reader next to the door and tried Hawkins's key card. The reader buzzed and blinked red. Moe reached out to rip off the cover panel to expose the wiring beneath, but was interrupted by a door opening beside the elevator.

Moe shook his head wearily as fifteen airmen armed with M4s poured through the door, each one barking a variation of the order to drop his weapons. A gray-haired man wearing the uniform of a four-star Air Force general stepped briskly through the doorway and gave the Replodian a confident smirk.

"It's over, young lady," said the general. "Give it up."

Moe looked from the general's face to the ID badge clipped to his left breast pocket, then looked over his shoulder at the card reader set into the wall next to the barricaded door and returned the smirk.

"I don't think so," said Moe. "And you know what, General? *You're* going to let me out."

The general scoffed, "And just how do you imagine that will happen?"

Moe smirked. "You're going to give me your ID card."

"Drop your weapons now!" shouted one of the airmen standing at the front.

Moe looked at the man. "Sure thing. Catch!"

He tossed the plasma pistol into the air and, as the airmen looked up to follow its arc, delivered a sidekick to the man's chest, knocking him back into the throng. With his leg still in the air, he twisted and swatted the airman to his left in the head with a hook kick, sending him sprawling to the ground. The Replodian turned and drove his left elbow into another airman's solar plexus, doubling him over as the wind was forced from his lungs. The man wheezed as Moe's knee struck him in the face and he was thrown headfirst into a nearby wall, leaving a deep dent in the drywall.

Moe turned to look at the others, who stared at the intruder's incredible speed. "Three," Moe said.

"Fire!" the general bellowed.

The deafening report of automatic weapons filled the air, and Moe sidestepped a hail of bullets from a nearby airman. He swept his left hand out to block the rifle and struck the man's nose with the back-side of his fist, loosening the man's grip on the rifle. His left hand gripped the rifle's barrel while his right took hold of the man's fatigues, and with a twist of the hips, he threw the airman onto his back. With the rifle in hand, Moe covered the distance between him and the next closest airman with a long, low stride and sidekicked the man in the chest, sending him crashing back into the first airman, who was now attempting to stand.

"Five," Moe said as he turned to strike another airman across the side of the head with the rifle butt. "Six."

A young, green-looking airman ran forward for a better shot, and Moe threw his rifle at the man's legs, tripping him. The boy slid across the tile at Moe's feet and immediately tried to stand, but Moe stopped him with an axe kick between the shoulder blades. "Stay down!" he said.

Bullets whizzed past the Replodian's head, and Moe jerked his head out of the way. He ducked another barrage, spun, and launched himself into the air, bringing the heel of his boot into the back of the assailant's skull. As he landed, he deflected the nearest airman's rifle and swept his arm into the man's throat, clotheslining him and throwing him off his feet.

"Nine," he said.

The searing barrel of an M4 pressed against the back of his skull. "Freeze," the weapon's owner commanded.

Moe raised his hands slowly, then kicked blindly behind him, driving his boot into the man's gut. The rifle discharged harmlessly into the floor. "Ten," Moe said, correcting himself.

His hands still raised, the Replodian cartwheeled out of the path of a stream of bullets and swung his leg around in a devastating wheel kick that sent his target spinning to the floor. The airman who'd fired ejected his magazine, and felt his bandolier for a fresh one. Moe stalked forward and kicked the man in the stomach, interrupting his task and doubling him over. The man sank to one knee, clutching his aching gut, revealing two more airmen behind him leveling their weapons at Moe.

The Replodian leapfrogged over the moaning man and launched himself into the air. He kicked out with both legs, striking both men in the faces. Their weapons discharged as they fell back, striking the ceiling and raining plaster dust onto Moe's hair and shoulders.

"Fifteen," Moe said. "Wait... or was that—"

A single shot rang out, and a searing pain tore through the Replodian's right shoulder. He looked down at the smoking hole in his fatigues, and the stream of glowing blood flowed onto the fabric. He turned and locked eyes with a trembling young airman. The boy stared at the yellow substance dribbling from the wound in his shoulder while an altogether different yellow substance dribbled down his leg.

"Fourteen," Moe growled.

The airman squeezed the trigger. The weapon clicked in response, and he flinched.

Moe glowered at the sweating human. "Reload, boy."

The airman ejected the spent magazine and fumbled to slam the fresh one home as the alien terror wearing Hawkins's face stalked toward him. Finally the magazine locked in place, and he cocked the weapon.

"Ready?" said Moe, still coming.

The airman raised the M4 to fire again, but was far too slow. Moe slapped the weapon aside and punched him twice in the ribs, then reached up to grab the back of his head and drove his knee into his opponent's face.

"Fifteen," Moe said as the airman collapsed to the ground.

He turned and saw the general huddled in a corner, whimpering. His eyes grew wide as the bullet wound in Moe's shoulder closed and healed; the flesh and uniform material mended seamlessly, leaving no trace of the wound. Moe held out his hand and smiled as the gibbering general obediently dropped the ID card into his waiting palm.

"I knew you'd see things my way." Moe paused to read the name on the badge. "Have a nice day, General Brinkmann."

Moe bent to collect his plasma pistol as he strode toward the door. He slid the badge through the reader and the door slid open, the barrier receding into the ceiling. He pushed the glass door open, and then paused to look back at Brinkmann.

"On second thought..." Moe smirked as his features and clothing morphed into those of the quaking general. "There *is* one more thing you can do for me."

Brinkmann pressed his back against the wall, his eyes wide and nostrils flared as the pretty young woman before him transformed into his own mirror image. Moe fired his last stun ball at the general's forehead, knocking him unconscious in a wave of blue lightning. Brinkmann slumped to the floor, his hat askew.

Moe knelt beside the general and plucked the hat from his balding head. He put it on, adjusting it until he had a snug fit, then patted the sleeping man on the cheek and smiled. "Thanks, Chief."

He stepped outside into the oppressive Nevada sunshine and strode toward a small parking lot adjacent to the building. He climbed into the closest vehicle, a black Ford SUV, and immediately checked the ignition, the center console, and flipped down the visor. No keys.

"No," he said. "Course not. That'd be too easy."

He pressed his index finger against the ignition, his upper lip curling in revulsion as the digit compressed and conformed to the mechanism's inner workings. One by one, the Replodian's finger pushed the tumblers aside until he heard a final, soft click. With a turn of his wrist, the engine rumbled to life, and Moe withdrew his finger, returning it to its normal shape and wiping the grime onto his leg.

As he steered the SUV toward the guardhouse at the edge of the base perimeter, Moe could see two sentries inside it. One man stepped out in front of the gate and held up his hand. When the MP saw Moe—or rather General Brinkmann—he snapped to attention and saluted.

"General, is everything all right?" the sentry said. "I heard the alarm."

Inside the guardhouse, a telephone rang.

"Everything's fine, Airman." Moe tried to look indifferent as he watched the sentry inside answer the phone. "In fact, if I were you, I'd forget I ever heard that alarm. Understood?"

"Understood, General!"

As the sentry turned to raise the wooden guard gate, his partner burst from the guardhouse and drew his sidearm. "Hands where I can see them!"

Moe cursed under his breath and took his hands off the wheel slowly.

"Are you out of your mind?" said the first sentry. "That's General Brinkmann!"

"Negative," said the second, stepping up to the SUV's window. "This is an imposter."

While the other sentry fumbled with his own sidearm, Moe reached out and snatched the pistol from the guard's hand, then slammed his foot down on the gas. The tires spun on the loose sand littering the pavement for a moment before the SUV surged forward, snapping the gate arm in two. Bullets peppered the rear of the vehicle, and Moe grinned as the SUV sped into the desert.

# FIFTEEN

*TDC Command*
*Bonaparte, Iowa*
*September 26th*

THE TDC COMMAND CENTER LOCATED BENEATH THE WALKER FARM was quiet; all of the machinery was silent. The only sound was the soft snoring coming from the chair in front of the large observation monitor. Lamont sat wrapped in his leather jacket, chin tucked to his chest to ward off the morning chill. While he slept, a large red blip on the monitor's satellite image drew closer and closer to home.

The door leading to the well shaft slid open and the artificial female voice resonated through the room, "Welcome, Alex Walker."

Alex stepped into the main chamber, his footsteps echoing softly. In the past three years since the aliens came into his life, the boy had grown into a strong young man. He was dressed in blue jeans, a white T-shirt, and a well-worn black leather jacket. After his brush with death outside Delmar's Barber Shop, he'd sworn off haircuts, leaving his hair long and slightly wavy, ending between his shoulder blades.

He held a box of day-old doughnuts from the gas station in Bonaparte while two Styrofoam coffee cups floated around his head like orbiting satellites. Alex crossed the room and placed the box on the console in front of his sleeping friend. He looked up and breathed a sigh of relief as the red tracking blip drew closer. Moe was coming home, and soon.

Alex plucked one of the steaming cups out of the air and waved it under Lamont's nose, who snorted and jolted awake. He shook his head to chase away the lingering grogginess and squinted up at the teen.

Alex held out the cup. "Morning."

"Good morning." Lamont accepted the cup and eagerly gulped the scalding liquid.

This type of behavior had taken Alex a long time to get used to. Due to Replodia's harsh climate, his friends were immune to extremely hot temperatures. In fact, they reveled in them. During the cold Iowa winters, the Replodians tended to drink copious amounts of coffee and take long soaks in boiling water inside the infirmary's rejuvenation tubes. Alex had soon learned never to take a Replodian's word for it that "the water's fine."

The sound of someone clearing their throat rumbled through the chamber.

Alex looked toward the ceiling and smiled. "Morning, Father."

"Good morning, Alexander," the computer replied. "Good morning, Lamont."

Lamont lowered his cup. "Good morning, Father."

Since the unexpected treason of their science officer three years before, the remaining members of the TDC had come to depend heavily on the base's central computer, affectionately naming it "Father." Amaadoss had been very pleased with the designation.

Lamont gestured toward the cup orbiting Alex's head. "That's a neat trick."

"Look, Ma, no hands!" Alex waited for the cup to pass in front of his face and let it float into his waiting hand. "Seriously, you ever try to carry two cups of coffee and a box of doughnuts down a ladder?"

Lamont chuckled.

Alex took a careful sip of his own cappuccino and pointed at the screen. "I see Moe made it out safely."

Lamont picked a cherry doughnut from the box. "I just hope he left the place standing."

Alex flicked his wrist and a nearby chair rolled toward him. When it reached him, he rolled it next to Lamont's and the two enjoyed their breakfast in silence as they watched the blip. It slowed as it passed the Walker farm and turned onto the dirt road leading to the field. Finally the blip stopped moving.

"Here he comes," said Alex. "Three... Two... One...."

The hall door opened and the female voice rang out again, "Welcome, Moe."

"Bite me!" the Replodian snapped.

Moe stepped into the chamber, his eyes red and bleary. Clutched in his right hand was a red accordion file labeled "TOP SECRET" in big, white letters. Moe tossed the file and Alex raised his hand, suspending it in mid-air. He made a slow beckoning gesture, and the file glided smoothly into his hand.

"There," Moe said. "Everything you'll ever want to know about the American military's involvement with extra-terrestrials and their little exchange program."

Alex read the title on the folder. "Operation *Sleepover*? Are you serious? That's the stupidest thing I've ever heard."

Moe scoffed. "I know, right? And to think they actually *pay* people to come up with this stuff! Where do I apply for *that* job?"

"Sorry." Alex smirked as he handed the file to Lamont. "I don't remember seeing that booth on career day."

Lamont snapped his fingers. "Let's focus. Did you have any trouble?"

"Give me that!" Moe snatched Lamont's coffee cup and downed the remaining half in two quick gulps. "Oh, I don't know. It was only Area Fifty-*freakin'*-one. Oh, and let's not forget the lovely joyride through the desert where I had to ditch six Nevada State Troopers and a gunship. Yeah, Monty, I guess you could say there was *some* trouble. Which reminds me..." Moe slipped the communicator off his wrist and tossed it onto the console. The device sparked and emitted a short burst of static. "Sorry I didn't call. Please don't ground me."

Alex stood and offered the rest of his cappuccino to Moe. "I need to get to school. I'll see you guys later. We can go through the file when I get home."

Moe rolled his eyes. "Can't wait. Combat training first, Junior."

"Aww, Mom!" Alex wailed.

Moe pointed a warning finger at Alex, and the teen shot him a mischievous grin as the door slid shut between them.

Moe reached into his jacket and tossed his weapons onto an empty chair. "I'm going to go have a soak."

"Poached or hard boiled?"

"Hard boiled," Moe said. "Definitely hard boiled. Don't wait up."

"All right. You mind if I look through the file while you simmer?"

Moe gave the folder a grimace and stripped off his jacket, tossing it onto the back of his chair. "Knock yourself out."

As the door to the main corridor closed behind Moe with a light hiss, Lamont broke the seal on the file. The tearing echoed through the empty room.

Lamont looked up. "How about some music, Father?"

Pounding electronic music flooded the room, and Lamont winced. This was more Moe's speed. Lamont's tastes were more refined. He preferred something a bit more... organic.

"No," he said. The music immediately ceased. "Give me some blues."

A moment later, the sound of fingers on strings soothed his aching ears. Lamont grinned and nodded as "All Over You" piped into the room from every corner. While his brother lowered himself into a tube of boiling water down the hall, Lamont settled back in his chair and opened the file.

# SIXTEEN

*Arqo Jump Gate*

*"Interceptor-class vessel, Saber, this is Arqo Gate Control."*

Rene tapped a holo-key on the display projected in front of his face. "This is *Saber*. Go ahead, Control."

*"You are cleared for approach to the gate."*

"Acknowledged, Control," said Rene. "Altering vector now."

Rene swiped the holographic interface to chest level and entered a series of commands. The maneuvering thrusters kicked in and the ship glided into the marked pathway leading to the immense, circular jump gate. The ring, which dwarfed the *Saber*, was built to accommodate much larger battle cruisers.

*"Hold up, Saber."*

Rene slid a holo-key downward and the ship drifted to a halt.

To his right, Cherry shifted in her seat and rolled her eyes. "What now?"

Rene stabbed the air with his finger, passing through the holo-key. "What's the hold up, Control?"

*"Saber, I'm reading your destination as the Sol System."*

"Affirmative, Control," said Rene. "And we're *very* anxious to get there."

*"Sorry, Saber. Sol is a protected system. I'm afraid I can't allow you to pass through the—"*

Robert flicked his hand in front of him, activating a dormant holo interface. His fingers flew across the keys as he spoke. "Control, we have level seven clearance granting us immediate clearance to the Sol System."

*"I'm sorry, Saber, but without the proper—"*

Robert's fingers grabbed a file and dragged it over to Rene's display. The controller went silent as the file appeared on his own.

Rene glanced at Robert. "If you listen closely, you can hear them wetting themselves."

Robert smirked.

*"Saber, this is gate control. You are cleared for immediate departure. Have a pleasant journey."*

Rene signed off and restarted the maneuvering thrusters. "Not likely."

Cherry glanced at him. "You're not going to barf, are you? Because if you are, I'm getting out right now."

"Oh?" Rene buckled his safety restraints. "In that case, yes, I am most certainly going to 'barf' *all over* this cockpit."

"Children," said Robert, buckling his own restraints, "behave yourselves or no ice cream."

*"Mmmmmm."* Cherry closed her eyes and bit her bottom lip. "Ice cream."

"Keep your ice cream," said Rene. "The minute we land, I'm getting me a double order of onion rings. With ketchup! You remember ketchup?"

Robert smiled, indulging in his own Earth fantasies. He'd given up on returning there decades ago, but his companions' exchange stirred up long-forgotten desires. How much had Earth changed in the time they'd been away? He and Rene had both witnessed the advent of electricity, telephones, and television in their lifetimes; the possibilities seemed limitless—and exciting.

"Take us home, Rene," he said.

Rene grinned. "You don't have to tell me twice."

The ship slowed to a stop, her nose pointed at the center of the immense ring. The gate crackled with energy.

Rene looked at his companions. "Everybody strapped in?"

They nodded.

Rene keyed in a sequence and settled back in his chair. "Hold onto your stomachs. Here we go."

A low hum filled the air and the ship surged forward. As the Saber's nose passed through the ring, they all exhaled. Reality stretched around them for a brief moment before the universe vanished in a brilliant flash.

---

*Sol Jump Gate*
*Ceres*

RENE'S STOMACH LURCHED AS THE *SABER* PASSED THROUGH AND THE stars returned to normal. He gulped air and coughed. Gate travel was no picnic, but it beat the alternative. When the Seignso abducted him, he was placed in cryostasis for the duration of the yearlong journey. He preferred the temporary discomfort of jump gate travel to cryostasis, which always gave him hibernation sickness.

"Where are we?" asked Cherry.

Rene unbuckled his restraints and consulted the navigation computer. "We're orbiting the—"

A jarring impact rocked the ship and threw the Cajun from his seat. His head struck a console and warm blood dripped from his eyelashes.

Robert grasped the arms of his chair to steady himself. "What the hell was that?"

Rene crawled back to his chair and winced as the gash in his forehead knitted closed, leaving a light scar. He rubbed the new skin with one hand and consulted his holo display with the other. He cursed.

"What is it?" said Cherry.

"We're on the far side of Ceres," said Rene. "The damn gate brought us out in the middle of the Asteroid Belt!"

Cherry's eyes widened. *"What?"*

"Damage report," said Robert.

Cherry keyed up her holo-display and breathed a sigh of relief. "No hull breaches. Structural integrity is holding. Looks like the shields took the brunt of the hit. We're safe... *for now.* What idiot places a jump gate in the middle of an asteroid field?"

"It was a one-in-a-million shot," said Robert. "If you think about it, there's no better place to hide a gate. Lots of flotsam floating around, but not so close together that it can't be avoided. Just a case of being in the wrong place at the wrong time."

Rene sighed and rubbed his forehead. "Story of my life."

Robert watched him. "You all right?"

"He'll be fine," said Cherry. "It was only his head. Not like he was using it or anything."

Rene slammed his fist down on his armrest and let loose an incomprehensible string of Bayou French.

"Enough!" Robert grabbed Rene's holo-display and swept it into his own, merging the interfaces and taking helm control away from the Cajun. "Rene, you go check the cargo bay and make sure the reserve fuel rods haven't ruptured."

"Why me?"

Robert tapped keys, laying in their new course. "Because if I leave the two of you alone, the ship might not be in one piece when I get back."

Rene stood and cast a venomous glare at Cherry as he left the bridge. "Fine."

---

RENE DESCENDED THE LADDER TO THE SHIP'S SUB LEVEL AND— hunched to avoid banging his still-pounding head on the low ceiling —walked the short path to the cargo hold. He pounded the access panel with his fist and the door slid open to reveal the darkened hold.

"Lights," he said.

The room was instantly illuminated and Rene cursed as one of the overturned supply canisters rolled past the open doorway. He touched a comm panel by the door and opened a channel to the bridge. "We've got loose cargo."

Robert's voice crackled over the channel, *"Salvage what you can, just in case. You never know what we might need down there."*

"Roger that." Rene signed off.

He stepped inside to survey the damage and did a double take when his eyes fell on a pair of legs clad in standard-issue Hunters Union black sticking out from behind a fallen barrel. He ran to the canister and pulled it away. What he saw turned the air in his lungs to ice. There, on the floor, with his face covered in blood and his eyes closed, was—

"Quintin!" Rene shouted.

The boy's eyes snapped open, and he sat up. He gasped, his lungs burning for that first breath of life.

Rene grabbed the boy's shoulders. "Quintin! Are you all right?"

Quintin coughed and nodded, blinking away the tears welling in his eyes.

"Dying," the boy gasped, "hurts."

Despite his concern, Rene smirked. *"Now* you are a man."

"I think I'd rather be a kid," Quintin paused for breath and coughed again, "if this is what it takes to be a man."

Rene helped the resurrected teen to his feet. "What in God's name are you doing here? You should be halfway to Glynfyl by now."

"I heard you and Jiri talking yesterday," Quintin said, his breathing finally starting to level out.

Rene rolled his eyes.

"And I wanted to come to Earth. I want to meet my brother."

*"Merde!"* Rene stamped his foot. "This isn't some pleasure trip, boy. This is a dangerous mission we're on. And it's *no* place for you."

Rene turned his back and muttered in Bayou French.

"This is where I belong," Quintin said.

"No!" Rene turned. "The *academy* is where you belong."

At these words, Quintin began to cry. He tried wiping the tears away with his sleeve, but only succeeded in smearing the blood on his face. Rene sighed, and his shoulders slumped in defeat. He reached out to lay a comforting hand on the boy's shoulder.

*"Rene?"* Robert's voice resonated from the wall comm. *"We're coming up on Earth. You might want to get up here."*

Quintin looked up and choked back a sob. "Earth?"

"Come on, kid." Rene grabbed Quintin by the arm and led him out into the corridor. "We'll discuss this with the others."

---

"YOU'RE A BIT TOO HARD ON HIM, YOU KNOW," ROBERT SAID.

Cherry crossed her arms over her chest. "He's an ass."

Robert nodded. "Sometimes. But he cares."

She glanced at him from the corner of her eye. "He has a funny way of showing it."

Robert shrugged. "You're not entirely blameless in that department, you know."

She sighed. "I know. I just...."

"It's not just Rene that's bothering you, is it?"

Cherry sniffled, and a tear streamed down her nose. She shook her head, and the tear fell into her lap. She wiped her face with her sleeve.

"Quintin?"

She nodded.

Robert held out his hand over Rene's empty chair. She took it, and their eyes met.

"Quintin's safe," he said. "A billion miles away from here."

Cherry smiled mirthlessly. "And Alexander?"

Robert's grasp on her hand tightened. "No harm will come to him. I *swear* it."

"Robert, we should—"

The bridge door hissed open, and Cherry let go of Robert's hand. He nodded. This discussion would have to wait.

Robert shifted his gaze to the front window, and the blue orb slowly filling it. "So how's everything down in the hold?"

"Fine," Rene replied. "Except for one tiny problem."

"What?" asked Cherry. "Did you break the fuel rods?"

"No," said Rene. "Look who I found *dead* in the cargo hold under a supply barrel."

*"Dead?"* said Cherry.

"Well, dead-ish."

Robert and Cherry exchanged confused glances and turned in their seats. They expected to see the Cajun holding some flattened stowaway rodent the sanitation crawlers had missed, but instead—

"Quintin!" Cherry struggled to unbuckle her restraints.

But the boy wasn't looking at her. His eyes were locked on the growing blue ball in front of the ship. White wisps of cloud floated across the planet's atmosphere. He stepped toward the window. "You always told me that Earth was green."

"Quintin!" Cherry shook him. "What are you *doing* here?"

The boy finally tore his eyes away from the beautiful planet and met Cherry's worried gaze. "I wanted to come with you to meet my brother."

"Your *brother?*"

"He overheard us talking to Jiri yesterday," Rene said.

"Well that's just *great*," Cherry snarled. "Turn this ship around, Robert. We're taking him back to Moebius."

"What?" Quintin protested. "Robert, no!"

Suddenly the ship pitched, and a shrill alarm filled the cockpit.

"Too late," said Robert. "We've entered the planet's atmosphere. Everyone strap in!"

Cherry ushered Quintin to one of the empty chairs, and then both she and Rene strapped themselves in for the bumpy ride to come. Bright orange flames spread across the nose of the ship and obscured their view.

"TDC Command, this is the interceptor-class vessel *Saber*," said Robert into the long-range communicator. "Do you read?"

Loud static filled the bridge.

"TDC Command, this is the interceptor-class vessel *Saber*," Robert repeated more urgently. "Do you read? Respond, TDC."

Again static filled their ears.

"It's no good," said Robert. "That collision must have knocked out the communications array."

"Well now," said Cherry. "Who do we have to thank for that?"

"Not now, woman!" Rene pointed a warning finger at her. "This is *not* the time!"

"Hang on tight." Robert adjusted the heading. "This could get rough. They don't know we're coming."

# SEVENTEEN

*TDC Command*
*Bonaparte, Iowa*

MOE STEPPED INTO THE MAIN CHAMBER, DRYING HIS HAIR WITH A towel. Lamont was still at the console with the open file in his lap, his back to the open door. Moe peered over his brother's shoulder as he examined a photograph of twelve humans, all dressed in Air Force uniforms.

"So," he said, draping the damp towel over his shoulders. "Is it a good read?"

Without looking up, Lamont replied, "It's incredible."

"How so?"

"Sit down," said Lamont gravely. "You're not going to believe this."

Moe sat, grabbed an open bag of Sterzing's potato chips laying on the terminal, and put his feet up. "After all the work I went through to get that file, it better contain something more earth-shaking than a Seignso cookie recipe."

"It does," said Lamont. "After the crash at Roswell in 1947, the U.S. Air Force began attempts to reverse engineer alien technology recovered from the crash site. They were, for the most part, unsuccessful, but they were able to create a crude communications device capable of transmitting simple signals to planet Sorua. There were two survivors of the crash. One died on the operating table less than eight hours after extraction from Roswell, the other survived and accompanied twelve humans to Sorua in 1983 as part of an exchange program codenamed Operation Sleepover.

"The team consisted of ten men and two women, a combination of various military personnel, doctors, and scientists. One team member died of unknown causes during the voyage. The team lived on Sorua for nearly a year until something completely unexpected happened."

"Oh yeah?" Moe popped a chip into his mouth. "What?"

"While on a research expedition, the Seignso hovercraft experienced a mechanical failure and crashed, injuring the humans aboard," Lamont explained. "Three team members were killed, but during the cleanup after the accident one of the dead opened their eyes and sat up."

Moe straightened in his chair, letting the chip bag fall to the floor. *"Sat up?"*

"That's what it says." Lamont pointed to the file. "Apparently a Dr. Cheryl Sadler, one of the team's medical personnel, just got up a few minutes later and seemed to be in perfectly good health. After this incident, the Seignso stopped being hospitable to the team and seized Dr. Sadler, subjecting her to numerous physical examinations against her will. When the team's commanding officer attempted to put a stop to the examinations, he was placed under arrest. The team had brought a few weapons along on the mission—a couple of pistols and a rifle apiece, but the Seignso quickly quashed the rebellion and sent the humans back to Earth. Without Dr. Sadler."

Moe snorted and retrieved his chips. "Typical Seignso crap."

"That's not all," said Lamont. "Upon dropping off the team at your favorite Air Force base..." Moe smiled cynically. "...and describing Dr. Sadler's unique 'condition,' they were then shown three human subjects the military had under observation. These three apparently exhibited the same traits as Dr. Sadler while serving in Vietnam. Private Remy Benoit, Sergeant Shawn Avery, and Lieutenant Jack

Maddock were all taken into custody after either reviving or mysteriously healing from severe wounds in the field. They were being held at Area 51 for observation and study; scientists labeled them as 'Homo immortalis,' a new sub-species of human."

"Bizarre," Moe mumbled through a mouthful of potato chips.

"Shortly after," Lamont continued, "the Seignso abducted these humans as 'compensation' for damages to their home planet during Operation Sleepover."

*"Damages?"*

Lamont nodded. "Among the damages cited by the Seignso were the air car involved in the accident that 'killed' Dr. Sadler and the environmental damage caused by the building of a facility to dispose of the team's excessive bodily wastes."

"Wait, wait." Moe waved a hand. "You're telling me the Seignso held a grudge because humans *poop* too much?"

Lamont shook his head with a smile and pointed to the file again. "You can't make this stuff up. It's all right here in black and white."

"Father," said Moe. "You been listening to this?"

"I have," said Father. "Some of this information I was already aware of, but this file presents new pieces to the puzzle. Apparently the Seignso had the same idea as I, but were thankfully too late to utilize the *Homo immortalis* genes in their plans for Temujin. However, if they were to continue experimenting on their reluctant specimens, they could create the perfect genetic soldiers for their war with the Federation, thus accelerating their plan."

Moe held up his hand. "Wait, 'same idea?' Does that mean Alex—"

A piercing klaxon filled the chamber.

Moe covered his ears and groaned. "Oh, what *now?*"

"Father," Lamont shouted over the noise, "are we under attack?"

"It is the early warning system," said Father. "The orbital sensor drones have detected an alien vessel entering Earth's atmosphere."

"Hostile?" asked Moe.

"Uncertain," said Father. "They are not responding to hails in any Federation language or frequency. However, I have plotted the vessel's course."

"And?" asked Lamont, even though he already knew the answer.

"The alien craft is on a direct course for TDC Command."

---

ALEX FELT HIS EYELIDS GROWING HEAVY AND FOUND IT INCREASINGLY difficult to focus on his textbook as the gray-haired, bespectacled man at the front of the room droned on about the judicial branch of the United States government. The caffeine rush from the cappuccino had worn off an hour ago, not that it would have made any difference. Nothing could keep Alex awake during Mr. Butters's fourth period government class. So he waited, his head nodding, for the lunch bell to ring so he could go eat with Crystal.

The digital display on his wristwatch emitted a sudden pulsating red glow. Alex's heart skipped as he stared at it. Something was wrong. In three years, the guys had never triggered the alarm.

::Alex,:: Lamont's voice echoed in his mind.

::Lamont,:: said Alex. ::What's wrong?::

::I think you'd better come see for yourself. Father says we're about to have company.::

::Are we under attack?::

::We don't know yet,:: said Lamont. ::You'd better come quick.::

::On my way.::

The connection was severed. Alex shut his textbook and raised his hand. "Mr. Butters!"

The teacher looked at him over the rims of his glasses. "Yes?"

Alex stood and gripped his stomach. "Can I go see the nurse? I don't feel so hot."

"Nice try, Walker," said Mr. Butters. "I'm not falling for that one again."

Alex's classmates snickered and whispered amongst themselves as he slumped down in his seat and sighed. Quietly, he reached into the side pocket of his book bag and felt around until his fingers closed around a small, green capsule. Alex grimaced at the pill, but steeled his resolve and popped it into his mouth, then bit down hard.

A foul-tasting liquid filled his mouth and trickled down his throat. Alex gagged and bolted out of his seat toward the teacher's desk. He fell to his knees and wretched into the wastebasket.

Several of his classmates uttered various expressions of disgust, and Mr. Butters looked as if he might follow Alex's example at any moment. Alex groaned miserably and looked up at Mr. Butters, his eyes pleading and watery.

"Go see the nurse, Walker."

"Thank you, sir." Alex got up to collect his bag and leave the room.

"Take the bucket!" yelled the teacher.

Alex turned to snag the wastebasket and ran for the door. Once outside the classroom, Alex dropped the foul-smelling receptacle and ran for the front doors as fast as his aching stomach would allow. He stepped out into the cool autumn air and breathed two big gulps before running for his car. When he reached the red 1984 Monte Carlo, he looked up and saw an enormous fireball falling westward.

"Whoa," he whispered.

He regained his composure and wrenched the car door open. The Monte roared to life with the twist of the key before he was even fully in his seat. Alex backed it out of the parking space and slammed the gearshift into drive. The tires smoked and squealed, leaving black marks all the way to the road.

---

MOE LED THE WAY UP TO THE SURFACE. THE CHEST-HIGH YELLOW GRASS whipped wildly in the wind created by the descending ship. Rocky was already on the scene, barking and snarling up at the intruder. Moe stared in awe as the ship, roughly seventy feet long, sank closer to the ground. Lamont pulled himself out of the well and readied the plasma rifle in his hands, the weapon's hum drowned out by the ship's engines.

The Replodians also never heard the roar of the Monte Carlo barreling down the dirt road and coming to a skidding, dust-kicking halt at the entrance to the pasture. Alex stepped out of the car with a plasma pistol in hand and ran toward his friends. Moe covered his eyes with one hand to block the dust and grass while clutching his rifle against his chest. Alex ran to his side and yelled, "Who are they?"

Moe shook his head. "We don't know. They wouldn't pick up the phone."

The ship's landing gear came down and sank into the ground under the ship's weight. Slowly, the engines wound down and the wind subsided, leaving the Walker farm frightfully quiet, save for Rocky's incessant barking.

"If they wanted a fight, they'd have opened fire on us from the air." Alex sighted down the barrel of his pistol. "Right?"

"Maybe." Moe raised his own rifle. "But I'm not taking any chances."

"Be ready for anything." Lamont raised his own weapon.

Finally a hatch opened in the belly of the craft and a long ramp extended to the ground. The TDC agents held their breath as they waited for the visitors to appear, their bodies tensed as the first footsteps clanked down the ramp. To their amazement, four unarmed humans in black coveralls stepped off the ship and into the wind-flattened grass.

"They're human?" said Alex.

"Oh, my God, Moe." Lamont lowered his rifle. "Look—that woman. That's Cheryl Sadler, the woman from the file—the one the Seignso took prisoner. And those men—"

"Benoit and Maddock?" Moe asked.

Lamont nodded.

Moe swallowed the lump in his throat. "That's nothin'. Get a load of the kid."

At these words, Alex's eyes fell on the youngest newcomer, who was attempting to wipe congealed blood from his face. When the boy noticed Alex, he adopted a similar expression of shock. Aside from their attire, it was like looking into a blood-streaked mirror.

Introductions were understandably short. Fearing somebody might come looking for the object that fell from the sky, Moe directed Maddock—who identified himself as Robert Long—to move the ship to a pond a little over a hundred yards north of the well entrance. Once the ship was in position, hidden pipes pumped the muddy water out and a large metal iris at the bottom of the basin slid open, revealing an empty bay. As soon as the ship's landing gear touched the deck, the iris closed and the pond refilled, sealing the craft away from prying eyes.

Now they all found themselves in the main chamber. Alex and Quintin stared at each other curiously, each one uncertain of what the other might do next. It was Quintin who finally broke the silence.

"Are you my brother?"

Alex flinched. "Brother?"

Father's booming voice filled every corner of the room, "I'm afraid I owe both of you an explanation."

Quintin began looking frantically around the room. *"Father?"*

"Yes, Quintin," said the computer. "I am here, although not in body."

"What do you mean 'not in body'?"

Cherry placed a comforting hand on the teen's shoulder, "Quintin, before he died, your father uploaded a copy of his consciousness into the TDC's central computer. He's not really here. It's just his essence."

"I don't understand," said Quintin.

"In order to provide the TDC with the proper technical support and to give your brother a chance to know the father he never knew, I integrated myself with the computer," Father explained. "I'm sorry, Quintin. I should have told you."

Tears welled in Quintin's eyes. "So you really *are* dead?"

For a moment the computer was silent, but finally answered softly, "I'm afraid so, Son."

Alex went to his brother's side and put a hand on his shoulder, "He's not dead. He's just in a different form. One that's immune to disease and death."

This statement brought a small smile to Quintin's lips, and he nodded.

"Father," said Moe. "Where did Quintin come from? You never mentioned him to us before."

"Quintin was an unforeseen side effect of the process used to create Alexander," said Father. "Jiri and I attempted to combine the resilience of a Methuselan with the telepathic abilities of the Seignso. During gestation, the embryo split, creating twins. One twin Methuselan, the other a human/Seignso hybrid. To compensate for losing the immortality gene in Alexander, I purchased three Replodian embryos for implantation."

"Right," said Moe. "That would be us."

"And the third's really gone AWOL?" prompted Rene.

"Correct," said Father. "And he is now in the employ of our enemy."

Rene cursed under his breath.

"Father, why didn't you tell me any of this before?" asked Quintin.

Again the computer hesitated before answering, "You are a strong-willed young man, Quintin. You always have been. I feared you might try to join the fight I reluctantly sent your brother into. I couldn't bear the thought of losing one—or both—of you. Perhaps it was a mistake to ever split the two of you up in the first place. I only hope that one day the two of you can forgive me."

Lamont took a tentative step toward Cherry. "Dr. Sadler, forgive me for asking, but what happened to you on Sorua after your capture? How did you manage to escape?"

Cherry took a deep, rattled breath. Rene quickly wrapped his arms around her and whispered softly in her ear.

Robert answered for her, sparing her the pain of having to tell the tale again. "We were rescued by the Federation when they raided a genetics lab on one of the Seignso's colony moons. The Federation wasn't willing to return us to Earth, so they offered us jobs with the Hunters Union when they discovered our... unique abilities."

"It was their genetic material I utilized to create you, my sons," said Father. "When Jiri and I outlined the project to them, they volunteered to donate cells to Project Alexander."

"We wanted to pay those Seignso bastards back for what they did to us," said Rene.

"Well at the rate we're going, we'll be lucky to even survive," said Moe. "I'm not sure how much payback we'll be able to offer you at this point."

"I'd say our chances just doubled," said Alex, indicating the new arrivals.

"Great," said Moe, crossing his arms. "We just went from 'up the creek without a paddle' to 'a snowball's chance in Hell'."

Rene smirked. "I like those odds."

# EIGHTEEN

Above ground, Alex went about the task of trying to fluff up the grass where the *Saber* had landed. Quintin trailed along behind him, observing his long-lost brother's strange behavior.

"It's just so bizarre," said Alex, tugging at a stubborn clump of grass.

"What is?" asked Quintin.

"This." Alex pointed to the flattened grass and finally at his twin. "All this."

"You know," said Quintin. "I'm really not all that shocked by it."

"You're not?"

"No." Quintin furrowed his brow. "I think, somehow, I always knew. All my life, I've felt pulled toward Earth, even though I'd never seen it. And now that I have, it's the most beautiful place in the entire galaxy."

Alex paused. "Seriously? Come on! There have to be cooler planets than this one. It's a big universe. What could possibly be so special about this *rock*?"

Quintin shrugged. "I guess I just knew there was something here for me... or someone."

Alex nodded.

"When I met the others," Quintin continued, "I thought I'd finally found what I was searching for. I had other humans to be with, but it still wasn't enough. There was still something missing. A home. *Our* home."

As they approached the Monte Carlo still parked by the gate, Alex fished for his keys. "I don't know about you, but I could really go for a chocolate shake. What do you say?"

"A what?"

"A shake," said Alex. "You know. It's a drink made with ice cream."

"What's ice cream?"

Alex sighed and opened the driver's side door. "Come on, space man. You've got a lot to learn. Hop in. I've got some clothes you can borrow. Lord knows they should fit."

"Lord who?"

Alex rolled his eyes. "Just get in."

After a few moments of Quintin's inexperienced fumbling with the door handle, Alex let him in and started the engine. Thus, the boy-from-another-world's education in Earth culture began.

———

QUINTIN STOOD IN FRONT OF THE FULL-LENGTH MIRROR MOUNTED ON Alex's closet door and stared at his reflection, dressed in native clothing and hair still damp from the washing he'd given it in the kitchen sink. Alex had provided him with a pair of socks, blue jeans, and a black short-sleeved T-shirt with a grotesque decaying human skull printed on the front and a strange word above it.

"M-E-T-A-L-L-I-C-A. *Meta Licka?* Alex?"

"Yeah?" called Alex from the stairwell.

"Is this English?"

A moment later, Alex appeared in the doorway with a pair of scuffed sneakers in one hand and a brown leather jacket in the other. "Is what?"

Quintin turned and ran a finger along the strange word.

"Metallica?" Alex tossed the shoes and jacket onto the bed. "It's a band."

Quintin cocked an eyebrow. "Band?"

"Yeah. They're musicians. They perform music. That's their job."

Quintin's expression brightened. "*Earth* music?"

"Yeah," Alex scoffed. "Only the best."

Alex crossed the room to the stereo on top of his dresser and inserted his iPod into the docking station. He searched the menu for a moment and pressed the PLAY button, filling the small room with thunderous heavy metal. Quintin flinched at the sudden noise, covering his ears as his brother began head banging along with "The Shortest Straw."

Slowly, Quintin uncovered his ears and began nodding along with the beat. He tried to say something to Alex, but the words were drowned out by James Hetfield's roaring vocals.

Alex turned the volume knob down ever-so-slightly. "What?"

"I said it reminds me of *Yerxak*," repeated Quintin, a little louder than necessary.

"What the hell is *Yerxak*?" asked Alex, thoroughly butchering the pronunciation of the word.

"They're my favorite musicians back home on Phaedaj," Quintin explained. He retrieved his ear buds from the bloody jumpsuit wadded up on the floor and handed them to Alex. "Here."

Alex turned the wireless earpieces over in his hands. "So... I just put them in my ears?"

"Yeah." Quintin shrugged. "Pretty primitive, I know. Jiri says I'm too young for implants."

"There's no iPod or anything?"

Quintin cocked his head to one side. "Eye pod? No, these are only for your ears."

"Never mind." Alex raised the buds to his ears.

"No," Quintin said, grabbing his brother's wrists. "That's the wrong way. You've got to switch them."

"Like this?" Alex swapped the buds in his hands.

"Yeah," said Quintin. "Otherwise it'll sound really weird."

"Okay." Alex secured the buds in his ears. "Now what?"

"Just press the big button on the side of the right unit," said Quintin.

"This one?" Alex pressed the button and immediately his ears were filled with a loud, grinding, screeching cacophony that resembled nails on a chalkboard with cowbells and garbage can lids to keep rhythm. "Whoa!"

"Isn't it great?" yelled Quintin, still nodding his head to Metallica as the previous song gave way to "Creeping Death."

Alex jerked the buds out and probed his right ear with his little finger. He looked at Quintin as if the small devices had just bitten him. "Are you *sure* I had them in the right way?"

Quintin opened his mouth to say something, but was cut off by an angry voice from downstairs.

*"Alex!"*

"Oh no!" Alex pressed the power button on the stereo, cutting Hetfield off mid-lyric. "My mom!"

"Alexander James Walker," Janice Walker called as she stomped up the stairs. "What have your father and I told you about playing that music so—"

Janice reached the top of the stairs and rounded the corner into the doorway of her son's room. The twins stared back at her like a couple of deer caught in headlights.

"Loud?" she said, her jaw slack with shock.

"Uh," Alex stuttered, trying to find the words. "Mom, this is—"

"Alan!" she cried weakly as her eyes rolled back and she fainted.

Alex rushed forward to catch her and, cradling her in his arms, finished his sentence. "...Quintin."

---

ALAN WALKER SLUMPED INTO HIS CHAIR AND SHOOK HIS HEAD. "I JUST can't believe it."

He sat with Janice at the kitchen table with Alex while the other members of the TDC stood in various locations throughout the kitchen. Lamont knelt beside Janice, checking her pulse. Quintin stood in the corner of the room by the refrigerator, putting as much distance between himself and Janice as possible for fear that the mere sight of him might put her back into shock.

At first, the Walkers hadn't recognized Moe or Lamont, but it didn't take them long to make the connection once they began telling their tale.

"It's just too incredible," said Alan.

For a moment, everyone was silent. It was Janice who finally broke the silence. She looked at Alex and whispered, "How long?"

"How long, what?"

"How long have you known all of this?"

Alex took a deep breath. "Since that night I was attacked in the alley."

"Three years."

Alex nodded. "Yeah."

Janice laughed. There was no joy in the sound. "I suppose there's no point now in telling you you're adopted."

Alex got out of his chair and knelt by his mother's side. "I don't care about all that. You'll always be my mom... Mom."

Janice laughed, this time genuinely happy, and hugged Alex tight. She looked over his shoulder at Quintin, who was still trying desperately to melt into the refrigerator. Janice held out her hand to him; he stared back nervously, but finally knelt beside his brother and allowed Janice to touch his cheek.

She smiled. "You have beautiful eyes."

Quintin's eyes glowed slightly. "Thank you."

"It's a shame you and Alex didn't come to us together."

Quintin thought about this for a moment and said, "I'm here now."

Alex smiled and placed his arm around his brother.

"We have a lot of catching up to do," said Janice.

Quintin nodded. "I'd like that."

Alan cleared his throat and addressed Lamont. "Excuse me, but there's still the issue of Alex's safety. Exactly how much danger is my son in? How much danger are *we* in?"

Lamont shuffled his feet. "Sir, our job is to ensure Alex's survival, no matter the cos—"

"That's not an answer!"

"Dad!" said Alex sternly. "Don't yell at them. They've already saved my life twice."

Moe spoke up for the first time since entering the room, "As long as we live, no harm will come to your son. You have our word on that."

"What about this man?" asked Janice. "The one that wants to kill Alex?"

Moe started to answer, but Alex cut him off. "Don't worry, Mom. He's on the other side of the world."

"We think," Lamont confessed. "There's been no contact in three years. If he was nearby, he'd surely have made an attempt on Alex's life by now."

Robert shifted against the doorframe. "What's more, he's limited in what he can do to us. During the trip here, I reviewed Samrai's file. There's a hidden subroutine in his programming preventing him from revealing sensitive information about Alex. So even if he truly *has* defected, Temujin will get nothing from him."

"See, Mom?" said Alex with a comforting smile. "Temujin can't find us here. We're perfectly safe."

Lamont and Moe exchanged worried glances.

# PART FOUR

# THE BATTLE OF EAST VAN BUREN HIGH

# NINETEEN

*Temple of the Golden Horde*
*Gobi Desert, Mongolia*
*October 20th*

TEMUJIN STRODE DOWN A CORRIDOR TOWARD THE ALIEN'S LABORATORY, a folded satellite map clutched in his right hand. His spies in Beijing had brought it to his attention earlier that morning. Apparently, an unidentified flying object had been briefly sighted in a small farming community in the American Midwest a few weeks before. The craft had disappeared without a trace.

Or had it?

The alien, despite its infuriating inability to supply him with intelligence of any significant value, had hinted on various occasions that he came from a small farm in the Midwest near the banks of a river and the borders of two states. The UFO had last been sighted in Van Buren County in southeast Iowa, not far from the Des Moines River, and the borders of Missouri and Illinois were only a short distance away.

Temujin stepped up to the laboratory doors and they opened automatically; one of the many "improvements" the alien had made to the existing structure. He stepped inside and saw the creature standing at a worktable in the center of the room, tinkering with a strange-looking silver helmet. Although he found the alien's presence irritating, he also found its mechanical ability astounding. The Replodian never slept, but rested in a tube filled with boiling water and drank the same. It also ate ravenously, no doubt to maintain its extreme body temperature.

The creature tirelessly designed and manufactured countless weapons for the eradication of the TDC and the impending war using materials smuggled by train from the Khan's followers in Ulaanbaatar. The Americans, so smug in their military prowess, would never know what hit them. The alien looked up at him with those strange blue eyes and straightened. It pointed to its work on the table.

"Hey, Khan," said Sam. "I think you'll really like what I have here. Check this out: it's a self-contained battle armor suit for your troops. The entire unit is contained in the helmet until activated, at which point the armor envelopes the wearer, granting him increased strength, speed, agility, and an array of onboard weaponry. I've already completed six other prototypes. Want to see a demonstration of what they can do?"

The Khan was silent.

"What? *Oh!*" Sam leaned in close and clapped a hand on Temujin's shoulder. "I know what you're thinking, but this is *nothing* like last time. I promise. Hey, c'mon, who knew humans were so... What's the word? Squishy."

Temujin wiped his robes where the alien had touched him with one gloved hand. "The time has come, Samrai."

"The time? Time for what?"

Temujin slapped the papers down on the table, and the Replodian peered closely at the location circled on the map. He studied the alien's face, and when he saw its eyes widen, he snatched the papers away.

"Ha!" he exclaimed. "I *knew* it. This is the location. Isn't it?"

Sam gave the Khan a confused look. "But the farm isn't circled."

"Yes," said Temujin. "I know that. Do you know what *is?*"

Sam's brow furrowed. Finally he answered, "It's a school."

Again, the Khan smiled. "Indeed, it is."

"I don't understand."

"It's simple." Temujin turned to leave. "Since you cannot provide me with the exact location of the TDC's hidden base, I shall have to search for it myself. I already know the child's name is Alexander. I also know he would be approximately sixteen years of age. Logic dictates that if I search the school for sixteen-year-old males named Alexander, I will find the one I seek."

Sam nodded. "I guess."

The Khan stepped through the door. "I must take my leave to make the final preparations for the attack."

"Wait!" Sam held the door open with his hand. *Attack?*

"Of course," said Temujin. "I've ordered a full battalion and six of your new Death Walkers. This should make for an excellent field test for them."

*"Mechs?"* cried Sam. "They're only kids!"

"The Death Walkers are insurance," said Temujin. "My search for the child shall not be hindered by any interference from the local authorities."

"But those mechs are equipped with .50 caliber guns and rocket launchers," Sam protested.

"Your point?"

"The kids—"

"What of them?" barked Temujin. "What are children in the path of *God?*"

Sam glared at the man he had served faithfully for three years. "You are *not* a god, Temujin."

"Once Alexander is dead, I *will* be."

Temujin turned to leave and called over his shoulder, "I expect you in the hangar in ten minutes to conduct the final inspection of the mechs."

Sam hung his head and, with slumped shoulders, whispered, "Yes, my Khan."

AN HOUR LATER, SAM STOOD IN FRONT OF A BIPEDAL ROBOT TWICE HIS height. He tapped a series of commands into a tablet computer and watched the diagnostics program scan the mech's critical systems. Lines of code and flashing diagrams danced across the display, flashing green as each system confirmed optimal functionality.

He glanced up at the Death Walker's weapons—twin .50 caliber miniguns attached to razor-clawed arms and two shoulder-mounted rocket launchers. He'd named the machines well; all they did was walk and spew death. The robot's black, oblong sensor eye mounted on the front of its body glared down at him accusingly.

The tablet beeped, signaling the completion of the diagnostics and drew his attention back to the task at hand. He nodded to a waiting soldier, and the final Death Walker was loaded into the *Ragnarok's* cargo bay.

*The Ragnarok*, an immense troop transport the length of a football field, was undetectable by radar or satellites and shielded with a light-bending apparatus that rendered it practically invisible to the human eye. Unfortunately, to Samrai's frustration, he was still unable to prevent it from casting a shadow, but the Khan was unconcerned.

Nearby, Temujin and Chuluun oversaw the boarding of the troops. Each Horde soldier, clad in new plasma-resistant body armor, received an assault rifle before stepping up. Sam felt a pang of guilt as he watched them. Although he didn't agree with the Khan's plan, it did seem to be the most efficient way of tracking down and elimi-nating the TDC. And that was his goal, wasn't it?

Sam shook his head and whispered, "What have I done?"

He was so absorbed in his thoughts, he didn't notice the modified loading mech walking straight toward him. The robot ambled dumbly on its path, both unaware and uncaring of the high-voltage charging cable stretched taut along the ground to the transport's power cells. One of the mech's clawed feet, designed to cling to even the roughest terrain, came down and sliced the heavy cable in two. One half recoiled and flailed toward Sam, who turned in time to see it but was unable to react.

The severed cable, spouting violent yellow and blue sparks, connected with Sam's chest. The Replodian screamed as an immeasurable amount of energy surged through his body. His screams died in his throat as the pain overpowered him and he was simply held up by the current. He was dying; he was sure of it.

One of the technicians flipped the emergency shut-off lever on the breaker and cut the current. Sam fell to his hands and knees; his body shuddered uncontrollably and his teeth chattered from the surge of energy leaving him. Smoke curled lazily from his clothes and hair. He sucked in a rattling breath as the electricity tingled through his bloodstream.

The shrill blast of the departing supply train's whistle sent new waves of pain through his skull, cutting through the fog of random sensations assailing his brain. He clutched his hands over his ears until the sound subsided.

Frantic soldiers and technicians called out all around him. Through the muddled din, he picked out one familiar voice – Temujin's. Slowly, Sam remembered where he was. He remembered the mission, and the innocents who would be caught in the crossfire in order to destroy his enemies.

He furrowed his brow.

*Whose* enemies?

The terrible hate he had always felt for his brothers was gone, replaced by deep, heart-wrenching sorrow. When he looked up, his eyes were filled with the most intense hatred he had ever known, but not for his brothers or for Alexander.

For Temujin.

As he glared at the warlord, he realized the terrible mistake he had made. He had allowed his programming to manipulate him into handing a madman the power to destroy *billions* of lives. But no longer. Sam realized he was unique; he was the first of his kind. Out of millions of Replodian mercenaries who had come and gone before him over the millennia, he was the first to have the gift of free will. Sam had a choice.

And he made it.

A technician rushed to his side and touched his shoulder, recoiling as the intense heat radiating from the Replodian burned his fingertips. Without so much as a glance, Sam threw the man aside with a swipe of his arm, sending the man sailing into a stack of crates several yards away.

The Replodian rose to his feet, his fists clenched so that his finger-nails dug deep into his palms. Hot, yellow blood dripped onto the filthy cement floor, sending tiny billows of steam into the frigid air.

*"Khan!"* he roared.

---

THE ALIEN'S CHANGE IN DEMEANOR DID NOT GO UNNOTICED BY THE Khan. Its rage was almost tangible, suffocating. The air became thick with it. For the first time in his life, Temujin was afraid.

"Onto the ship," he said.

Chuluun turned. "My lord?"

"Onto the ship," the Khan repeated more urgently. "Now! Get us in the air."

Chuluun obediently followed Temujin onto the bridge of the *Ragnarok.* The alien leapt onto the boarding platform and ran down the ramp toward the door, which slammed shut just before he could reach it. He crashed into it and pounded his fists against the armored shell, screaming as loud as his parched throat would allow.

---

"TEMUJIN!" SAM BELLOWED. "OPEN THIS DOOR!"

The Khan's voice rang out over the hangar's P.A. system, "I can't do that, my friend. I don't know what has come over you all of a sudden, but I cannot allow you to stand in my way."

"You son-of-a-bitch," yelled Sam. "They're only children! Leave them out of this."

"How does the old saying go?" The smile in Temujin's voice was quite apparent. "Oh, yes. One cannot make an omelet without breaking some eggs."

"No!" Sam screamed. "You can't!"

"Goodbye, Samrai."

The warlord's words were punctuated by the transport's engines igniting. As the *Ragnarok* lifted off the ground, Sam clung to the guardrail to avoid being blown back by the thrusters.

Sam watched, helpless, as the *Ragnarok* rose out of the building and disappeared into the low bank of clouds drifting over the temple. He turned, sprinted down the platform, and shoved a sentry aside as he burst through the exit into the corridor. Someone had to stop Temujin, and he knew just who could do it, but first he had to warn them... and collect something from his lab.

---

IN THE COMMUNICATIONS ROOM, CAPTAIN SÜKH'S HAND MOVED TO THE pommel of his sword as he watched the alien flee the hangar on the monitor. The *Ragnarok* lifted to safety, and he breathed a sigh of relief. Lord Temujin was out of danger.

The Khan's voice came over the radio, *"Captain Sükh."*

Sükh keyed the communicator while tracking the alien's progress through the base on the row of monitors. "I am here, my Khan."

*"The alien is no longer of any use to me. Destroy it."*

Sükh smiled. "Yes, my Khan. It shall be done."

*"Do not fail me, Captain."*

Sükh watched the alien turn into the north wing. There was only one place it would go.

"Have my elite guard meet me at the alien's laboratory," he ordered one of the communications officers. "Fully armed."

"Yes, sir!"

SAM STEPPED THROUGH THE DOOR TO HIS LABORATORY AND SCANNED the room, making a quick mental inventory of its contents. He grabbed two pistols, one plasma and one gel, and stuffed them into his belt. Next, he collected a plasma rifle from a wall rack and checked the magazine. Full charge. He slipped the rifle's shoulder strap over his head and collected several grenades from a nearby bin.

As he turned to leave, his eyes fell on the main worktable. He slowly approached the silver prototype helmet and brushed his fingers against the cold, unfinished metal. Temujin could never be allowed to possess these weapons.

*Never.*

He crossed the room and rummaged through the clutter underneath a workbench until his fingers closed around an oversized canvas duffel bag. He opened a cabinet door beside the weapons rack and six helmets identical to the one on the table stared back at him, their black visors lifeless and sinister, just as he'd designed them. One by one, he shoved the helmets into the bag, finally collecting the prototype on the table and shoving it into the bag as well.

He slung the bag over his shoulder and walked toward the exit. Just as he approached the doors, they slid open and he came face to face with Captain Sükh and his elite guard.

The captain smiled. "I've waited a long time for this, freak."

Sam took a step back and adopted a defensive posture.

"Kill him," barked Sükh, moving out of the way of the troops behind him.

Immediately the air was filled with bursts from both plasma and double-barreled corrosive gel rifles. Sam jumped above the blasts, drawing the plasma pistol from his belt and firing on the advancing troops, but the bolts bounced off the soldiers' armor. Sam fired into a rack of gel rifles and the weapons exploded, spraying a few of the soldiers with lava-hot purple gel that burned slowly through their armor and melted their flesh like marshmallows to a flame.

He bolted to the left, pelting the soldiers with plasma fire as he ran, and slid behind a barrel. Enemy fire shredded the barrel as he scanned the room, looking for any means of escape. His eyes came to rest on the grenade bin, and he remembered the ones stashed in his pocket. Sam grabbed the bin and flung it into the center of the room, spilling grenades across the floor.

He dug in his pocket for a single grenade and popped the top off with his thumb. "Hey! Captain *Suck!*"

Sükh looked up in horror at the alien's hand. "Stop him!"

"Let's play a little game." Sam thumbed the primer plunger and tossed it into the cluster on the floor. "One of these things is not like the others."

"Get out!" Sükh dove into the hallway.

Sam jumped onto a worktable and ran across it, bypassing the scrambling Horde troopers, and leapt over their heads toward the open doorway. The grenade exploded, triggering a chain of explosions. Sam cleared the door just as the resulting fireball reached it and slammed into the opposite wall. He cringed at the sound of screams from within as the fire from dozens of weapons exploding engulfed the room.

Sam stood and turned to see Sükh staring back at him, the right side of his face badly burnt and his sword drawn.

"Don't try it, Sükh," Sam warned.

Sükh rushed forward to strike, but the corridor was rocked by another explosion from inside the lab, and the supports holding up the rough stone ceiling began to buckle. Sam aimed his pistol at the support beam and fired, causing it to snap under the strain of its burden. Sükh and Sam dove for safety as the ceiling collapsed between them, raining down chunks of steel and stone.

Sam took advantage of the diversion and turned to run toward the nearest emergency exit. Shaken but unharmed, Sükh climbed to his feet and keyed his communicator.

"This is Sükh," he yelled over the deafening fire alarm that was now blaring throughout the temple. "Deploy the Death Walkers to destroy the alien."

"*How many, sir?*"

"All of them, you *fool*," Sükh roared. "Do it now!"

***

SAM CLIMBED THE LADDER TO THE EMERGENCY HATCH AND PULLED THE release lever. Tiny charges detonated around the circular opening, and the cover flew off in a shower of sparks. He crawled out of the smoking hole and found himself standing in the middle of a derelict airstrip. He pulled his jacket tight against his body, his teeth chattering from the below-freezing temperatures, and looked around for any means of transportation; a car, a truck, a damned bicycle —anything!

"The train," he breathed. "Train, train, train. Where's the goddamned train?"

A door set into the front of one of the hangars lining the runway split open. As the sunlight poured inside, twelve Death Walkers jerked awake, their postures straightening, and lumbered toward him.

Sam's shoulders slumped. "Oh, *balls*."

The mechs homed in on his voice and scanned him. Sam felt his heart jump into his throat when the lead mech raised its arms and trained the twin guns on him. The cannons spun, spewing fifty rounds per second while Sam flipped nimbly out of the line of fire, but the robot continued to track his movements. The other robots followed suit, sending plumes of sand into the air as their projectiles narrowly missed their mark.

Over the din of gunfire, Sam heard the distant sound of a whistle. The train was already nearly half a mile away, but it was his only chance. Sam turned his back on his deadly creations and ran northward into the Gobi Desert.

The robots stopped firing to pursue their prey. Powerful, clawed legs propelled them over the sand and rocks with great speed as they closed in on their target. One of the mechs locked onto the Replodian and fired a shoulder-mounted rocket. It missed the mark by a mere three feet, but still threw sand and rock flying in all directions and sent Sam sprawling to the ground.

162

As they came within range, the mechs opened up again with the .50 cals, their barrels glowing bright orange from the heat. Sam rolled out of the way and half-crawled, half-ran toward the tracks until he was able to regain his footing. He ran parallel to the tracks, straining to catch up to the rear car.

He dug in his pocket for a grenade, the rapid rise and fall of his body making the action difficult. Finally he found one, mashed the plunger, and counted to three before chucking it over his shoulder. The grenade detonated under one of the robots' feet, sending it teetering onto the mech beside it. It fell hard against the other's rocket launcher and the weapon exploded, critically damaging but not neutralizing the robots.

Sam ran as hard as his legs would allow until he came right alongside the rear railcar. As the train began to slip away from him, he jumped and reached out, snagging the ladder on the back. One of the mechs swiped at him with its clawed hand, but the fingers closed on empty air as the Replodian climbed to the top. Once there, Sam primed his rifle. He sighted down the barrel at the closest mech and opened fire, sending white-hot plasma bolts through the air in a steady beat.

The plasma bounced harmlessly off of the robot's armored shell. The mech raised its arm cannon to fire again, and Sam aimed for the barrels. As they began to spin, Sam fired a plasma bolt into the cannon, which exploded, sending shrapnel into the electronic eye. The mech's movements became erratic, smacking into the others until another robot slapped it aside and continued the pursuit.

"Damn," Sam said. He'd have been proud if only his creations weren't trying to turn him into Replodian road kill.

Sam reached into the breast pocket of his coveralls and pulled out a roll of electrical tape. Placing it between his teeth, he searched for more grenades and found three. He ducked the bullets whizzing past his head and hastily lashed the grenades together with the tape, tearing off the excess length with his teeth. He plucked the safety tops off, mashed down all three plungers, counted to four, and pitched the bundle over the side of the car.

The grenades plopped onto the rocky sand just a few paces ahead of the charging robots. Sam covered his head the instant before they detonated. The railcar teetered from the force of the blast but managed to stay on its wheels. The explosion created a deep crater, and Sam laughed as the three leading mechs fell into it, kicking and flailing their metal limbs. The rest of the robots were caught in the pileup, and Sam cheered as the train steadily pulled away from them.

When he was confident that the mechs could no longer pursue him, Sam collapsed onto his back and closed his eyes, mentally preparing for the two-day journey ahead. Khan's transport ship, while advanced, was mercifully slow.

At least he'd done *something* right.

As the train carried him north toward Russia, he prayed to whoever would listen that he was not too late.

# TWENTY

*East Van Buren High School*
*Farmington, Iowa*
*October 21st*

Crystal Hammond looked up from her Spanish notes and gazed across the table at Alex, who was frowning at his algebra book with his pencil poised over a notebook covered in half-erased and botched equations. She giggled as he growled and scratched out a long sequence of numbers and letters. He looked up and gave her a rueful smirk.

The room grew dark. Alex looked out the window and saw a shadow creeping over the cars in the parking lot.

Crystal groaned. "Please tell me it's not going to rain!"

Alex looked up. Blue sky and lazily drifting white clouds filled the skylight. He shrugged.

Crystal tore her gaze away from the window. "So, have you got a date for the homecoming dance?"

Alex grinned and began to rework the equation. "I think I just might."

"Really?" Crystal feigned indifference. "Anybody I know?"

Alex's pencil scratched across the paper. "Oh, I don't know."

"Is she pretty?"

Alex nodded, still not looking up. "Gorgeous."

"Where's she from?"

"Salem."

"Really?" Crystal raised an eyebrow. "What a coincidence."

"Yup."

"Sounds an awful lot like me," Crystal teased.

"Kind of," said Alex, "except this girl does my math homework for me."

Crystal gasped and kicked his shin underneath the table. "Alex Walker!"

Alex grinned as he rubbed his leg. "You have something better to offer?"

Crystal grinned suggestively. "I might."

"Ah." Alex returned to his work. "Then I'll take it into consideration."

This earned him a kick to his other shin, and Alex laughed despite the pain.

"You're terrible!"

Alex grinned. "But you love me."

"Maybe."

"*Maybe?*"

Crystal leaned in close and smiled. "I'll have to take it into consideration."

"Oh ho," said Alex. "So that's how it is?"

"Yep. That's how it is."

"Walker! Hammond!" barked Ms. Fremont, the study hall monitor. "You two lovebirds knock it off over there."

"Sorry, ma'am," said Crystal.

Alex muttered under his breath as he began to doodle in the margins of his notebook.

"She's just jealous," whispered Crystal.

"Yeah," said Alex. "Dinosaurs went extinct sixty-five million years ago and she hasn't been able to find a date since."

Crystal giggled, and then after a moment of silence sighed. "I'm bored."

"Gee," said Alex as he sketched an angry-looking Ms. Fremont. "Now I really *do* feel loved."

"Not like that, silly." Crystal slapped him playfully on the arm. "I just wish something would happen."

Alex added Stegosaurus back plates to his doodle of Ms. Fremont and murmured, "Like what?"

"I don't know," said Crystal. "Something. Anything. Nothing *ever* happens around here."

At that moment, the cafeteria doors were violently thrown open, and a squad of more than thirty armed Horde troopers surged into the room and surrounded the students. A group of students at the far end of the room attempted to escape through the other door, but found the hallway filled with more soldiers. The troopers raised their weapons, particularly nasty alien-looking rifles, and the teens cowered in their seats and under tables.

Ms. Fremont tried to protest, but one of the soldiers fired his double-barreled rifle at her face and she fell to the floor screaming as smoking purple gel covered her head. The students closest to the action screamed in terror and pushed back into the crowd, away from the body. Through a gap in the crowd, Alex could see Ms. Fremont, still kicking as the flesh melted and fell off her exposed skull. Crystal screamed and buried her face in his shoulder.

A large bald man entered the room from the hall and shouted something in Mongolian at the soldier who had shot Ms. Fremont. Alex struggled to hear them over the shouting and whimpering of the other students, but he did catch one word that the large man said.

*Alive.*

As part of his training in the TDC, Alex underwent extensive language training in many Asian dialects, but still had problems with some of the bigger words. He cursed himself for leaving his translation ear bud in his locker; it had remained there ever since the time Lamont scolded him for using it to cheat in Spanish class. The meaning of the exchange was instantly cleared up, however, when the troops began ushering the panic-stricken students down the hall toward the gymnasium.

Along the way, Alex saw other groups of students being ejected from their classrooms by more gunmen. Mr. Gibson, the algebra teacher, tried to play hero and got a rifle butt to the teeth for his trouble. Alex started to step out of line to help him, but Crystal grabbed him by the arm and stared pleadingly at him with tear-filled eyes. One of the Hordesmen shoved them forward with his rifle, and Alex stared at the floor as he walked, trying not to look at the group of soldiers mercilessly kicking the downed teacher. Slowly, so as not to attract attention to himself, Alex pressed the small red button on the side of his wristwatch.

And he prayed.

---

"GOT ANY FIVES?" ASKED ROBERT.

Moe shook his head. "Go fish."

Robert grimaced and drew another card from the deck, adding it to his hand.

"Got any twos?" asked Moe.

Robert grumbled under his breath as he pulled out the two of spades and flicked it across the workstation to Moe.

"I hate this game," he muttered.

Suddenly a long string of muffled French cursing spewed forth from behind them. Moe looked over his shoulder at the pair of legs sticking out from the open access hatch on the bottom of the long-dead hologram projector.

"Problems?" asked Moe.

Rene crawled out of the machine and wiped the sweat from his forehead with the back of his hand, smearing it with dust and grime. His hair was held in place with a black bandanna wrapped around his head. In his left hand he held a small, strange-looking piece of alien hardware.

"Can you fix it?" asked Robert.

"No," said Rene. "These parts were manufactured on Phaedaj, but they've been out of production for about ten years give or take. I doubt there's a junk shop in this corner of the galaxy that would carry one."

"So much for our lifetime warranty," said Lamont from his chair where he sat watching Robert and Moe play cards.

"Isn't there an Earth equivalent?" asked Robert.

Rene shook his head. "I highly doubt it. Besides, I don't think it would fit anyway. Any piece of Earth tech that does the same thing as this would be the size of an engine block. Sorry, I just don't think it can be fixed."

Lamont got up from his chair and began to pace angrily. "Samrai knew *exactly* what he was doing when he shot that projector."

Rene nodded and turned the alien component over between his fingers. "I'd say so."

"Well, that's that," said Moe, turning back to his cards. "Got any threes?"

"Damn," growled Robert, passing Moe another card from his hand.

Suddenly the lights began flashing red and a blaring klaxon filled the room. A few moments later, Quintin and Cherry entered through the door leading to the gym, their shirts and hair drenched with sweat and their hands encased in boxing gloves.

"What's going on?" yelled Quintin.

Father's booming voice filled the room. "Alex has activated the personal distress beacon on his wristwatch. I'm afraid the school is under attack."

"Attack?" asked Moe. "Are you sure? Maybe he just bumped it."

"I am monitoring the police band," said Father. "The sheriff's department and highway patrol are responding to a hostage situation at the school."

"*Hostage?*" Cherry shouted.

"Everybody gear up," ordered Moe. "Grab as many weapons as you can carry."

"Moe!" called Lamont.

Moe turned and looked at his brother, and the look of grave concern on his face. "What?"

"I've been trying to contact Alex telepathically," said Lamont.

"And? What's he saying?"

"Nothing," Lamont replied. "He's not answering me."

Moe's eyes narrowed for a moment in intense concentration, then widened in horror as he came to the same conclusion. "Double time it, people!"

———

CRYSTAL SLIPPED HER HAND INTO ALEX'S AND FOUGHT BACK THE TEARS stinging her eyes. Ever since the students were first ushered into the gym, Alex had been calmly scanning the room as if looking for someone among the gunmen. He squeezed Crystal's hand reassuringly and continued his search of the room, not looking at her. Finally the last of the students and teachers were forced into the room and the doors closed, locking the students in with the gun-toting intruders.

A minute later, the doors opened again and a tall Asian man stepped into the room, followed by the bald man who had been giving orders back in the cafeteria. The new arrival had long black hair underneath a horned helmet and sported a long black mustache and neatly trimmed goatee. A cold shudder ran through Crystal's body when she looked at him. When the tall man entered the room, Alex's eyes finally stopped moving.

The man stepped to the center of the basketball court, removed his helmet, and in a commanding voice said, "Good morning. I apologize for intruding upon your studies, and I promise to be brief. I am here for one person and one person alone. If you cooperate, you will be released. If you do not—" The soldiers all cocked their rifles in one unified and unnerving motion. "—there *will* be consequences."

The crying became louder, and Crystal could hear the occasional whispered prayer around her.

"Bring me the headmaster," said the man.

Two of the troopers dragged the principal to the center of the floor and forced him to his knees in front of the tall man.

"Good morning, Mister..." The man paused and looked at him pensively before continuing with a queer smile on his lips. "Hoskins."

"Who are you? What is it that you want?"

"My name is Temujin, Mr. Hoskins. And what I *want* is the world, but today I'm going to settle for a child. I want you to turn over to me all male children in this room with the first name Alexander."

Crystal gasped and cried into Alex's shoulder. Alex continued to stare at Temujin while he ran his fingers through her hair.

Mr. Hoskins shook his head, astounded by Temujin's request. "I will *not!*"

Temujin sighed. "I will only ask one last time. *Please* turn over to me all of the boys in your school with the name Alexander."

"You must be insane to think that I would hand *any* of these children over to you," said Hoskins defiantly.

"Unfortunate." Temujin shook his head in disappointment. "Chuluun."

The bald man drew his sword and the blade came down on the back of Mr. Hoskins's neck, severing his head and sending it rolling across the basketball court. Screams issued from every corner of the gym. One of the boys, a freshman whose name Crystal didn't know, vomited.

"Bring me a teacher," said Temujin. "Now!"

"Yes, my Khan." Chuluun motioned to a nearby trooper.

Two more soldiers dragged the Spanish teacher, a frail and frightened woman, to the center of the gym. When they deposited her at the Khan's feet, she tried to scramble away, but was stopped by Chuluun's blade at her throat.

"Again," said Temujin. "Turn over to me all boys named Alexander."

The teacher, completely overcome with fear, buried her face in her hands and sobbed uncontrollably.

"Two more minutes," Alex whispered.

Crystal looked up into Alex's eyes. "What?"

"Just two more minutes," he repeated, more to himself than to Crystal. "Don't hurt anybody else for two more minutes."

———

SHERIFF CHALLIS BROUGHT HIS PATROL CAR TO A SCREECHING HALT alongside Chief Deputy Tim Barker's vehicle and jumped out as fast as his fifty-four-year-old legs would allow.

"What the hell is going on in there, Tim?" he yelled over the approaching sirens of other responding deputies.

"I'm not sure, Keith," said Barker. "Apparently a secretary got to a phone and called in a report of gunmen in the school. I can just see two of them guarding the front doors there."

"Have they made any demands?" asked Challis.

"None."

"State Police coming?"

"I called 'em," said Barker. "A couple of troopers in the area are on their way now with more coming from Mount Pleasant."

"Good," said Challis. "Have we got a line of communication into the school yet?"

Barker shook his head. "Dottie's working on it, but no one's answering in there."

"Well, you tell her to ring that damn phone off the hook if she has to," shouted Challis over the growing noise. "I want to know what these bastards want."

"You got it, Keith."

Challis walked back to his car, grabbed the microphone for his radio, and switched it to loudspeaker mode. "This is Sheriff Challis. We are willing to listen to any demands you may have. Come out with your hands in plain sight and no one will be...."

The ground beneath his feet began to shake and the sheriff's voice trailed off. He watched as a discarded soda can at his feet rattled on the pavement.

"What the hell?"

The first of the Death Walkers stepped around the east corner of the building and lumbered slowly toward the bewildered cops. The mech was followed by a second, and a third, until all six were lined up in front of the school, barring the police from entry.

The mech in the center raised its arm cannons, aiming them directly at Sheriff Challis, and in a menacing electronic voice said, *"No access."*

"What the hell are those things?" one of the young deputies behind Challis yelled.

As if signaled by some silent electronic cue, the other five mechs raised their arms, bringing the .50 caliber guns to bear on the pistol-packing cops.

"Everybody back, now!" Challis ordered.

The first mech opened fire and shredded the hood of Challis's cruiser into scrap metal; oil and antifreeze spewed onto the ground. The other mechs opened fire and riddled both the police cars and students' vehicles with armor-piercing rounds. The cops ran for cover as the mechs advanced, spewing white-hot lead with every step. The lead mech stepped down onto the ragged remains of Challis's patrol car, plunged one of its clawed hands through the roof, and ripped the back seat out with one deft tug. The mech hurled the seat at the cowering cops, missing both Challis and Barker by mere inches.

*"No access,"* the mech growled a second time.

"Barker," Challis yelled over the sound of heavy gunfire. "Do you have your phone?"

Barker looked up in time to see his patrol car explode in an immense fireball as one of the high-caliber bullets found the gas tank. "Not anymore!"

"Jesus Christ!" Challis shielded his face from the intense heat with his arm. "Somebody get me the god damned National Guard!"

# TWENTY-ONE

Moe white-knuckled the steering wheel of Alan Walker's red and white pickup. Although the school was only a few miles from the farm, this had easily been the longest drive of his short life. He looked up, saw the first plumes of black smoke rising from behind the trees, and buried the accelerator. When the school came into view, the carnage was far worse than he could ever have imagined.

"What are those things?" yelled Quintin from the back of the pickup.

Moe watched in horror as one of the Death Walkers brought its massive clawed foot down on a deputy. The cop fired his service revolver into the robot until it clicked empty. Moe felt his lunch coming up as the mech shoved its arm cannon into the screaming man's face and opened fire.

"*Mon Dieu*," cried Rene. "We have to get in there!"

"Working on it!" Moe jerked the wheel to the left and swung the pickup into the parking lot. "Hang on!"

Moe aimed the truck right for the mech and stepped down on the accelerator. The mech turned and brought its weapons to bear on the approaching vehicle. Moe did not swerve, but kept the truck aimed right for the center of the mech. Beside him, Lamont grabbed his door nervously.

"Uh, Moe," he yelled. "What are you doing?"

Moe tightened his grip on the wheel and snarled, "I'm going to ram this truck right down its god damned throat!"

Lamont stuck his head out the window and shouted to the others sitting in the back, "Everybody, grab ahold of something!"

A moment later, the truck collided with the mech at nearly seventy miles-per-hour in an explosion of grinding metal and sparks. The mech let out an electronic screech as the impact tore the cannons from its arms and one of the missiles detonated inside the launcher, taking the right arm off at the shoulder. The front end of the truck wrapped around the mech's sturdy body and Moe grunted as the steering wheel collided with his chest. The truck sat there for a moment, entangled with the burning wreckage of the mech as Sheriff Challis stared in disbelief.

Moe kicked the driver's side door clean off the hinges and hopped out, a "paintball" rifle clutched in his hands. The others followed suit, jumping out of the back and brandishing weapons. Challis stared in awe at the completely intact people walking away from a wreck that should have left every last one of them in body bags. One of the deputies raised his shotgun at the armed strangers, but Challis put out an arm and lowered the gun.

"Who the hell are you people?" he yelled.

Moe cocked his rifle and smirked. "We're the good guys. We'll take it from here, Sheriff."

The sound of grinding metal drew their attention and they turned in time to see the wounded Death Walker swipe the wreckage of the truck away with a single swing of its remaining arm. It turned to face the bewildered TDC agents and growled.

"I think you pissed it off, Moe," said Robert.

The mech stepped forward and a red laser flashed out from its electronic eye, passing slowly over each of the TDC agents in turn before finally blinking out again.

The mech took another step forward and in its electronic voice said, *"TDC."*

"I take it we're expected," said Cherry.

"Samrai," Lamont growled as he twisted his grip on the rifle stock.

*"Objective altered,"* said the mech, flexing the razor-sharp claws on its remaining arm. *"Destroy TDC."*

The other mechs immediately ceased their assault on the police and focused their attention on the six new arrivals. Lamont raised his rifle and fired a plasma bolt at the nose of the damaged mech, but the blast bounced harmlessly off its armored shell.

"We're in trouble!" he yelled.

Moe fired three paintballs from his gun and the sticky purple substance adhered to the mech's shell, bubbling and smoking as it began to do its work, but after several seconds, the metal was still intact. Only a dark stain showed the corrosive gel had ever been there.

"You ain't kidding," said Moe.

The others immediately opened fire, but it had no effect. As the other mechs approached, they unloaded their arm cannons at the TDC, sending them scattering to various areas of the parking lot. Quintin ran toward the school, firing continuous bursts of automatic plasma fire, and took cover behind a demolished and burning police car. He turned and looked at the school, praying to the Great Mother that his brother could hold out just a few minutes longer.

---

TEARS STUNG ALEX'S EYES AS TEMUJIN KICKED THE SPANISH TEACHER'S lifeless body aside. The poor woman had shown no defiance, only immobilizing fear—something the Khan had shown no patience for. Temujin strode forward, away from the spreading pool of blood at his feet.

"You're only prolonging the inevitable, boy," he taunted. "How many more have to die? Maybe your peers should be next to suffer."

Alex ground his teeth together in anger.

In the distance, an explosion rocked the school. Dust rained down from the rafters, and the students huddled together and screamed. Temujin smiled.

"Are you that much of a coward that you will let others die in your stead?" the warlord asked.

Alex took a deep, calming breath.

"I tire of this," said Temujin. "Separate them."

The girls shrieked, clinging both to each other and their boyfriends for protection.

"If they resist," Temujin shouted to be heard over the screams, "shoot them. The girls are of no use to me."

Slowly, the soldiers picked the girls out of the crowd one by one. Alex held onto Crystal's hand until a Horde trooper finally tore them apart, his fingers reaching for that one last touch as she was pulled away, sobbing hysterically and struggling not to cry his name and reveal him to the invaders. Finally, the girls were herded to the other side of the gym, and Temujin approached the boys, examining them carefully. Alex tried to empty his mind, not giving the Khan anything to lock onto with his mental powers.

"Reveal yourself, Alexander," said Temujin as he passed. "Spare these innocent children. Prove to them just how much of a hero you *really* are."

Alex's anger reached the boiling point. ::Bastard.::

Temujin turned, but the brief projection wasn't enough for him to lock onto his prey. He smirked.

"I had hoped we could be civilized about this, but it seems you leave me no choice." Temujin turned to address the soldiers guarding the girls. "Shoot one of the girls. Pick a pretty one."

The boys shouted with outrage as the soldiers pulled one of the sophomores, a raven-haired girl with braces named Lindsey, out of the group and shoved her to her knees. Lindsey cried and screamed as a Hordesman placed the barrel of his plasma rifle against her head. Alex tensed and prepared to surrender himself when a voice rang out from the group of boys.

"Wait," said the voice. "My name is Alexander."

Alex looked over and saw one of the seniors, Alex Ross, stepping out into the open. Ross was tall and muscular; being captain of the football team and an avid bodybuilder, he actually looked the part of a hero. Temujin strode over to him and looked long and hard into Ross's eyes.

"He is not the one," he said. "Kill him *and* the girl."

"No!" screamed Ross and Lindsey in unison.

Chuluun raised his sword toward Ross and the soldier across the room squeezed the trigger.

"Khan!"

Temujin turned slowly and looked doubtfully at the pale, long-haired young man stepping out of the crowd toward him.

"I'm the one you want," Alex said. "*I'm* Alexander."

The Khan sneered. "Prove it. Chuluun, kill the boy."

Chuluun swung his sword, but an unseen force stopped the blade in midair, just short of Ross's neck. A dark laugh escaped the Khan's lips as he looked at Alex. The teen's hair ruffled in the wind created by the psychic energy around him.

Temujin clapped slowly and took two steps toward his adversary. "Impressive... for a mere child."

"That's nothing," said Alex. "Wait until you see *this!*"

Alex raised his arm and Lindsey's captor was flung into the air. The angry teen swiped his arm across his body and the Horde trooper sailed across the room. The man struck the wall with a sickening crack that silenced his shrill screams and fell to the floor, his neck broken.

Temujin laughed. "A child with toy soldiers."

Unable to contain his anger, Alex stepped forward and, focusing all of his rage into a single burst of energy, thrust it forward at Temujin. The blast struck him hard in the chest, knocking him off balance, but the warlord kept his footing and sneered.

"Very good." Temujin nodded with approval. "My turn."

Temujin thrust his hand into the air, and Alex felt the ground abruptly pulled out from under him as he was lifted into the air by the superior power of the Khan's mind. Temujin curled his fingers together in a half-fist, and Alex screamed as his body was wracked with terrible pain, suspended helpless, over fifteen feet in the air. His body became enveloped in searing hot, blue waves of electricity and his screams grew louder. The lightning poured from his eyes like electric tears.

*"Yes,"* Temujin roared. *"This* is the one! *You* are the child I seek!"

"Lamont!" Alex screamed, unable to project his call through the intense pain. "Moe! Help me!"

"Scream all you want, boy." The Khan laughed and closed his fist tighter, sending new waves of pain into Alex's body. "No one is coming to save you. You are alone now!"

"Quintin!" The tears streaming down Alex's cheeks boiled and evaporated in the heat. *"Father!"*

Through the pain, Alex heard Crystal crying out his name, her voice hoarse from the screaming. Suddenly the pain ceased, and Alex fell to the floor in a moaning, smoking heap.

"Help... me," he groaned. "Please."

A shadow fell over him, and Alex looked up through burning eyes to see the cloudy form of Temujin standing over him.

"How does it feel, boy?" Temujin jeered. "True power? The power of God! Perhaps you would have attained it if you lived long enough."

Across the room, Crystal fought against the holds of several girls trying to restrain her and cried out, "Alex!"

::Crystal,:: Alex projected desperately. ::Don't!::

But Temujin intercepted the mental message and turned to look at the girl. "Crystal? Come to me, my dear."

One of the soldiers grabbed Crystal by the hair and dragged her to where the Khan stood waiting and Alex rolled on the floor in agony. Crystal sobbed as she drew closer. The smell of burnt flesh and hair hung heavy in the air. She tried to run to him, but the hand tangled in her hair jerked suddenly, yanking her away, even as she reached out to touch his prone form. Temujin took hold of her by the arm and pulled her closer to him.

"See your beloved hero?" he whispered in her ear. "See how far he has fallen?"

The putrid stench of yak's milk lingering on the Khan's breath reached her nostrils, and Crystal tasted bile rising in the back of her throat. "A-Alex!"

"She's not part of this," Alex moaned.

Temujin sneered. "She's *yours*."

"Let her go!"

"Or what, hero?" Temujin mocked.

His muscles burning, Alex reached behind his back, drew a plasma pistol from the waistband of his jeans, and aimed it at the Khan's head with a trembling hand. The captive students gasped.

"I'll kill you," Alex croaked. "You son-of-a-bitch, I swear to God I'll kill you."

"Put that away, boy." Temujin swatted the air with his hand and sent the pistol flying. "You might hit the girl."

Alex watched the pistol fly from his hand and skitter under the bleachers, hopelessly out of reach. He reached out to try to retrieve it, but he was too weak. His powers were gone.

Temujin sneered as he brushed his gloved fingers through Crystal's mussed hair. "I wouldn't want you to damage the newest addition to my harem."

"No," Alex growled. "Don't you *touch* her!"

Temujin brushed his lips against the sobbing girl's ear. "Perhaps I'll let you watch before you die. Would you like that?"

"No!" Alex rose awkwardly to his hands and knees and prepared to lunge at his enemy.

Chuluun kicked, striking Alex square in the jaw with his boot. Alex tumbled over backwards from the force of the impact and fell hard onto his back, unconscious before he even hit the ground. Temujin shoved Crystal into the arms of the nearest soldier.

"Take her," he said. "Prepare the *Ragnarok* for departure. We have what we came for... and more."

"No!" Crystal shrieked and struggled against the soldier. "Alex! Oh, God! Alex, wake up!"

Temujin shushed her with a finger to her lips. "Hush, child. It will all be over soon."

"What of the boy, my lord?" asked Chuluun.

Temujin turned to leave. "Bring him, of course."

"And the TDC?"

Temujin paused and smiled at the general. "I don't think they will be a problem, Chuluun. The alien saw to that for us."

"What if he shows up here, my lord? Captain Sükh reported that he escaped to the north on one of the supply trains."

Temujin smirked. "Let him come. What can he possibly do to stop us now?"

---

SHANIA TWAIN POURED OUT OF TINNY SPEAKERS, FILLING THE CAB WITH insufferable, inane lyrics. Sam rolled his eyes. At least it was a change from his traveling companion's flood of questions.

The truck driver, a chatty fellow named Floyd, had picked him up hitchhiking a few miles south of Cedar Rapids. Floyd, glad to have someone to talk to while hauling hogs to a slaughterhouse in northern Missouri, had been more than happy to pick up the ragged hitchhiker. The Replodian couldn't decide which was more offensive to his senses: the music or the stench. He wondered if he had just enough evil left in him to kill the man.

Floyd pointed to a sign beside the road and, through a mouthful of beef jerky, said, "That's it, ain't it?"

Sam sat up straight and nodded. "Yeah. Yeah, that's it. Turn right here."

"You got it." The trucker turned the smelly rig off of the interstate onto the two-lane country road. "How much farther?"

"About ten miles."

Suddenly Floyd looked into one of his side mirrors and shouted, "Whoa, lookit that!"

Sam looked over as five Iowa State Troopers whipped around the eighteen-wheeler with their lights flashing and sirens blaring. The engines roared as the cars rocketed to the west toward East Van Buren High School.

"I'm too late," Sam whispered.

"Huh?" Floyd twisted the volume knob on the radio, silencing Shania. "You say somethin'?"

The Replodian disappeared into the back.

Floyd twisted in his seat, taking his eyes off the road to watch his passenger. "Hey! Where you goin'?"

Sam returned a moment later with his oversized duffel bag and unzipped it. After a moment of shuffling the contents, he pulled out his stolen plasma rifle and pressed the energy primer, bringing the weapon to life.

"Whoa," Floyd shouted, pressing his body against the door. "What the hell is that thing? Hey, I don't want any trouble, Sam!"

"Shut up, Floyd," said Sam, using the man's name for the first time in nearly a hundred miles. "Put the hammer down or whatever you guys do, and follow those cops."

"But, I—"

Sam cocked the rifle and a loud hum filled the cab. "Do it!"

"All right!" Floyd shifted gears and stepped on the accelerator. "No need to get testy, pal."

Floyd pushed the rig to its limit, passing several other vehicles as they barreled down the road toward the school. It didn't take long before they saw the thick black smoke rising in the distance. Sam slammed the butt of the rifle into the dash and cursed.

Floyd chanced a brief glance at his passenger. "Mind tellin' me what's goin' on, partner?"

"Just drive the truck, Floyd." Sam fought back the tears flooding his eyes. "Just drive the damn truck."

A few agonizing minutes later, the school came into view, and Sam ordered Floyd to pull over in front of the driveway. The truck had barely come to a complete stop when Sam threw the door open. A rocket fired by one of the mechs destroyed one of the highway patrol cars, sending it into the air in a long arc before it nearly fell on a group of cops firing futilely at the robots.

Floyd cringed. "Sweet Jesus!"

Sam jumped out of the truck and ran down the long driveway toward the parking lot.

"Wait," Floyd yelled. "You can't go out there! You're goin' to get yourself killed!"

"I'm the only one who can stop them," Sam shouted. "Get as far away from here as you can, Floyd!"

"You don't have to tell me twice!" Floyd reached over and pulled the passenger door shut.

As the truck pulled away, Sam ran as fast as his legs would carry him; the heavy bag on his back banged against his body with every footfall. He skidded to a halt as one of the mechs flung an overturned car aside to reveal three deputies and the sheriff huddling behind it. Two of the deputies ran while the older sheriff tried desperately to drag the severely wounded third deputy out of harm's way.

"Stay back," the sheriff yelled as he dragged the man by his shirt collar with one hand and fired his pistol at the robot with the other. "I'm warning you!"

The mech tore the deputy from the sheriff's grasp with one clawed hand and flung him aside into a lamp pole, breaking his spine. The robot then raised one of its feet and brought it down on Challis's legs, crushing them. The sheriff cried out as it leaned down and examined him curiously like a dog with a wounded grasshopper.

In a desperate act of defiance, the sheriff spat on the robot's black sensor eye. The mech brought back one of its arms to strike the finishing blow.

Sam leapt into the air as the mech brought its claws down toward its prey. His foot struck the sensor eye, and the robot stumbled back slightly from the impact. It sent out its scanning beam to scrutinize the Replodian, then stepped back, its arm cannons trained on its new target.

"*Samrai*," the mech growled.

"That's right, you convoluted pile of scrap," Sam snarled as he raised his own weapon. "Come and meet your maker."

The mech stepped forward and opened fire with its arm cannons, but Sam sidestepped and unleashed his own barrage of plasma bolts, which bounced off the advancing Death Walker's armor. Sam leapt into the air over the line of fire, landed on top of the mech's body, and clung to the hot metal. His fingers dug into a ridge in the robot's armor, and he braced his legs below the sensor eye.

He pressed the barrel of the plasma rifle against the eye. "Scan this, you son-of-a-bitch!"

He squeezed the trigger and the air between him and the mech became a strobe of red plasma fire. Sam screamed as some of the blast fragments ricocheted back and tore through his body, leaving ragged, glowing yellow holes in their wake.

"Crack, you mother," he growled. "Crack!"

Finally the eye cracked, and the Death Walker recoiled, bucking wildly. Sam tossed the rifle aside, punched his fist through the broken eye, and dug his hand around inside while the mech tried desperately to shake him off. Finally his fingers closed around a bundle of wires, and he savagely wrenched on them.

"Shit. Ought. Not. Resist. Me!" He pulled out the handful of multi-colored wiring.

The Death Walker convulsed, and Sam fell to the ground, landing on his feet and still clutching the bundle of wires in his fist. The mech teetered and flailed its mechanical arms.

"Fall," Sam said. "Fall!"

The robot fell forward onto the pavement, caving in its armored nose. Smoke poured out of the shattered sensor eye, and the mech shuddered for a moment before it became permanently still. Sam tossed the wires to the ground and ran to Sheriff Challis, who was convulsing and clutching his broken legs.

Challis gaped at Sam as his glowing wounds began to close. "What are you?"

"Don't talk." Sam knelt to examine the sheriff's injuries. "You're going into shock. You need medical attention now."

"No paramedics," Challis's voice grew weaker. "On their w...."

"Don't worry." Sam gingerly scooped the wounded lawman into his arms. "I know the best doctor on the planet."

Sam turned and scanned the parking lot for any sign of his brothers. "Lamont! Where are you?"

# TWENTY-TWO

Q<small>UINTIN POPPED UP FROM BEHIND A POLICE CAR, FIRED THREE QUICK</small> shots at the back of a nearby Death Walker, and quickly dropped back down before the robot's retaliatory fire shredded the car's front end. He checked his weapon and cursed. Half a blast pack and he hadn't put so much as a scratch on the metal bastard.

He pulled a grenade out of his jacket pocket, mashed the plunger with his thumb, and counted to three softly in Phaedojian before chucking it over the top of the car. The mech locked onto it with its sensor eye and fired a short burst from its arm cannons. The grenade exploded in mid-air, and the shockwave hit Quintin like a hammer even behind the burned-out husk of the squad car. Sensing no movement, the mech turned and focused on other activity.

Quintin dug three more grenades out of his pocket and stood to shout at the departing mech, "Hey! Don't you turn your back on me!"

The Death Walker quickly swiveled at the waist to face him again and took aim, its legs stepping slowly to match the direction of the torso.

Quintin mashed the plungers and tossed all three grenades at the robot. "Think fast!"

The mech adjusted its aim accordingly and shot two of them out of the air, but the third went untracked in the explosions and detonated mere inches from the sensor eye. The mech staggered back a step, its stance unsteady on its sidestepping legs. When the smoke cleared, Quintin saw a scorch mark covering the robot's entire face, but more importantly, there was a hairline crack in the eye. The mechanical monster growled and flexed its claws as it advanced.

"Uh oh," said Quintin. "Now I've done it."

As he fumbled for his rifle, twin plasma blasts sliced through the air around his shoulders. The mech staggered back from the continuous string of impacts. Rene and Cherry appeared at Quintin's side, firing on the robot with their rifles.

"Quintin," Cherry shouted, "get out of there!"

"Move, boy!" said Rene.

Quintin nodded and looked around him for an escape route, but froze when his eyes fell on the entrance to the school and saw the two guards stationed there walking away.

"They're leaving!" Quintin shouted.

Rene cocked his head toward the boy, straining to hear over the gunfire. "What?"

"The Horde is leaving," said Quintin. "Now's our chance."

"Leave it to the Replodians, Quintin," said Cherry. "Now get out of here!"

"No." Quintin shook his head. "Alex needs me."

He slid over the cruiser's hood and ran for the front doors at full speed, deftly hurdling large chunks of debris along the way as bullets raked the ground.

"Quintin!" Cherry dropped her rifle to chase after him. "Come back!"

"No, Cheryl!" Rene grabbed her arm and pulled her back. "Cheryl, no! Don't draw attention to him!"

"You bastard! Let me go!"

"No!" Rene grabbed both of her arms and shook her. "Listen to me! It's time you let the boy become a man. The best thing we can do for him is keep these things busy so he can get away."

Cherry looked up at him through tear-filled eyes. "I hate you, Rene Boudreaux."

"I know, *cher*," he said. "But you can hate me later. Right now I need you to fight!"

"Rene..." Cherry's shoulders heaved as she sobbed. "He's my—"

The blind mech followed the sound of their voices and unleashed a salvo of heavy fire between their feet.

"Son of a bitch!" Rene shouted.

The two Methuselans raised their rifles and resumed their assault on the metal giant.

"Run, Quintin," Cherry called. "Don't stop!"

---

QUINTIN COULDN'T HEAR CHERRY'S CRIES OVER THE SOUND OF AN exploding grenade behind him as he jumped over an overturned garbage barrel near the entrance. He raised his rifle and fired a three-round burst at the doors, shattering the glass and twisting the steel frames. Once inside, he looked down both halls and chose the path to the right.

The gymnasium doors opened, and two Hordesmen entered the hall holding Alex's unconscious body by the arms, his feet dragging lifelessly along the floor. Quintin slung his rifle over his shoulder and ran toward the soldiers.

"Hey!" he shouted.

The soldiers turned and dropped Alex. While they fumbled for their weapons, Quintin leapt into the air, kicking one in the face and shoving the other's head into the brick wall. Both fell to the ground unconscious. Quintin rushed to his brother's side and carefully turned him onto his back. He winced at the burns and blood covering his face.

"Alex!" Quintin lightly slapped his brother on the cheek. "Alex, wake up!"

Slowly, Alex opened his eyes and blinked. "Quintin?"

"What happened?"

Alex struggled to sit up, and Quintin propped him up against the wall. "It's Temujin. He's here."

"Are you okay?"

"No," said Alex, holding his head. "He took Crystal."

"Took her where?"

"I don't know," said Alex. "He said he's going to make her part of his harem. We have to save her."

He struggled to his feet and fell to his knees.

"You can't fight in your condition," Quintin protested. "I'll go after Crystal. You go find Lamont."

"Quintin—"

"Shut up and go," said Quintin. "I'll bring her back to you, I promise. Now, take my rifle. You'll need it outside. And take my jacket."

Alex leaned against the wall and accepted the rifle, "What about you?"

Quintin stripped off his jacket and lifted his shirt, revealing the silver handle of a laser sword shoved into the back of his jeans. "I'll manage."

"Thank you," Alex said as he struggled to put the jacket on.

"Thank me later," said Quintin. "These guys are starting to come around. I'll meet up with you later."

Alex nodded and limped down the hall as fast as his burning muscles would allow. Quintin watched until his brother disappeared around the corner. He wiped a hand over his face, smearing it with Alex's blood. One of the troopers groaned, and Quintin quickly dropped to the floor and closed his eyes. He listened as they slowly got to their feet and began to chatter at each other in an unfamiliar language. His earpiece translated.

"What happened?" asked one.

"Somebody hit us," said the other.

"Where'd they go?"

"Who cares? Probably some kid trying to play hero. Just help me carry this punk to the *Ragnarok* so we can get out of this miserable place. These brats are driving me crazy."

*Yes, that's it, boys.* Quintin smiled. *Take me to your leader.*

———

LAMONT TOOK A COUPLE STEPS BACK AND FIRED THE LAST BURST FROM his rifle. The weapon fizzled, and he flipped it on its side. He cursed; the gauge now read empty. He flung the spent weapon aside, drew a plasma pistol from within his jacket, and fired. The small bolts bounced pathetically off the mech stalking toward him, not even making it falter in its gait. It loaded a rocket into its left-side launcher.

The Death Walker was too busy locking onto Lamont to notice the sound of a roaring engine rapidly approaching. Lamont looked between the robot's metal legs and saw one of the highway patrol cars bearing down on it from behind. He jumped out of the way and the mech turned to track his movements, but it didn't notice the car until it rammed into the back of its legs and sent it toppling over onto its back.

Moe crawled out through the driver's side window and ran to help Lamont to his feet. "You okay?"

"Fine." Lamont rubbed his shoulder. "You look like you're having fun."

"Time of my life," said Moe.

The ground shook as the twisted Death Walker slammed its claws into the concrete and righted itself. Its free arm leveled at the Replodians and the cannon spun. Moe crouched, ready to spring out of the line of fire, but the guns issued a rapid clicking. With its free gun empty, the mech swiveled its legs slowly until the feet found purchase, lifting it off the ground.

"This isn't working, Moe." Lamont stared wearily at the struggling robot. "We just can't smash these things enough to make them stay down."

"They've gotta run out of ammo *sometime*," Moe said. "Right?"

::Lamont.::

Lamont whirled toward the school. "Alex?"

His eyes fell on the smashed front doors. Alex stood leaning against the doorframe, wearing his brother's brown leather jacket and holding a plasma rifle in his right hand.

"Alex!" Lamont shouted.

::Help me.:: Alex collapsed onto one knee.

The Replodians ran to his side. Lamont laid Alex on his back while Moe covered them with his "paintball" rifle. Lamont felt along the teen's ribs, arms, and legs, and then took his pulse. He peeled back the teen's eyelids and frowned at how his eyes quivered.

He dug into the pack hanging over his shoulder. "What happened in there?"

"Temujin took Crystal," said Alex, his voice weak.

Moe looked over his shoulder. "He *what?*"

Alex's eyes flicked to him, barely visible under heavy lids. "I tried to stop him. He's too strong."

Lamont produced an injection gun and a large vial of bubbling green liquid. "How'd you get away?"

"Quintin," Alex rasped. He struggled to keep his eyes open. "He took my place. He's going after Crystal."

"Damn." Moe turned toward the door. "I'll go and get them."

"No!" Lamont shook the vial and pushed it firmly into the gun until it clicked. "I need you here. I can't treat Alex and fight those things off at the same time."

Moe pointed to Alex's rifle with the barrel of his own weapon. "Is that thing loaded, Alex?"

"I think so," Alex nodded.

Moe tossed his rifle down and traded it for Alex's. "Paintballs don't do squat to these things."

"Neither does plasma," Lamont observed, pushing up the sleeve of the jacket and swabbing the inside of Alex's elbow with alcohol. "It just pisses them off."

Moe checked the primer. "You almost done there?"

"Almost." Lamont picked up the injection gun. "All right, Alex, listen up. I'm injecting you with a cocktail of adrenaline, endorphins, and muscle enhancers. It'll give you a short boost in strength and stamina. You got that?"

Alex nodded weakly. "Just do it."

Lamont pressed the barrel of the injection gun against Alex's skin and squeezed the trigger. Twelve needles arranged in a circle pumped the green liquid into Alex's bloodstream, and he immediately curled up in the fetal position and grunted in pain.

"Jesus, Monty," said Moe. "You're supposed to fix him, not kill him."

"I never said it would be pleasant."

"Lamont?" said a voice behind them.

Moe whipped around and snapped the butt of his rifle to his shoulder. He sighted down the barrel, training the weapon directly at the newcomer's head. "Hold it right there, Samrai!"

At the mention of the traitor's name, Alex immediately snatched up Moe's discarded paintball rifle and sat up, aiming for Sam's head as well.

"Help me." Sam nodded at the wounded sheriff in his arms. "This man's legs are broken."

"No thanks to you," said Lamont.

"You think I don't know that?" Sam snapped. "Lecture me later! Right now this man needs help. He's going into shock."

Lamont nodded. "Get him inside. Everybody get inside, now!"

Moe whistled between his thumb and forefinger. "Fall back to the school!"

Lamont led Sam into the lobby and pointed to a spot on the floor free of broken glass. "Lay him down, gently."

Sam laid the sheriff on the floor and knelt at his side as Lamont rummaged through his pack on the opposite side.

"You've got a lot of nerve coming back here, traitor," said Lamont as he pulled out a blue vial and shook it. "Elevate his feet and keep him awake. Don't let him pass out."

Sam obeyed and lifted the sheriff's legs in his hands. "I came here to fight."

"Yeah," Lamont scoffed as he loaded the injection gun. "Well, those creations of yours are doing a real fine job out there. You should be proud."

Sam grabbed Lamont's wrist. "I came here to fight *alongside* you."

Lamont stared back, searching for the truth in his brother's eyes.

Moe pressed the barrel of his rifle against the side of Sam's head. "Why should we trust *you*?"

Sam looked up into his brother's angry eyes. "Because I'm the only chance you've got."

"Maybe we'll take our chances without you," said Moe. "We've done just fine without you for the past three years."

"I've already disabled one of them," Sam snapped. "How many have you taken out?"

The Replodians fell silent.

"That's what I thought," said Sam.

Robert ran through the door. "They're converging on the building!"

"We can't stop them," added Rene, right behind him and pulling Cherry by the arm. "We can't even slow them down."

Cherry doubled over and gasped for breath. "What are we going to do?"

Robert pointed at Sam. "Who's this?"

"This is our brother," said Moe, keeping the rifle pressed firmly against Sam's head. "Samrai."

"The traitor?" asked Rene.

"So you're the one responsible for those *things* out there?" asked Cherry.

Sam sighed and nodded.

"You *bastard*," said Cherry. "I hope you burn in Hell."

An explosion rocked the building, sending dust raining down on their heads.

"I'm already there," Sam whispered.

Lamont finished administering a dose of epinephrine to the sheriff's arm, unrolled two long plastic sleeves from his pack, and began sliding them over the man's legs.

"What are those?" asked Sam.

"Temporary casts until we can get him to a hospital," Lamont explained. He pulled out a metal spray can and shook it vigorously.

"That's not going to happen unless we can get past those robots," said Robert.

"Yeah." Cherry slapped the back of Sam's head with the barrel of her rifle. "Thanks a lot."

"Look," Sam snapped, "I'm sorry, okay? I didn't mean for this to happen."

"Shut up! Hold his legs still," Lamont snapped. He pressed the button on top of the can, and the sleeves filled with rapidly hardening pink foam. "Why the sudden change of heart, Sam?"

Sam sighed. "There was an accident. Somehow my programming—"

The thunderous sound of metal feet and the crumbling of bricks filled the air as one of the mechs tried to force its way through the much shorter doorway.

Lamont grabbed the sheriff by the shoulders and dragged him down the hall. "Fall back to the cafeteria!"

Once there, Lamont and Sam carefully laid the Sheriff on one of the long lunch tables while Rene knocked over a vending machine and pushed it up against the door.

"Oh, sure," said Cherry. "That'll stop them."

"You have a better plan?" the Cajun snapped.

"I do," said Sam.

Everyone turned and stared at the blond Replodian as he pulled the duffel bag off his shoulder and set it on one of the tables, brushing aside someone's abandoned biology homework. He unzipped the bag and pulled out one of the silver helmets.

"What is that?" asked Moe.

"It's something I was developing for the Horde," said Sam.

"What does it do?" asked Alex.

"It's a self-contained suit of powered armor," said Sam, tossing a helmet to each of his companions. "Everybody take one."

Lamont turned his helmet over in his hands and looked inside. "How does it work?"

"Just put it on," said Sam. "The helmet will do the rest."

Moe held up his helmet. "Kind of plain, aren't they?"

Sam rolled his eyes contemptuously. "I didn't have time to finish them while I was escaping from Temujin's compound. Why? Did you want pink?"

Moe took a step toward his brother, his hands balling into fists.

A distant crashing sound on the other side of the door made them all jump.

"We're running out of time!" said Alex.

The cafeteria doors rattled as the Death Walker bashed against them from the other side.

"Correction," said Rene. "We *are* out of time."

"They're coming through!" said Cherry.

"When you put the helmets on, you'll feel a slight prick on your neck," said Sam, raising his own helmet above his head. "The helmet will analyze your DNA and configure the suit to fit properly."

---

ALEX TOOK A DEEP BREATH AND PULLED THE HELMET OVER HIS HEAD. For a moment, everything was dark and silent, but then lights blinked inside and holograms of gauges and meters flashed across the visor. He felt the prick of a needle on the back of his neck, and he winced. The display on the visor changed to a rotating view of a DNA strand and then to a three-dimensional view of Alex's naked body in red. A white wire-frame helmet appeared over the head, and a stream of white crawled over the image of his body.

Suddenly a cold, liquid sensation began to flow from the helmet's collar down to the soles of his feet and the tips of his fingers. He panicked as the substance enveloped his entire body and the collar at the base of the helmet contracted, forming an airtight seal around his neck. The coldness encasing his body was replaced with a warm, tingling sensation, and he felt the substance harden. Alex flexed his arms and noticed they felt incredibly light. The image on the visor showed a completed suit covering his body.

A computerized female voice whispered in his ear, *"Transformation complete."*

The visor cleared, and he saw Sam standing in front of him, fully encased in metallic silver armor. Alex looked down and examined his hands—his powerful, *metal* hands. He flexed his fingers and marveled at the strength the suit gave his grip. He turned and looked at the others, who were examining their own suits in a similar manner.

"What do you know," said Sam in a synthesized voice. "They work!"

Lamont turned his head to look at his brother, his expression unreadable through the black visor, but the outrage in his tone was unmistakable, even synthesized. "What do you mean, *'They work?'*"

Sam shrugged. "I never got a chance to test them. I was afraid the alloy wouldn't harden."

"Oh, now I feel safe," said Rene.

"What was that stuff?" asked Alex.

"Nanobots," said Sam. "Trillions of 'em. Pretty sweet, huh?"

Lamont turned to check on the sheriff, who was now shaking with fear as much as shock as he stared at the armored figures gathered around him.

"What are you?" the lawman asked.

Lamont placed a hand on the man's quivering shoulder. "Rest now. We'll send help."

The doors behind them crashed again and the TDC agents turned, each adopting defensive stances. The doors parted against the toppled vending machine, and Alex could just make out the movement of the Death Walkers beyond.

"What's taking them so long?" asked Robert. "They should be through by now."

"They're too tall," said Sam. "These ceilings are too low for them to maneuver effectively."

"Will that stop them?" asked Cherry.

"Not a chance," said Sam gravely.

"Will these suits stop them?" asked Lamont.

"Our armor is made of the very same alloy as the Death Walkers," said Sam. "Ours isn't quite as thick as theirs, but I've equipped these babies with all-new miniature ion cannons. They should be powerful enough to pierce their shells if my calculations are correct."

"That's a mighty big 'if,' man," said Moe.

"Have I ever steered you wrong?" asked Sam.

Moe stared at him.

"Right." Sam nodded. "Don't answer that."

"Well it looks like we're about to find out." Rene pointed at the door. "Look!"

They watched as a mech—hunched over due to the low ceiling—ripped the doors off their hinges and swiped the vending machine aside with its one remaining arm. It was the same mech Moe had crashed the truck into when they first arrived.

"Hey there, Lucky!" Moe said. "Long time no smash."

"You did that?" Sam pointed at the Death Walker's ragged shoulder joint. "Nice work, little sister."

"Bite me."

A red scanning laser flashed from the sensor eye and scanned each of the suited figures individually. Finally, the laser blinked out.

*"Scanning subjects,"* the mech said. *"Subjects are hostile. Eliminate."*

Sam stepped forward and pointed a gloved finger at the damaged mech. "I'll show you hostile, tin man."

The Death Walker opened and closed its claws in answer to its creator's challenge.

# TWENTY-THREE

COLD STEEL BIT INTO CRYSTAL'S WRISTS. EVEN WITH HER SMALL HANDS, the handcuffs were too tight for her. She was in a dimly lit holding cell with a floor made of honeycomb steel grating.

Heavy boots thumped in the hall, coming closer. Crystal pressed her back against the wall as the door opened and two soldiers dragged a limp body between them. When the men dropped their load onto the floor, Crystal cried out, "Alex!"

One of the soldiers bound Alex's hands behind his back with a pair of hinged cuffs. Alex groaned, and one of the troopers stomped on his leg, barking at him in Chinese.

"Leave him alone!" Crystal shouted.

The men laughed at her. One of the soldiers cleared his sinuses and spat in Alex's hair. Crystal's nostrils flared in outrage as she fought against her cuffs. The spitter grabbed her by the chin and made kissing noises at her. Crystal tasted bile in the back of her throat as she caught the stench of sour milk on his rancid breath.

She fought back the urge to vomit as the soldiers left the room, laughing and taunting her until the door closed behind them. Alex groaned and tried to move. Crystal tried to walk on her knees, but lost her balance and fell onto her side. She squirmed along the floor, inching toward him.

When she reached him, she rested her head on his shoulder. "Alex," she sobbed. "Oh God, Alex, why are they doing this to us?"

"Crystal?"

Crystal recoiled. That voice! It was soft and accented. French maybe, but it definitely wasn't *her* Alex.

The boy turned his head, and Crystal got her first good look at his face. The resemblance to Alex was uncanny, but his eyes were all wrong. They shimmered like emeralds, catching what little light there was in the room. A dirty lock of auburn hair fell over the boy's face.

"Who are you?" she asked.

Alex's doppleganger winked. "Shhh."

---

THE MANGLED DEATH WALKER TOOK ANOTHER LABORED STEP INTO THE room and snapped its claws at the suited figures. Sam stepped forward and cracked his armored knuckles.

"I've got this," he said. A silver-clad arm flashed out in front of his chest.

"No, leave him to me," said Moe. "We're old friends. Aren't we, Lucky?"

The Death Walker snarled and lunged awkwardly at the Replodian. Moe rushed in and met the mech head-on, slamming his hands into the mechanical monster's nose and creating deep dents in its armor. The robot tried to push its way forward, but was unable to move the alien. Moe straightened his arms and grinned behind his faceplate as he slowly forced the larger machine back about a foot. The mech slashed at him with its claws, but the Replodian batted the arm aside effortlessly.

"All right, big guy..." Moe crouched to spring. "Let's take this outside, shall we?"

Moe lunged forward and was caught by surprise when rocket thrusters embedded in the suit's ankles ignited, propelling both him and the Death Walker out of the cafeteria and back into the lobby. The gymnasium doors opened, and a small group of brave students ventured out in time to see the mech smash into the trophy case, showering the corridor with broken glass and mangled awards.

"What the hell was that?" asked Moe, jumping back from the struggling robot.

Sam appeared at his side "You jumped too hard and engaged the boot thrusters. Try not to overcompensate for the suit so much. Just move normally."

"Now you tell me," said Moe.

Alex and Cherry rushed to the open doors where the bewildered students stood.

"Are you kids all right?" asked Cherry.

A girl near the front of the crowd sobbed, "They took Crystal Hammond and Alex Walker!"

"Don't worry. We'll get them back," said Alex. To his relief, his helmet distorted his voice enough that none of his classmates recognized it.

"Who *are* you people?" asked a boy in a red and white football jersey.

Alex tried to think of some response—any response—that didn't sound like a bad comic book cliché.

"I could use some help over here!" Moe was struggling to push the damaged Death Walker out the door as two others attempted to force their way inside.

One of the girls pointed at the mechs and screeched, "What are those things?"

"Get back inside!" Alex pushed his classmates back through the door and slammed it behind them.

Sam ran to Moe's side and grabbed the wounded mech by one foot. "Take the other leg!"

Moe grabbed it, digging his armored fingers deep into a joint.

"To the left," Sam grunted. "Swing!"

The Replodians spun around and swung the flailing mech in a long arc, releasing it in the direction of the entrance. The robot collided with its fellows in a cacophony of grinding metal. Another Death Walker appeared behind the pileup and loaded a rocket into one of its shoulder launchers.

"Down!" yelled Robert.

The rocket fired and, without thinking, Alex raised his right arm, bracing his elbow with his left hand. The armor along the forearm split open, and a flat, rectangular cannon slid out over his wrist. A burst of green energy exploded from the weapon and detonated the projectile mere feet from the entrance, loosening more bricks from the structure. Alex stood motionless for a moment, dumbstruck.

Sam cheered and gave him a thumbs up. "Nice shot, kid!"

Alex stared at the smoking barrel protruding from his forearm. "H-how did I do that?" The cannon retracted, and the mechanism folded itself flat against his arm.

"The suit knows what to do," Sam explained. "Just go with the flow."

"Guys," said Rene, "we're getting popular."

Outside, another Death Walker lumbered up to join the others, who were slowly regaining their footing.

"We have to lure them away from the building," Sam said. "The structure can't take much more pounding."

Lamont nodded. "All right, team, let's take out the trash!"

"Yeah!" Moe shouted as he leapt through the demolished doorway at "Lucky," who had just gotten to its feet.

Moe engaged his thrusters and crashed into the robot, sending them both tumbling across the parking lot and throwing sparks as their metal skins scraped across the cracked pavement. When they came to a rocking stop, Moe was on top, driving his fists into the robot's face until a gaping hole appeared in the armor.

"Say goodnight, Lucky!" Moe shoved his arms into the cavity and fired both arm cannons simultaneously.

Bright green light reflected off Moe's silver armor. Something deep inside the robot exploded, and it gave a final pathetic shudder before lying completely still.

"Let's see you get back up from *that*," Moe taunted, cracking his metallic knuckles.

Thick, black smoke billowed from the silent Death Walker. Lucky's luck had finally run out.

———

ROBERT STEPPED OUT INTO THE SUNLIGHT AND A RED FLASH ON THE RIGHT side of his heads-up display drew his attention. He turned as the Death Walker raised its arm and prepared to fire one of its Gatling guns, the barrels spinning. Robert ducked underneath the arm and pushed it skyward, riddling the front of the building with a vertical line of bullets. The mech jerked its arm away, carrying Robert with it. As the robot tried to shake him off, Robert felt the contents of his stomach beginning to rise.

"Hold on, Robert!" Rene aimed his arm cannon at the robot's shoulder joint. "I'll get you down."

Robert watched as the other mech reached a clawed hand for the Cajun. "Rene, look out!"

Rene turned just as the claws clamped down around his waist and picked him up. He wailed in surprise as the robot's other arm cannon pointed at his face.

"Hey!" Cherry delivered a crushing kick between the robot's legs, leaving a small dent.

The mech stared down at her.

"If anyone's going to kill him," Cherry snarled, "it's going to be *me*!"

Unimpressed, the Death Walker lowered its arm cannon to aim at her head.

"Hey," said Rene. "Look at me, you ugly bastard! We're not finished yet!"

The mech turned to look down the barrel of the Cajun's right arm cannon. The blast struck just above the sensor eye, and it staggered back. The mech released its prisoner to paw at the new hole in its face. Rene fell clumsily to the ground and turned around to find himself faceplate to faceplate with Cherry.

"Thank you," he said.

"For what?"

"For saving my life."

Cherry shrugged. "Everybody makes mistakes."

"Guys," Robert called as his Death Walker, now with a firm grip on his leg, swung him through the air behind them. "I could use a little help here!"

The two Methuselans ran forward to aid their comrade, but the mech swung Robert's body at them like a club. Cherry ducked, but Rene took the full brunt of the impact. Robert's armor struck his with a resounding, spark-throwing *clang*. Rene sailed through the air and landed on top of a relatively undamaged highway patrol car, shattering the windows and caving in the roof.

---

ACROSS THE LOT, SAM LED LAMONT AND ALEX IN A CHARGE AGAINST another Death Walker. The mech opened fire and Sam cartwheeled out of the way, barely avoiding being pelted with bullets.

Sam bounded off toward the last mech. "I'll take the next one."

"We'll handle this one," Lamont called. "Alex, go low."

"What am I supposed to do?" Alex ducked another volley from the cannon. "Bite its ankles?"

"Try to knock it down," said Lamont, jumping into the air.

The mech swatted him out of the air like an insect and swung at Alex with the other arm, but narrowly missed the teenager as he slid between the birdlike legs, throwing sparks on the pavement. The mech brought its hand down over Lamont's helmet, embedding its claws into the asphalt around his head. The Replodian snatched the flexing claws in his hands and fought against them as they tried to close around his helmet.

"Now, Alex!" he yelled. "Take it down!"

Alex kicked the robot's knee, but the mech only growled and kicked at him, unwilling to release its prey. He opened fire on the joint with his arm cannon in a continuous stream. His visor dimmed to protect his vision as the ion cannon cut into the armor like a torch. The metal soon began to drip away in great molten globs. The leg wobbled and the mech awkwardly looked between its own legs.

Alex kicked the lower half of the leg once, twice, and on the third blow, the limb broke apart in a splash of molten metal. "Timber!"

The claws released their hold on Lamont's helmet as the Death Walker toppled onto its side. Lamont scrambled away to join Alex. The robot thrashed and kicked the smoking stump of its leg in a futile attempt to right itself.

Alex examined his smoking forearm. "I love this thing. Sam's a genius."

"Speaking of which..." Lamont scanned the parking lot. "Where is the 'genius,' anyway?"

---

SAM RAN TOWARD A DEATH WALKER AS IT FIRED ON A GROUP OF retreating police officers. The Replodian came to a skidding halt behind the mech, looked up at the maintenance hatch on the robot's backside, and punched through the armor. The mech took a step back and turned, looking for Sam as he inserted his arm into the crude opening and began to root around.

"Don't worry, baby," he said, shoving his arm in almost to the armpit. "I'll still respect you in the morning."

The mech took another step back, but stopped dead as Sam's hand found the machine's central processing unit.

"Oh, you like that, do you?" he grunted, blindly interfacing with the CPU. "Let's see what happens when I do *this*!"

The Death Walker jerked to attention and turned toward the school. It raised both arm cannons and trained them on the mech still fighting with Cherry and Rene.

Sam opened the suit's comm channel and shouted, "Fire in the hole!"

Rene and Cherry looked over their shoulders and dove out of the way as Sam flexed his fingers. The shanghaied Death Walker unloaded both barrels at the other, turning it into Swiss cheese. Sam laughed as the bullets found the rocket launchers and blew the robot's torso into flaming shrapnel.

"Ha ha! Go boom!" Sam laughed as he directed his mech at the one still fighting with Robert, who was trying vainly to fire off a clean shot while the robot swung him like a rag doll.

Sam fired a series of controlled bursts at the shoulder joint, and the flailing arm was shorn off. Robert fell to the ground with the robot's claws still clenched around his ankle. He wrenched on the claws until one of them snapped at the joint. Freed, Robert scurried out of the line of fire after Cherry and Rene, who were taking refuge inside the school entrance. Sam's mech fired another burst, this time from both barrels, before finally launching a rocket at the one-armed robot. The Death Walker exploded as both Sam's rocket and those stored in its launcher detonated simultaneously.

Sam laughed. "Oh, baby, I *love* it when you get aggressive! You know how Daddy likes it."

"Sam!"

He looked over his left shoulder. Lamont waved his arms and pointed to a one-legged mech attempting to pursue and fire on him and Alex at the same time.

"Take it out," Lamont shouted.

Sam sneered as he brought the Death Walker's guns to bear on its crippled brother.

"Come on, baby," he whispered breathlessly to his captive weapon. "Almost there. Don't stop. Don't stop!"

The Death Walker loaded a fresh rocket into each of its launchers, and Sam flexed his fingers one final time, giving the order to fire. The dual projectiles exploded from the mech's shoulders in twin trails of smoke and sailed over Lamont and Alex's heads as they dove to the pavement. The wounded mech ceased its desperate barrage against its fleeing prey and looked up as the rockets flew toward it. It raised an arm to cover its eye an instant before the rockets connected and vaporized it, leaving only one kicking leg intact.

"Ha," yelled Sam. "Money shot!"

For a few moments, the only sound in the devastated lot came from the crackling fires consuming the demolished mechs and cars. Slowly, the cops and TDC agents got to their feet and ventured from their respective hiding places to inspect the damage.

Rene stuck his head out from the school's demolished doorway. "Is that all of them?"

"That's it," Lamont called back. "They're all dead."

Cherry stepped out and—upon getting a good look at Sam and the remaining mech—said, "Does he have his hand up that robot's *butt*?"

Sam slowly pulled his arm out of the jagged opening and grimaced at the hydraulic fluid dripping from his armor. He shook as much as he could away, and then slapped the lifeless mech hard on the rear end with an open palm.

"Call me, sweet cheeks," he said.

The Death Walker teetered precariously for a moment before crashing forward onto its nose. Black smoke billowed from the hole in its backside.

"Well," Sam said as the others assembled around him, "I'm spent. What's next?"

"We have to rescue Quintin and Crystal," Alex said.

"Who?"

"My brother and my girlfriend!"

Sam turned to Lamont. "The kid has a brother?"

"It's a long story," said Lamont. "We'll explain later. Right now we have to figure out how to rescue them."

"If Temujin took prisoners, he probably took them back to the *Ragnarok*," Sam said.

"The what?" asked Cherry.

"It's a ship," Sam explained. "A really *big* ship."

"If it's so big, then where is it?" asked Robert.

Sam looked up and scanned the sky. "The *Ragnarok* has a cloaking field. It's undetectable to the human eye and most surveillance technology."

"Great," said Moe. "Another one of *your* great inventions."

"It still casts a shadow," said Sam. "We can track it from the ground. Once we're underneath it, I can locate one of the emergency escape hatches and get us inside."

Sam scanned the parking lot but failed to see any shadows on the ground large enough to be cast by the *Ragnarok*. His eyes fell on a flipped, but otherwise relatively undamaged, blue Chevy pickup.

"Help me flip that truck," he said.

# TWENTY-FOUR

WHILE THE *RAGNAROK* CLIMBED PAST ONE THOUSAND FEET, THE KHAN stood in front of the full-length mirror in his quarters. The gleaming armor he had worn inside the school was gone, replaced with a red silk shirt and brown fur cloak. As he poured himself a drink, there was a knock on the chamber door.

"Enter," he called.

The door opened, and two guards, accompanied by Chuluun, ushered the captive teenagers into the room. Crystal struggled against her escort, kicking, bucking, and squealing wildly. The boy, on the other hand, simply walked ahead of his escort with his eyes directed at the floor, surely ashamed by his humiliating defeat. Temujin smiled as he finished pouring his drink.

"Welcome, children," he said. "That will be all, gentlemen. Chuluun, if you would please remain?"

Chuluun nodded. He closed the door behind the departing troopers and stood with his hands folded in front of him.

Temujin gestured toward the porcelain jug in front of him and addressed Quintin, "Sake?"

Still looking at the floor, Quintin shook his head despondently.

"My dear?" Temujin smiled sweetly at Crystal, looking every bit the part of the generous host.

Crystal scowled and fought the urge to spit on the plush furs beneath her skinned knees. The Khan shrugged and corked the jug with a sigh as he walked around the table to more closely scrutinize his prisoners.

"Shame." He swirled the clear liquid in his glass. "On the whole, I abhor the Japanese culture, but I must say their taste in spirits is superb. Wouldn't you agree, Chuluun?"

The general smiled. "I prefer their weaponry, my Khan."

"Ah, yes. Magnificent." Temujin leaned in close to Quintin. "But nothing compared to *Replodian* weaponry, is it, Alexander?"

Quintin remained silent.

"Why are you doing this?" asked Crystal. "What do you want from us?"

Temujin downed his drink in one gulp and smiled. "From you? Nothing."

He leaned toward Quintin again and whispered, "But *you*...."

Quintin continued staring at the floor.

"You," continued Temujin. "You are the only thing that stands between me and my ultimate goal."

"What are you *talking* about?" said Crystal.

"The world, my dear," said Temujin, spreading his arms in a wide, sweeping gesture. "I want *the world*! But your lover sees fit to stand in my way."

Crystal looked quizzically from Temujin to Quintin.

Temujin sneered. "So you've never told her?"

His question was answered with silence.

Temujin threw his head back and let loose a hearty, barking laugh. "The humble hero! You see, my dear, your beloved Alexander and I are merely pawns in an inter-stellar game of chess between two rival regimes. We were both bred for the sole purpose of spoiling the other side's plans."

*"What?"* Crystal blurted.

"Aliens, Miss Hammond," the Khan elaborated. He leaned in close to her, filling her nostrils with the overpowering odor of alcohol on his breath. "We are *gods* created by *men*—or rather extraterrestrials. To call them men would be an insult to even this lowly race, wouldn't it, Alexander?"

Quintin glanced up as Chuluun casually walked around them to stand closer to his master. Slowly, and making as little movement as possible, Quintin slipped his fingers beneath his shirt and fumbled for the handle of the concealed laser sword.

The Khan continued his speech. "What you saw in the gymnasium was only a small display of my power." He paused and looked over his shoulder at Quintin. "And yours as well, I'm sure."

Quintin feigned anger as his fingers wrapped around the handle and ever so slowly slid the sword out of his waistband.

"You see," said Temujin, turning his back on the teens once more. "Once our little war is over, my alien benefactors plan to march in and pick up the pieces. Then, once they have what they want, I will be obsolete. Outmoded. No longer required. They will claim what remains of humanity and forge it into their ultimate weapon to use against their enemies.

"But I have no intention of turning the world over to them. Why should I hand over what is rightly mine? My *birthright*? Thanks to our mutual acquaintance, I now have the technology to stand up to the Seignso and repel them from *my* kingdom."

"You're insane!" Crystal said.

Chuluun raised his hand to slap Crystal. Instead of recoiling, she clenched her jaw and readied herself for the strike. Chuluun grinned and lowered his hand.

The Khan turned and looked at Quintin. "But perhaps I am being too hasty. I had forgotten how alike we are, you and I. After all, we are both the bastard children of uncaring, selfish parents, Alexander. We should combine our forces. Imagine the power. Imagine the *fear*!"

The laser sword's hilt finally cleared the waistband of Quintin's jeans. His thumb caressed the igniter switch.

"Together we could crush the Seignso *and* the Federation," said Temujin. ::What say you, brother?::

Quintin continued to stare at the floor, unable to respond the way Temujin expected him to.

::It is where you belong. Do not deny it.::

Again Quintin remained silent.

::Insolent child!:: Temujin shouted inside Quintin's mind. ::Why do you not answer me?::

Slowly, Quintin looked up into the Khan's trembling eyes, his own eyes glowing an eerie emerald green.

"Who are you?" Temujin backed away from the teen. "You are not Alexander. Chuluun!"

Quintin flicked the sword's igniter switch and the white-hot blade hissed from its hilt. He flipped the handle in his fingers, and the blade sliced clean through the handcuffs binding his hands, instantly melting the metal on contact. With his hands free, he adopted an offensive stance with the sword.

"Don't move!" he shouted. "Hands in the air!"

Temujin stood his ground. "Who are you?"

"Cadet Quintin MacLaren," said Quintin. "I am hereby placing you under arrest for crimes against the Federation, conspiracy to commit planetary genocide, kidnapping, and murder."

Temujin and his general were silent for a moment, dumbstruck by the absurdity of the youth's declaration, but then the Khan chuckled. The chuckles erupted into hearty laughter as Chuluun joined in.

Suddenly the Khan stopped laughing. "Guards!"

The door behind Quintin was thrown open, and the two armed escorts stormed into the room. Caught off guard, Quintin barely noticed as the laser sword flew from his fingers and into the Khan's waiting hand. He looked down at his empty hand, baffled by the warlord's display of mental power.

Temujin looked at the guards. "Kill him."

The Horde troopers opened fire with their plasma rifles, and Crystal screamed as rapid-fire crimson beams tore through Quintin's body. Blood trickled from his mouth as he groaned and fell onto his back, dead.

Temujin roared with laughter and clapped his hands with delight. Crystal sobbed as the emerald glow slowly faded from Quintin's eyes.

---

"Faster!" Alex shouted over the suits' comm system.

Sam's armored fingers gripped the steering wheel so tight that it cracked. He pressed the accelerator, and the engine roared as the needle on the speedometer passed ninety, one hundred, and finally one hundred and ten miles-per-hour, a speed normally considered to be suicidal on the hilly country road with its regular traffic of tractors and horse-drawn Amish buggies.

"The road splits just up ahead," said Alex. "We can either go south toward Bonaparte or north toward Stockport."

"No," Sam said. "Temujin will most likely keep a westerly course. We need to do the same."

"This road doesn't *go* west," Alex insisted. "You either have to go south through Bonaparte and Bentonsport, or go across Highway 16 past Stockport."

"That'll take too long. We can't lose him," said Sam. "Aren't there any roads that go west?"

"Just a dirt service road."

Moe snorted. "More like a goat trail."

"Then that's what I'm taking," Sam said.

"Well, whatever you're going to do, do it fast," said Moe. "We're running out of road here."

Up ahead, the intersection came into view, and a small tractor pulling a load of hay bales crossed the truck's path.

"Sam," Alex shouted. "Sam!"

"I see it," said Sam. "Hang on!"

He pressed the accelerator against the floorboard. The needle climbed past one-twenty and buried as the engine roared like an irate dinosaur. For a brief instant, Sam could see the whites of the horrified farmer's eyes as the truck ran the stop sign and sailed through the air toward the hay wagon. The truck plunged through the hay and for a moment the world turned yellow until the windshield cleared and the front tires made contact with the muddy service road on the other side.

In the passenger seat, Cherry braced her hands against the roof and dashboard. Her helmet banged against the roof of the cab as the truck shuddered and pitched. "You maniac!"

"Oops," said Sam. "Did I do that?"

Robert brushed hay away from his helmet. "Now what, genius? We don't even know where we're going now."

"Sure we do," said Sam. "West."

"This road won't go on forever," said Alex.

"This truck's got four-wheel drive."

"You're going to get us killed!"

Sam shook his head. "Nah."

Sam ignored the cautionary signs on the side of the road, and the truck rocketed over a deep creek bed. The back tires barely made contact with solid ground on the other side and chewed the earth until they regained traction and propelled the truck forward again. The truck rammed through a fence and into a harvested cornfield. The back tires dug deep, muddy ruts into the soil and threw yellow, stubby corn stalks into the air. The truck's rear end fishtailed momentarily before straightening out and surging forward through the field.

"Dammit, Samrai!" yelled Moe. "Watch where the hell you're going!"

"Yes, Mom," said Sam.

The truck crested a hill and a line of trees at the end of the field came into view.

"All right, sweetheart, take the wheel," Sam said.

Cherry turned. *"What?"*

"Take the wheel," Sam repeated as he crawled out the driver's side window.

"Where the hell are you going?"

"I'm going to clear a path."

"You're *what?*" Cherry quickly scooted over to grab the wheel.

BIRTHRIGHT

Sam settled onto the ledge of the open window. "I'm going to need more firepower."

"How's this?" Rene hefted a minigun ripped off one of the disabled Death Walkers onto the roof.

Sam nodded. "Let's do it!"

Sam and Lamont each wrapped an arm around the truck's roll bar and leveled their free arms at the rapidly approaching tree line while Robert stood behind Rene, bracing himself between the Cajun and the tailgate.

"Ready," Robert said.

Moe and Alex flanked Rene and aimed their cannons. "Ready!" they said.

"Aim low and don't stop until you see blue sky," Sam ordered. "Fire!"

The armored soldiers unleashed a devastating barrage of green ion blasts and .50 caliber bullets at the base of the tree line, raising a dense cloud of dirt, charred wood, and leaves. Trees fell left and right as the truck penetrated the cloud, lurched, and jumped over the crudely severed stumps.

"I can't see!" cried Cherry.

"You don't have to!" Sam increased his rate of fire as he sprayed the forest. "Just go straight!"

A low branch appeared out of the cloud and smacked Lamont in the face, splintering the limb in two and sending the Replodian flying.

Alex reached for him but was too late. "Lamont!"

Lamont bounced out of the truck and clawed the air, but the tailgate was already out of reach. The suit's boot thrusters engaged, propelled forward at high speed. His fingers clamped down like a vise on the tailgate, and the thrusters disengaged, dropping his legs and causing the armored boots to dig deep furrows in the pulverized earth. Lamont scrambled up into the bucking truck while Alex and Robert pulled.

"Are you okay, lad?" asked Robert.

Lamont took three deep breaths and shouted, "No!"

Finally the truck cleared the timber, and the dust cloud slowly dissipated. Sam climbed back inside the cab and took the wheel back from Cherry, who was now shaking uncontrollably.

"Nice driving, babe," he said.

"You're insane!" she shouted. "How could you do that?"

"Oh, c'mon," said Sam. "It's not just a job, it's an adventure. Remember?"

"That's the *Navy*, you nitwit!"

"My bad."

Suddenly the truck was plunged into darkness.

"Hey, who turned off the sun?" said Moe.

Sam looked out the window into the sky and, despite the blackness enveloping the truck, saw only blue sky and sunshine above them, with the occasional cloud drifting lazily by.

"It's the *Ragnarok*," said Sam. "We're right below her."

"How do we get aboard?" asked Alex.

"Use your boot thrusters," said Sam. "Just push off the truck hard and the thrusters will engage automatically."

"That's all?"

"Happy thoughts wouldn't hurt," Sam said.

"Gee," said Alex, "thanks."

"No problem," said Sam. "Once we reach the ship, I'll locate an emergency escape hatch and unlock it."

"Everybody get ready," said Lamont.

Sam set the cruise control and climbed out the window again, this time crawling along the roof of the truck to the passenger side, where Cherry was climbing awkwardly out of her own window. She crouched on the roof and looked from the invisible ship to the shadowy ground rushing below her and back to the ship again.

"You okay?" asked Sam.

She shook her head.

"Now!" said Lamont.

Five sets of thrusters engaged one by one, and the others were propelled into the air.

Sam appeared at Cherry's side. "Just jump."

Sam laid a hand on Cherry's shoulder. His display lit up with diagnostics and charts. Everything was working properly. Her heart rate, however, was through the roof, and her breathing erratic.

"I can't," Cherry said, her voice shaky.

"Trust me," Sam said. "All you have to do is jump. The suit will do the rest."

"What if it doesn't?"

"Well then we'll probably crash into that tree."

"What?" Cherry turned her head.

Sure enough, a large oak tree was drawing dangerously close as the truck thundered onward. Cherry screamed as Sam wrapped his arms around her waist and leapt into the air, engaging his thrusters and rocketing away from the truck in a trail of jet exhaust. Less than a second later, the truck collided with the tree and folded like an accordion.

Cherry stared at the receding wreckage. Her chest heaved as she breathed, the armor's breastplate flexing with the motion.

"What's the matter?" asked Sam, his voice calm and cheery. "You're acting like we were in some kind of danger."

"Why, I—*Oof!*" Cherry grunted as they came to rest against the underbelly of the ship.

Sam hovered over to the others. "Find the edges," he said.

The others dispersed, feeling along the ship's invisible underbelly. Sam repositioned Cherry so that he held her under her arms. She panicked and kicked her legs.

"Okay," he said, "I've got you. Now, I want you to push down with your heels to ignite the thrusters."

Cherry shook her head. "But—"

"Hey," Sam said. "*I've got you.* You can do this. Just push down."

Cherry's body tensed, and she kicked down with both legs. Bursts of blue flame shot from the thrusters along her ankles, and Sam felt her rise up slightly in his grip. As she drifted away from him, she flailed her arms and grabbed his wrists.

Sam nodded. "Good. Don't worry about balancing. Let the gyroscopes do all the work."

Cherry nodded. Sam let her drift away until his arms were fully extended and then—despite her protests—let go of her hands. She reached for him as their fingers came apart and rocked forward, but she remained airborne.

"See?" Sam said. "Easy."

Cherry looked down at her feet. "I'm *flying!*" She laughed.

"I found the edge," Moe called.

Sam drifted toward his brother, and Cherry, still unsure of the suit, stayed within arm's reach of him.

Finally the others positioned themselves at the edges of the invisible ship and signaled to Sam. He did a few quick calculations in his head and hovered to an area toward the rear of the ship, feeling along the surface until his fingers disappeared into invisible grooves. With a turn of his wrists, a circular panel the size of a manhole cover came away and the cloaking failed, leaving the panel in his hands a dull black color. Sam dropped the panel and stared up at the conspicuous black hole in an otherwise flawless sky.

"This is it," he said.

One by one, the others followed Sam into the ship and found themselves in a vast, albeit mostly empty, cargo hold. Sam tapped the side of his helmet and the view on the inside of his visor switched from shadows to green night vision. He scanned the room, looking for any signs of human life, but the display remained green. He turned to the others, giving a nod before leading the way to the exit. Once at the door, he turned and switched his helmet's communication settings to radio only, silencing the external speakers.

"Okay," he said. "The corridor outside this door will take you all the way to the bridge. Just keep going straight. Temujin's quarters are on Deck C. There's an elevator about fifty yards ahead."

"We should split into two teams," Lamont said. "One to take control of the bridge, and the other to rescue the prisoners."

"Good idea," Sam said. He turned and walked away.

Moe grabbed his arm. "Where do you think you're going?"

"To the engine room," said Sam. "Somebody has to bring this behemoth down."

"I'll go with you," said Moe.

"No." Sam shook his head. "They'll need you to take the bridge."

Moe stepped toe to toe with his brother. "I still don't trust you. Your track record still stands... Traitor."

"I got you this far, didn't I?"

"You got Alex on this ship," said Moe. "Which is exactly what your boss wanted. Isn't it?"

"It's not like that, Moe," said Sam, his voice barely over a whisper.

"You bring this ship down, and I'll believe you," said Moe.

"Guilty until proven innocent, eh?"

"That's the idea."

"Fine," Sam growled. "Just try not to slow me down."

"Okay," said Lamont. "Alex and I will go after Crystal and Quintin. Can I count on you three to take the bridge?"

"Sure," said Robert. "But are you sure the two of you can handle Temujin alone? I mean, he's sure to have all kinds of security up there. Maybe I—"

"No," said Sam. "Temujin keeps his security to a minimum. He doesn't like being surrounded by his followers. He thinks they smell bad... well, he's right. But, no, the most resistance will probably come from Chuluun and Temujin himself."

"Let's do it, then," said Alex. "My girlfriend's up there with that lunatic."

"All right," said Sam with a curt salute. "See you on the ground."

"How will we know when you've disabled the engines?" Alex called as Sam and Moe disappeared into the gloom.

"Oh, you'll know," Sam said.

# TWENTY-FIVE

Sam could almost feel his brother's gaze boring through the back of his head as he led the way through the darkened corridor. The silence between them was suffocating. Only the clanking of their boots and the whisper-soft whirring of servos inside their armor filled the air between them.

"You got something you want to say to me, little sister?"

"Yeah," said Moe coldly. "Why the sudden change of heart?"

"The kids."

Moe stopped dead in his tracks at these words. "What?"

Sam sighed and stopped. "The kids. When Temujin told me he planned to attack the school, I tried to change his mind, but he wouldn't listen. I wanted to stop him, but I just couldn't bring myself to do anything about it."

Moe remained silent.

"But then there was an accident on the loading platform," Sam said, "and suddenly everything became clear. It was like a haze was lifted from my mind, and everything I've done for the past three years became pointless and wrong. Then I remembered the children, and the Death Walkers he was planning to use against them. I got angry. First with myself, but then I realized I was really angry with *him*.

"I tried to stop him," Sam continued, "but I wasn't fast enough. So I stole the armor prototypes and escaped. You know the rest."

Moe took a deep breath, his armored shoulders rising and falling with the action. Finally he slapped his brother on his arm, their armor connecting with a dull *clang*. "Let's go. The others are counting on us."

Sam allowed himself the smallest of smiles and nodded to his brother. They continued down the corridor, finally coming to a large circular door.

Sam patted it. "The coolant delivery system is on the other side. Past that is the engine room. Let's just hope they didn't change the access codes."

"Leave that to me."

Sam touched a pad on the wall and the door slid open like an iris. The Replodians stepped inside and surveyed their surroundings. Lining both walls were six thick pipes, all crusted over with a layer of frost. Moe shuddered involuntarily even though his suit kept his body temperature constant.

"Whatever you do, don't fire your weapons in here," Sam said. "That isn't Kool-Aid in those pipes. You nick one of those and you can kiss your butt goodbye."

"What's in them?"

"Liquid nitrogen," said Sam. "Now let's go."

"After you," Moe grumbled, giving the coolant pipes a wide berth.

They followed the corridor to a narrow, single-paneled door equipped with a keypad, the numbers an iridescent blue. Sam reached out and tapped in a long sequence of numbers on the keypad. The keys flashed red, and Sam punched the wall.

"Damn it!"

"They changed it?"

Sam nodded.

Moe forced his way past his brother. "Step aside."

"Be my guest, but you can't crack it."

"Oh, ye o' little faith," said Moe, carefully pulling the face of the keypad off the wall.

"Hey! Be careful with that. You could set off the alarm."

"No, I won't," said Moe patiently, sorting wires into separate bundles between his fingers.

"Hell, *I* could do that," said Sam.

"Too late," said Moe. "It's my turn now. You had your chance."

"I designed this system, and I know it better than anybody," said Sam. "You don't know what you're doing."

"Please," Moe scoffed. "Anything you can do, I can do better."

"No, you can't."

"Yes, I can."

"No, you can't," said Sam, his voice becoming childish.

"Yes," Moe growled through gritted teeth. "I *can*. Now shut up and let me work."

"Can't crack it," said Sam stubbornly.

Moe sighed. "This would be a lot easier if you weren't breathing in my ear."

"Fine!" Sam walked away.

"Ah ha!" Moe said triumphantly. "I see what you did. Tricky, tricky. Not bad, actually. Kind of impressive as a matter of fact, but all I have to do is pull these five wires here, and—"

"Fire in the hole!"

Moe's head snapped up. "What?"

He turned and saw Sam walking toward him, carrying a long, cylindrical gas canister. Sam raised an armored fist and brought it down hard on the valve, snapping it clean off and releasing a stream of white vapor. Moe dove out of the way as his brother sprayed the door from top to bottom with liquid nitrogen. After a few seconds, the door was encrusted with a thick coating of ice. Sam tossed the spent canister over his shoulder and kicked the door dead center, shattering it into a million frozen shards.

Sam stepped over the threshold and paused midstride. "Or would that be 'ice in the hole?' 'Fire in the hole' just doesn't seem appropriate in this context."

Moe peeked out from around a corner. "Damn it, Samrai! I had it!"

"Tick tock, little sister." Sam stepped through the steaming doorway. "Let's go."

Moe started to follow his brother through the doorway, but paused and looked down at the keypad, still dangling by the wires. He reached out to pluck the five wires he had been prepared to pull before Sam's stunt. The keys flashed green.

"Son-of-a—" Moe tossed the keypad aside and stepped over the threshold. "Jerk."

He stepped onto a railed catwalk, barely wide enough for even one person. The catwalk ran between two giant turbines, both roaring deafeningly as they spun. Moe was so engrossed in the colossal machinery that he almost bumped into his brother. Sam gave him the briefest of over-the-shoulder glances and returned to gazing at the turbines.

"Are these the engines?" asked Moe.

Sam nodded. "Part of 'em. The rest is in another room farther back."

"So what are we waiting for?" Moe wrenched a piece of pipe from the railing and brandished it like a club. "Let's get to breaking stuff."

Sam sighed. "Three years, Moe. I spent the first three years of my life building this monstrosity, thinking it was my purpose, that it was the *right* thing to do. I'm responsible for everything that's happened today. It's my fault. All of it."

Moe nodded. "Well, you can't change the past, but I do know what will make you feel better."

"What's that?"

Moe held out the pipe. "Senseless and wanton destruction of private property."

Sam took the pipe, hefted it in his hand for a moment, and then threw it into the turbine to his right. The pipe slipped between two blades and—like a stick in a bicycle's spokes—the turbine caught and groaned to a reluctant halt. The air was filled with the grinding of metal on metal and the whine of straining machinery. A flash of light flickered inside the stalled turbine, followed by an immense fireball erupting from between the blades. The ship pitched, and the Replodians grabbed the railing.

"Will that do it?" Moe yelled over the roar.

Sam nodded. "The other engine will fail under the strain. We only have a few minutes to get clear."

Moe turned and ran toward the door. "Well then, let's blow this joint."

Sam started to follow, but he slowed and looked back at the smoking turbine.

"It's not enough," he muttered.

As they crossed the threshold into the corridor, Sam stopped and looked at the frosty coolant pipes lining the walls. "Hey, Moe."

Moe stopped running and turned toward his brother.

"Remember what I said about firing our weapons in here?"

"I don't think I like where this line of questioning is going," said Moe.

Sam raised his arms and primed both ion cannons. "Fly."

"Oh, hell," Moe breathed. He ran a few steps and pushed off the ground, engaging his boot thrusters.

Sam engaged his own thrusters, twisted in the air onto his back, and aimed his arm cannons at the pipes lining each wall behind him. He opened fire, spraying the hallway with alternating rapid-fire green ion blasts. Thick, white vapor erupted violently from the pipes with every blast. He twisted in the air again and surged forward to catch up to Moe, clearing the door with the sub-zero cloud right on his rocket-powered heels.

On the other side, Moe punched the pad beside the door. As the iris closed, he shouted, *"Comeoncomeoncomeon!"*

A thin plume of vapor escaped just before the iris closed on it, sealing off the gas. The Replodians watched as the door slowly frosted over.

"Wooooo!" Sam hooted with delight. "Let's go on that ride again!"

"Let's not," said Moe, his eyes locked on the expanding crust of ice.

Suddenly, a floor grate near the door exploded upward, and a column of the frigid vapor erupted into the room. The Replodians jumped as a second grate, this one directly in front of them, was thrown into the air and unleashed yet another cloud.

"What's happening?" Moe shouted.

Sam pulled his brother to his feet and dragged him down the hall, narrowly avoiding a third grate blowing. "No time to explain. Just run!"

Sam cursed himself as the hall behind them filled with nitrogen gas. In his brashness, he'd forgotten the liquid-to-gas expansion ratio of liquid nitrogen and had inadvertently started a chain reaction that would soon fill the *Ragnarok* with the only substance on Earth lethal to Replodians, not to mention humans.

Sam opened a comm channel to the other teams. "Out! Everybody out, now!"

The ship pitched again as the second engine failed, and he nearly lost his balance. Sam engaged his boot thrusters and Moe quickly did the same, trying to keep up with his brother.

"What's happening?" Moe shouted.

"The coolant system's gone critical," Sam explained as he passed through the door to the cargo hold. "The ship's filling up with nitrogen gas."

"What?" Moe shouted. "What about the others?"

# TWENTY-SIX

HEAVY, ARMORED BOOTS CLANKED LOUDLY ON THE STEEL GRATING OF the corridor leading from the *Ragnarok*'s cargo bay. Alex scanned the hall for any sign of the elevator Sam had mentioned, but so far only unlabeled, featureless doors lined the walls every twelve feet.

"These must be barracks," Rene observed.

"Yeah," said Robert. "Which begs the question, where are all the soldiers?"

A door several yards ahead opened and a dozen troopers strode down the hall toward them. For a moment, they were lost in boisterous, celebratory conversation, but stopped dead in their tracks when they noticed the armored figures.

Rene looked at Robert. "You were saying?"

"Now what?" asked Cherry.

"Take them," Lamont ordered. "Before they raise the alarm!"

One of the soldiers tried to key a nearby wall-mounted intercom, but Rene beat him there and slammed his fist into the man's face. The trooper collapsed to the deck, unconscious before he hit the floor.

Taking their cue from the Cajun, the others rushed into the fray. One Horde trooper got off a lucky shot with his plasma rifle to Cherry's chest, knocking her down, but she was back on her feet immediately and drove her boot into the soldier's throat. Another soldier, unable to draw his weapon in the middle of the suffocating battle, punched Alex in the face and broke his hand on the unyielding metal. The trooper screamed and cradled his hand while Alex countered with a roundhouse kick to the side of his head.

The momentum of the kick brought Alex around and he finally realized what sort of door the soldiers had exited. "Lamont! The elevator!"

Lamont delivered a bone-crushing headbutt to a soldier attempting to shoot him with a corrosive gel rifle and whirled around to face Alex, his faceplate splattered with blood. "Get in!"

Alex pressed the "call" button and muttered to himself impatiently for a moment before the door slid open.

Lamont ran for the elevator and slapped Robert on the shoulder as he passed. "This is where we part ways."

"You can count on us," Robert said as he dodged a stray plasma blast. "Go save those kids."

"Good luck," said Lamont as the elevator doors closed, cutting him off from the battle and his teammates.

"You too," Robert whispered.

To Robert's left, Rene snapped a trooper's neck and dropped the corpse unceremoniously to the ground with the others. "There. That's the last of them."

"Then let's go." Robert slapped him on the back and broke into a run. "Before more of these goons show up."

Cherry wrinkled her nose as she stepped over the pile of unconscious and dead soldiers. Even with the suits' air filters, the stench was unbearable. "God, they stink."

"Obviously the Khan cares nothing for the health of his minions," said Rene, running alongside her.

"Showing sympathy for the man whose neck you just broke?"

"Look," Rene said, "I take no pleasure in killing, but the Germans showed me no mercy on Omaha Beach, nor did the Yankees offer me any kindness at Antietam."

Cherry ran in silence for a moment, letting this sink in.

"War is unpleasant, *cher*," the Cajun continued, "but we have a job to do, just as those men back there had theirs. We just did ours better."

Robert nodded to himself as he ran. The life of a soldier may have been new to Cherry, her military service limited to being a peacetime medic, but he and Rene knew it well. In the centuries that he could remember, Robert Long had seen conflict ranging from the Battle of Waterloo to the Vietnam War. He'd still been coping with the horrors of 'Nam when the Seignso came and took him and his comrades to that sweltering planet in the Zeta Reticuli system. Now, he found himself in a new war, but for the first time in a very long time, he actually *believed* in the cause he was fighting for.

"How much farther?" asked Cherry.

"It can't be much," said Robert. "We've been running forever."

"Remind me to give that new Replodian a swift kick in the ass when we see him again," said Rene. "That guy needs a hobby."

"This *is* his hobby," Cherry grumbled.

"I mean like stamp collecting."

"There!" Robert pointed toward the end of the hallway. "It's just ahead."

They came to a halt in front of a large circular door at the end of the corridor. Rene raised his arm to fire his ion cannon, but Robert grabbed it at the last second and shook his head.

"Why not?" asked the Cajun.

"If they hear weapons firing, who knows what they'll do?" Robert explained. "We need to think of something else. We need to surprise them."

"Oh, for Pete's sake," Cherry pushed past the two men. "Just ring the friggin' bell."

"I like it," said Rene. "Subtle, but effective."

Cherry shook her head and pressed a green button on the intercom beside the door.

A few seconds later, a gruff, impatient voice filled the hallway and the helmets' earpieces instantly translated, *"Yes? What is it?"*

"Boudreaux's Pizza," called Rene in a singsong voice.

Cherry slapped her hand hard against the back of the Cajun's helmet.

*"What?"* asked the voice.

"Did you order the large sausage and mushrooms with extra goat cheese?" Rene said.

Cherry slapped him again. "Stop screwing around, you idiot."

*"I'm coming out,"* said the voice.

A few seconds later, the door's iris spun open and a portly Mongolian holding a double-barreled gel pistol took a half-step through the door before stopping to stare at the TDC agents with their arms raised and ion cannons primed.

"Hi there," said Rene. "You can keep the tip. We just want your ship."

Slowly, the Mongol lifted his pistol.

"Don't even think about it, Porky," Cherry warned. "Drop it!"

The man continued to raise his pistol, obviously not understanding the English being shouted at him.

"Stop!" Rene fired a warning burst past the man's head.

The green ion bolt screeched past the man's ear and crashed through the *Ragnarok*'s windshield, filling the bridge with icy, whistling wind. The Mongol promptly dropped the pistol and thrust both hands into the air. The other six crewmembers wheeled around from their stations to watch the commotion.

"I think we have a little language barrier here," said Rene. He stepped over the threshold and kept his aim on the bridge commander. "But you understood that just fine didn't you, fatty?"

The Mongol grinned sheepishly and nodded his head.

"The rest of you get away from those consoles," snapped Cherry. "Move it!"

With near zombie-like slowness, the unarmed technicians shuffled to the center of the room.

Cherry kept the techs covered with her arm cannon. "Now what do we do with them?"

Robert felt along his forearm with his fingers and scanned the heads-up display on his visor. "How the hell do you engage the stun function on these guns? Please tell me that lunatic included a stun function."

Rene lashed out with a knife-hand strike to the base of the chubby Mongol's neck and stood back as the man collapsed to the deck. Cherry and Robert stared at the fallen man for a moment before looking up at Rene.

Rene crossed his arms. "There's your stun function."

Cherry shook her head. "Barbarian."

Rene merely stared back in silence.

"What?" said Cherry. "No clever comeback?"

"I'm trying to think of a really good one," said Rene. "'Nag' just doesn't seem to cover it anym—"

A huge explosion rocked the ship and the bridge was suddenly filled with flashing lights and blaring klaxons. The technicians erupted into a panic and ran back to their posts, chattering so fast the suits' translators couldn't keep up.

"What's happening?" Cherry yelled over the din. The ship pitched, and she nearly lost her balance.

"The engines!" Rene exclaimed.

A few moments later, a panicked transmission filled their helmets and confirmed Rene's theory. *"Out! Everybody out, now!"*

"Evacuate," Robert ordered. "Move it, people! Double time!"

Rene promptly fired his arm cannon into the long windshield, melting large holes in the thick glass. "Let's go!"

"Wait!" Cherry grabbed him by the arm and pointed at the technicians. "What about them?"

But the crew wasn't interested in being rescued as they ran screaming from the room.

"Forget them," said Rene. "Get moving!"

The Cajun pushed off the deck, and his boot thrusters roared to life, launching him out of the *Ragnarok* with the others on his heels. Once above the rapidly descending ship, they watched as fire and smoke poured from the rear of the ship. With systems failing all over, the *Ragnarok*'s cloaking field flickered erratically until it was fully visible.

"I hope Moe and Samrai got out in time," Robert said.

Just then, two silver-clad figures flew out of the emergency hatch on the bottom of the ship mere inches ahead of a spewing white cloud.

"Look!" Cherry pointed at the rapidly approaching figures. "It's them!"

Moments later, Sam and Moe hovered in front of the Methuselans.

"*Wooo!*" Sam cheered. "Do I know how to throw a party, or what?"

"*Mon Dieu!*" Rene pointed over the Replodian's shoulder. "Look!"

"Yes," said Sam smugly. "It *is* impressive, if I do say so myself."

"Not that," Rene shouted. "Look!"

"What is it *now*, Frenchy?" Sam turned, following the Cajun's gaze. What he saw made his blood run cold.

The *Ragnarok*, smoking and spewing both flames and ice, was heading straight for the small town of Keosauqua, or more specifically the bridge on the south side of town. A school bus—the driver oblivious to the crippled monstrosity bearing down from above—approached the bridge from the north.

"What have I done?" breathed Sam.

"We've got to do something," said Cherry.

"Damn straight." Sam engaged his boot thrusters.

"We have to keep traffic off the bridge," said Robert. "Rene, Cherry, you come with me."

---

Sam landed on the street in front of the bridge and waved his arms at the bus, but the driver was too busy reprimanding rowdy children to notice the armor-clad alien until the bus was practically on top of him. The driver slammed on the brakes, but it was far too late. The front of the bus struck the Replodian and knocked him flat on his back before coming to a skidding halt on the bridge.

The driver opened the door and ran to the front of the bus, sputtering, "Oh, my God! I didn't see you. Are you all r—What the hell?"

Sam got to his feet and pointed at the bus. "Back this bus up! Get it off the bridge now!"

The deafening roar of the descending *Ragnarok* filled the air, and the ship struck the bridge in an explosion of concrete and twisted metal. One of the wings swept the northernmost support out from under the bridge, and the ground beneath Sam's feet dropped sharply. The shrieks of over thirty terrified children joined the cacophony created by the *Ragnarok*, which was still grinding along the bed of the Des Moines River. Sam fired his boot thrusters and pushed against the front of the bus, trying to push it back onto level ground. The bus driver screamed as the road slanted and he slid on his back toward the river, which was now nothing but flaming, jagged debris.

Sam reached for the driver, his fingers mere inches out of reach. *"No!"*

A silver streak swooped through the air and grabbed the flailing driver under the arms.

"I've got you," said Moe. "Don't worry."

"Y-you g—" the driver stuttered, looking down at the ground whizzing past below his kicking feet. *"Huh?"*

Sam grunted as the section of bridge under the bus's front wheels fell away, leaving the full weight on his shoulders. Slowly, the bus slid farther down, the bottom of the frame scraping against the jutting concrete ledge. The Replodian boosted the power to his thrusters, and watched the power gauge drop steadily from the exertion.

The sound of breaking glass drew Sam's attention up to the windshield. A little blond-haired girl of around six years old was lying against the glass, shrieking as the crack in the window slowly spiderwebbed outward. Several yellow dots lit up Sam's heads-up display: stress points in the glass.

"Hang on, sweetie," Sam said, trying his best to sound calm. "Everything's going to be okay."

Just then, the thrusters failed momentarily, and the bus dropped another few feet. The girl shrieked as the force of her second impact against the safety glass caused it to bow outward. Tiny fragments of glass rained on Sam's armor.

"Hold on!" Sam shouted, increasing the thrusters' power to maximum.

*"I'm coming, Sam,"* Moe's voice rang out over the comm channel.

"Hurry!"

The back tires bumped against the edge of the concrete, briefly stopping the bus's descent. The jarring impact caused the windshield to pull free of its frame, sending the shrieking girl plummeting, but this time, Sam was faster and snatched the girl's wrist.

"I've got you, sweetheart," he gasped, holding the entire bus up on one shoulder. "I've got you."

Suddenly, the weight lifted slightly from his shoulder and a welcome and familiar voice sounded in his ear, *"I've got your back, bro."*

The little girl squealed and kicked in the air, her little fingers clinging desperately to Sam's forearm. Stinging sweat dripped into his eyes. The girl's wrist slipped between his fingers, and Sam knew he couldn't hold both her *and* the bus much longer. Then a pair of silver hands appeared in front of his eyes, and the bus lifted up a little bit more.

"Take the girl," said Cherry. "I'll hold the bus."

Sam considered this, taking note of the rapidly dropping power levels of his thrusters, but decided against it. Cherry's inexperience with the armor's functions was a liability. No one knew the suits better than him.

"No," he said. "You take her and get her somewhere safe."

"You're hurt," Cherry replied. "I can tell."

"I'm fine," he insisted. "Don't argue. Just do it. I can hold it."

Cherry hesitated, trying to read him through the black visor.

"Hurry," he grunted, his voice tired and pleading. "Please."

Reluctantly, Cherry released the bus, settling the weight back onto Sam's shoulder, and dropped down to hover beside the frightened girl.

"Come here, sweetheart," she said, holding out her hands.

The girl's eyes widened as she stared at the flying woman reaching for her and she looked up at Sam questioningly.

Sam nodded. "It's okay, sweetie. She's my friend."

Cherry wrapped an arm around the girl's waist, and the child settled onto her hip. With his arm free, Sam slammed his hand back onto the front of the bus. The suddenness of the movement startled the girl, and she squealed, clinging to Cherry's neck.

"Go," Sam grunted. "I don't know how much longer we can hold this."

"You said you could hold it!" Cherry said.

"I lied. *Go!*"

In a flash of thruster fire, both Cherry and the little girl were gone.

Sam opened a private comm channel. "Moe?"

*"I'm here, Sam."*

"Listen to me very carefully. I want you to grab the children. Take them out through the emergency exit on your end and get them the hell out of here."

*"I won't leave you,"* Moe answered.

"God damn it, Moe, get the children out, now!"

There was silence over the channel for a moment, and then Moe responded, *"No. We're doing this together."*

Moe increased the power to his thrusters, slowly lifting the bus up and back onto the street. Sam pushed against the front, inching the bus over the concrete. An alarm rang out inside his helmet, and a synthesized female voice said, *"Warning. System failure imminent. Thruster power: ten percent."*

"Moe," he shouted. "I'm losing power!"

---

MOE INCREASED THE POWER TO HIS THRUSTERS TO MAXIMUM AND pulled with his arms simultaneously, combining the armor's power with his raw alien strength. He snarled as the joints in his suit groaned and popped under the strain. He blinked away the sweat and ignored the icons flashing in his visor.

Finally the bus leveled out and the rear tires touched solid ground. Moe disengaged his thrusters and pulled the bus back onto the street.

Finally, after what seemed like an eternity of pulling, the front tires rolled onto the pavement and the bus sat stationary.

Moe ripped the back door off its hinges. "All right, kids. Everybody out."

The words barely passed his lips before a stream of crying and screaming children exploded from the back of the bus. When the last child climbed down, Moe stepped out from behind the bus and walked right into Sam. He stared at Moe for a moment and punched him in the shoulder, throwing sparks.

"Hey!" Moe exclaimed.

Sam staggered and pointed at his brother. "I told you to leave me and get those kids out!"

"We're a team, Sam. *No one* gets left behind."

Sam's exhaustion caught up to him, and he sank to the ground. "I don't know about you, little sister, but I could really use a hot one right now."

Moe laughed and sat next to his brother. "Roger that."

A crowd gathered on the sidewalk. None were brave enough to approach the gleaming, armored men reclining against the bus tire. Camera flashes danced across the brothers' vision as the onlookers held up their phones to document the event.

"Smile, little sister," Sam said, nudging Moe with his shoulder. "You're on YouTube."

Moe laughed.

The crowd of onlookers parted, and Cherry and the little girl—her fingers still wrapped tightly around Cherry's index and middle fingers —stepped out into the street.

Sam stood and stepped away from the bus to meet them. He knelt in front of the little girl. For a moment, she only stared into the blank, black visor covering his eyes, but suddenly she darted forward and wrapped her arms around him as tight as she could. Hesitantly, Sam returned the embrace, placing one armored hand gently behind her tiny back.

"Thank you, Mr. Robot Man," she said, her voice soft and timid.

Warmth flooded the Replodian's body as he closed his eyes to fight back the tears welling up in them. "You're welcome, angel. You're very, *very* welcome."

One of the onlookers began to clap, a contagious sound that spread throughout the crowd. Moments later, Rene and Robert arrived to renewed shouts of awe and curiosity from the assembled crowd. Sam noticed the ion cannons on Robert's arms were smoking and looked across the river. Through the smoke, he could just make out the giant oak laying across the road, as well as the crowd of curiosity seekers clamoring over it for a closer look at the carnage.

Robert took in the damage. "What a mess. Where are Lamont and Alex?"

Sam looked at him over the girl's shoulder. "They're not with you?"

# TWENTY-SEVEN

"Good luck," said Lamont to Robert.

The elevator doors slid shut, sealing Alex and Lamont off from the sounds of battle raging in the corridor, and they began their ascent to the Khan's private chambers. Alex's pulse thumped in his ears, and a bead of sweat trickled down his nose, triggering a blast of cool air inside his helmet that brought the temperature to a more tolerable level.

Alex's eyes flicked to the translucent display on his visor:

**SYSTEM STATUS:**
*WEAPON SYSTEMS: 95%*
*ARMOR INTEGRITY: 98%*
*THRUSTERS: 92%*

So much power. How much differently would the day's events have gone if they'd had them from the beginning, or not at all for that matter? Without them, he and his friends would have been red smears in the school parking lot.

And Crystal would be lost forever.

The thought made Alex's breathing quicken. When he got his hands on Temujin—

Lamont laid a hand on his shoulder. "Calm down. Focus. Remember what Moe taught you and you'll do fine."

Alex took a deep breath and nodded.

As the lift slowed and came to a complete stop, Lamont primed his arm cannon. "Ready, Alex?"

Alex primed his own and flexed his fingers. "Let's do this."

The doors slid open, and they stepped out, training their weapons ahead of them at the open door leading to the Khan's chambers. They could hear laughter from within. Two Horde troopers stood just inside the doorway with their plasma rifles aimed at something on the floor.

"Hey!" Alex shouted.

The sentries whirled around and raised their weapons to fire, but were caught off guard by the bizarre suits. Alex fired an ion blast into the chest of the closest soldier; he was dead before he hit the floor.

A girl's scream rang out from the room as the second sentry fired, pelting Alex's armor with plasma bolts. The shots pushed him back slightly, but he kept his footing and raised his arm cannon to return fire. Lamont was already on the move, however, and delivered a bone-crushing uppercut into the man's chin. The force of the blow slammed the soldier into the top of the doorway and he crumpled to the deck.

With the soldiers down, Alex finally had an unobstructed view of the chamber. His heart jumped in his chest when he saw his girlfriend cuffed and crying over the bleeding body of his twin.

"Quintin!" He rushed to their side.

Alex knelt beside Crystal and examined his brother's injuries. His pulse throbbed in his ears louder than ever as his fingers grazed the deep, smoking wounds.

He turned to look at Crystal. "Are you okay?"

Crystal sniffled. "They killed him."

"No," said Alex, not believing his ears. "That's not possible."

He placed a hand against his brother's bloody chest and a holographic image of a human heart appeared in the middle of his visor; it wasn't beating. The E.K.G. below the image was flat-lined and unresponsive. The steady, high-pitched tone ringing in his ears confirmed the terrible truth before his eyes.

"Quintin," he sobbed, tears burning at the corners of his eyes. "Lamont, do something!"

Lamont knelt beside him and placed his fingertips against Quintin's throat, but pulled his hand away an instant later, shaking his head despondently.

"I'm sorry," he said, barely above a whisper. "There's nothing I can do. He's gone."

"No!" Alex sobbed as he hugged his brother's limp body and tears splashed against the inside of his visor. "Quintin! Quintin, come back!"

"Who are you people?"

Alex froze. He knew that voice. His sorrow faded, replaced with a burning hatred. His head snapped up to face his enemy, his brother's blood smeared across the front of his helmet.

"*You.*" He pointed at Temujin with an accusing, armored finger. "You did this."

"Who are you?" Temujin pointed the unlit laser sword at Alex and Lamont in turn. "How did you get on this ship?"

"We had a little help from a mutual friend," said Lamont, standing and moving away from the body. "We made him a better offer, one that doesn't involve the slaughter of innocent children."

"Samrai," Temujin whispered vehemently. "Then that must make you the infamous TDC." He emphasized each letter with an air of contempt.

Alex flexed his fingers, itching to wrap them around the Khan's throat.

Chuluun drew his sword. "Infidels!"

While this exchange was going on, Alex didn't notice the E.K.G. monitoring his brother's pulse—now minimized in the bottom left corner of his visor—had begun to register a steady beat. He didn't see Quintin's fingers slowly inching toward the discarded sword belonging to one of the dead sentries. Slowly, Alex stood and clenched his fists.

"You killed him," he growled, taking one slow step toward his enemy, his hands shaking with grief and rage. "You killed my *brother*! You son-of-a-bitch, I'll kill you!"

Temujin took a cautionary step back from the armored terror slowly advancing on him. "Your brother?"

::You should have killed me when you had the chance,:: Alex projected, sending waves of wrath with the message.

As the words reached the Khan's mind, the room began to shake. Ornaments and paintings fell from the walls as the very metal plating they were made of creaked and buckled. The air around them hummed with the energy being released.

*"You,"* Temujin breathed. "Chuluun, it's the child! Kill him!"

At these words, Quintin's eyes snapped open, glowing a fiery, radioactive green. His fingers wrapped around the handle of the sword, and he sprang to his feet, meeting Chuluun halfway; their swords clashed and threw sparks as they collided. Chuluun's eyes widened as he fought back against the youth's blade, their strength evenly matched.

"Quintin," Alex cried gleefully. The shaking immediately ceased as the teen's concentration was broken.

Shocked by Quintin's inexplicable resurrection, Crystal's eyes rolled back and she collapsed to the deck. Alex knelt at her side and snapped the handcuffs binding her wrists.

"Impossible," Chuluun grunted. "I *saw* you die."

"Believe it," Quintin replied. "You'll have to aim a little higher if you want to get rid of me, pal."

"I will keep that in mind," Chuluun snarled, pushing off of Quintin's blade and preparing to strike. "Freak!"

Suddenly the ship pitched, and the floor beneath them shook violently, sending everyone sprawling to the deck, but the disruption did not slow the swordsmen, who continued to fight even on the ground.

Alex cradled Crystal in his arms. "What the hell was that?"

"The engines," said Lamont, holding out his arms to maintain his balance. "Sam did it!"

"You *fools*," Temujin shouted, spit flying from his lips. "What have you done?"

As the battle between Chuluun and Quintin raged on, a panicked transmission filled Alex and Lamont's helmets, *"Out! Everybody out, now!"*

"Quintin!" Alex scooped Crystal up into his arms and rose to his feet shakily. "We have to go now! This ship's about to crash!"

"No one is going anywhere," Temujin snarled. He thumbed the igniter switch on the hilt of the stolen laser sword and swung it in an arc directly in-line with Quintin's neck.

Alex saw the beam flash out. "Quintin, look out!"

Another explosion rocked the *Ragnarok* as the second engine exploded, and the Khan was thrown off balance. The white-hot blade missed its target, but instead sliced deep into Quintin's left cheek. Quintin cried out as both he and Chuluun were thrown to the deck by the force of the explosion. Quintin's hand flew to his cheek and felt the hot, gaping wound. He grimaced as the wound knitted and healed, leaving a thick white scar in its wake.

Temujin stared at the fresh scar. "Impossible."

Quintin's eyes glowed with renewed intensity as he stared back into Temujin's. "You'll *pay* for that."

Chuluun regained his footing and charged the enraged Methuselan. "My Khan!"

Quintin spun, bringing his blade into the Mongol general's face and slicing across his left eye. Chuluun screamed and dropped his sword, his hands flying to his ruined face. A third explosion, more powerful than the first two, rocked the ship and smoke began to fill the chamber as Lamont staggered to Quintin's side.

"We have to go. The ship's about to crash."

Quintin pointed at the two Mongol leaders scrambling on the floor. "Not until I see them dead."

"They're dead already," said Lamont. "Come on."

"How do we get out of here?" asked Quintin.

Lamont pointed toward the ceiling. "Up."

"Up?" asked Quintin, looking at the large glass-domed skylight above the chamber. The blue sky outside was thick with black smoke. "What do you mean, 'up'?"

Lamont wrapped his arms around Quintin's waist. "Cover your eyes!"

"What are you do—"

Lamont ignited his thrusters and surged into the air, cutting off Quintin's words and rocketing toward the skylight. The glass shattered on impact with the suit, and Lamont and Quintin disappeared above the smoke.

Alex turned to face Temujin with Crystal in his arms. "How does it feel, *old man*? True power? The power of friendship. Perhaps you would have attained it if you had lived long enough."

The room trembled with the Khan's rage as his own words were chewed up and spat back out at him by the youth he thought he'd crushed. Every piece of glass in the room left untouched by the explosions shattered as Temujin roared a single word like a curse, *"Alexander!"*

Alex directed his gaze at the broken skylight and ignited his thrusters, disappearing through a gap in the framework.

Temujin scanned the room for any means of escape. His eyes finally fell on the silver sarcophagus, knocked off its pedestal by the explosions.

"Chuluun," he shouted. "The coffin!"

Weakened by pain and loss of blood, Chuluun crawled along the floor toward the sarcophagus. "Yes, my Khan."

"Hurry!" Temujin lifted the heavy lid.

Moments later, the casket lid slammed shut on both the Khan and his general, sealing them both inside.

"They will pay for this, Chuluun," Temujin said. "I swear it."

"Yes, my Khan," Chuluun rasped, his words drowned out by the rumbling of the *Ragnarok* crashing to Earth.

"GREAT MOTHER'S BEARD!" QUINTIN WAILED, REVERTING TO HIS NATIVE Phaedojian tongue in his panic. "Put me down!"

Lamont swooped low over the river and deposited the kicking youth on the southern bank. He turned to look as the *Ragnarok* crashed into the bridge. In hindsight, he thought, maybe bringing the ship down hadn't been such a hot idea after all. He watched the ship plunge into the river, trailing thick black smoke and incongruous white vapor behind it.

"I hope everyone's all right," he said.

"Okay," said Quintin. "I don't know who you are, pal, but I had everything under control until you two showed up."

"Relax, kid."

Lamont reached up to his helmet, thumbing a hidden switch in the collar. The helmet emitted a soft hiss as the airtight seal was broken. He slowly lifted the helmet off his head, revealing his face, his dark hair matted against his head.

Quintin squinted in the afternoon sun. "Lamont?"

"Howdy, kid," said the Replodian, setting the helmet down on a log.

Quintin snatched up the helmet and turned it over in his hands. "Wow! Where did you get this armor? This is some serious hardware!"

"It's a long story," said Lamont. "Right now, we need to meet back up with Alex and the others and get the hell out of here before the military shows up."

"Alex?" said Quintin, realization slowly dawning in his voice. "Was that Alex with you on the ship? In the—"

"In the other suit?" Lamont said. "Yeah, it was."

Quintin scanned the sky for any sign of his brother. "Where is he?"

Lamont looked up and smiled as he caught a distant metallic glint high up in the sky. "I think he's got some important business to attend to."

---

ALEX BOOSTED THE POWER TO HIS THRUSTERS, PULLING AWAY FROM THE ship and breaking through the dense layer of black smoke. He climbed higher, far away from the fireballs erupting from the enemy craft. As the air around them grew cold, Crystal stirred in his arms. He slowed his ascent and shook her gently.

"Crystal?" His voice was soft and tender even through the voice synthesizer.

Slowly, she opened her eyes and looked around her. She panicked as she saw the ground hundreds of feet below them. She wrapped her arms around Alex's neck and shrieked.

"Oh, my God!" she screamed, clinging to Alex's body. "Oh, my God! Please, don't drop me! Oh, God, please don't let me fall!"

"Crystal."

At the mention of her name, Crystal stopped struggling and slowly looked into her rescuer's faceplate.

"Remember when we went ice skating at Gabe Hamilton's pond?" asked Alex, his head tilting slightly to the side. "I promised I'd *never* let you fall."

The fear in her eyes faded, replaced by confusion. "Alex?"

The black visor on Alex's faceplate retracted into the helmet, revealing his familiar green eyes. "Hey, babe."

Crystal shook her head. "I don't understand. What's going on? What are you *wearing*? Who were those people?"

"Crystal... I have something I need to tell you. Something I should have told you a long time ago."

She looked into his eyes expectantly.

"But it can wait," he said. "Are you all right?"

She nodded.

"Thank God," he sighed, wrapping his arms around her tighter.

He carefully repositioned her so that she was standing on top of his armored toes, the thrusters keeping them airborne as they shared a long embrace.

"I thought I'd lost you," said Alex.

Crystal choked back a sob. "I thought you were dead."

"Shh." Alex stroked her hair. "Everything's going to be okay, Crys. It's all over now."

She rested her cheek against his armored chest. "I love you, Alex."

He closed his eyes, savoring the words he thought he'd never hear pass her lips again. "I love you, too, Crystal."

They stayed there for a few minutes, holding each other before Crystal finally broke the silence. "Umm, Alex?"

"Yeah, babe?"

"Put me down."

"Oh." Alex grinned sheepishly. "Sorry."

# TWENTY-EIGHT

*TDC Command*
*Bonaparte, Iowa*

"GOD *DAMN* IT," SAM GRUNTED. HIS CURSE ECHOED IN THE CONFINED space underneath the hologram projector in the deserted main chamber.

He turned a small piece of alien hardware over between his fingers, the same piece Rene had been examining only a few hours prior, and sighed despondently. He could fix it, but it would take time. Sam didn't like taking time. He slipped the module into his breast pocket and inspected the central imaging processor, humming to block out the sounds of revelry drifting down the hall from the commissary.

It hadn't taken long for his guilt to get the better of him. The damage he'd caused those three long years ago was at the front of his thoughts from the moment he stepped over the threshold, and partying was the farthest thing from his mind. And so there he was, lying on a mechanic's creeper, waist-deep in the charred and long-cold guts of the central computer's hologram projector.

Faint footsteps echoed through the main chamber, and Sam

paused to listen. He smiled and called out softly, "Borrowing the car, Junior?"

The footsteps stopped.

He slid the creeper out and looked up at Alex, who was holding his power-armor helmet underneath his arm. The teen looked like he'd just been caught with his hand in the cookie jar.

"Don't worry, kid," said Sam. "I'm not gonna rat you out. Just have it back by midnight or it'll turn into a pumpkin."

Alex nodded nervously. "Thanks. I owe you."

"Oh, shut up," said Sam. "You do not. Now get out of here before someone else sees you."

Alex turned and ran for the well entrance. Sam chuckled and slid back into the machine. A minute later, he heard another set of footsteps approaching the projector.

"Did you forget something?" he called out.

A well-worn boot thumped against the side of the creeper and pulled him out into the open air. Cherry looked down at him, smirking

"Cheryl! Hi."

*"Cherry,"* she corrected him. "You didn't like the party?"

He shrugged. "It's not that. I just have a lot of work to do."

"Busy man."

Again, he shrugged. "I like to keep busy."

An awkward silence hung in the air for a moment, but Cherry's smile never faltered. Sam grabbed the edges of the access panel and prepared to pull himself back under the machine. "Well, back to work."

Cherry's foot pulled the creeper back out before he could completely disappear. The Replodian blinked nervously as she stepped over his body and sat down on top of him, straddling his hips.

"That was a very brave thing you did today," she said.

"It was nothing."

"Hmm." She smiled. "Modest, too."

"Me, modest?" He laughed nervously. "Lady, you obviously don't know me very well."

She placed her elbows against his chest and rested her chin in her hands. "Well, what do you think I'm doing here if not trying to get to know you better?"

"Umm," he replied, trying to think of a response not typical of a grade-schooler. "I... I, uh... Well, I—"

"Let's see," she said, ticking off points on her fingers. "Brave. Modest. *Cute*. And glib. Am I forgetting anything?"

He grinned. "I'm good with my hands."

She leaned closer and whispered in his ear, her voice low and throaty, "I'll remember that."

Sam swallowed the lump in his throat as her breath tickled his ear and neck.

"I never got a chance to thank you properly for saving me on the truck earlier," she said.

"Oh, well, that was n—"

She crushed her mouth against his, cutting off his words and filling both his mouth and body with warmth he had never felt before. He reached up and ran his hand along the small of her back as her fingers curled through his hair. When she finally pulled away, she couldn't help but giggle at his bewildered expression.

"How was it?" she asked, her lips a mere inch from his.

He licked his lips. "Wet."

She laughed. "Is that a good thing?"

He grinned, regaining a little of his composure. "Lady, I'm a Replodian. Wet is *always* a good thing."

"Well then," she said, sitting up and slowly unzipping the front of her coveralls, "you're *really* going to like what's coming next."

---

ALEX HOVERED OUTSIDE THE SECOND-STORY WINDOW AND PEERED inside. Crystal was sitting on her bed, dressed in her red satin pajamas. A recent comedy movie played on the television, but Alex could tell she was uninterested in it. Just background noise.

He tapped lightly on the glass, but his metal fingers made the noise louder than intended, and Crystal jumped with a small squeal. She looked over at the window, but couldn't see clearly in the reflected light from the bedside lamp. Alex tapped again, this time a little softer. Slowly she approached the window and opened it, startled by the silver figure.

Alex gave a little wave. "Hi."

"Alex?" Crystal whispered, looking first at him and then down at the ground. "What are you doing here?"

"Can I come in?"

Crystal looked outside once more, and then gestured for him to come inside. "Hurry up before somebody sees you."

Alex climbed through the window awkwardly, struggling to disengage his thrusters without falling into the bushes below. He left a small burn mark on the windowsill.

"Sorry," he said. "I'm still getting the hang of it."

Crystal sighed. She was obviously having a hard time adjusting to this, not that he could blame her. Alex brushed a cold metal hand against her cheek. She recoiled from the touch.

Alex pulled back. "What's wrong?"

"I just..." Crystal pointed at the armor. "That *thing* creeps me out."

"Oh." Alex looked down at his body. "Right. Um... just a sec."

The armor melted into a featureless mass of liquid silver metal that crawled up Alex's body, disappearing into the helmet's collar. When the armor was fully retracted, Alex lifted the helmet and shook out his hair. Crystal relaxed.

He touched her cheek again, this time with his own skin. "Better?"

Crystal nodded.

Alex took a step closer and planted a kiss on her lips, which she returned.

"So..." Alex placed his helmet on the floor. "How'd your parents take it?"

Crystal rolled her eyes and began to pace around the room. "What do you think? They *freaked out*! I just got home from the hospital an hour ago."

"The hospital?"

"Yeah. My mom is so paranoid. And my dad scheduled an appointment for me with a psychiatrist on Tuesday."

Alex winced.

"I know, right? I'm scarred for life." She rolled her eyes again.

Alex shrugged. "Most people would be."

She sighed. "I guess."

"Look..." Alex pulled her into an embrace. "You don't have to worry about anything anymore. Temujin's dead. It's all over."

The tension in Crystal's shoulders faded. "Thank God."

"*Crystal!*" a male voice called from downstairs. "Who are you talking to?"

Crystal gasped. "My dad! Alex, hide!"

Alex looked around frantically as Mr. Hammond's heavy footsteps thumped up the stairs. As the doorknob turned, Crystal kicked the helmet underneath her bed. Alex slipped behind the door as Mr. Hammond threw it open and stepped into the room.

"Who are you talking to?" he demanded.

Alex held his breath and willed his heart to beat more quietly. Crystal's eyes flicked past her father's shoulder at him.

"Crystal," Mr. Hammond said. "I said, 'Who were you talking to?'"

"No one, Daddy."

"I heard talking."

"No you didn't."

But Mr. Hammond wasn't buying it. He ripped her closet door open and parted the clothes hanging inside. When he found it empty, he knelt beside her bed and lifted the bed skirt. Crystal looked at Alex and saw the look of horror on his face that mirrored her own. When she looked back down, her father was holding the helmet in his hands.

"What's this?"

"It's... Alex's..." Crystal began slowly, trying to come up with a suitable cover story. "Motorcycle helmet! He forgot it when he was here the other day."

"Motorcycle hel—" Mr. Hammond sputtered. "Are you telling me that Walker punk has a *motorcycle* now?"

Alex gaped and mouthed the word *"Punk?"*

Crystal shrugged and gave her father a sheepish grin.

Mr. Hammond slowly turned toward the door. One didn't have to be a mind reader to know what he was thinking; the gears turning inside his head were so loud Alex could hear them over his own pounding pulse. As Mr. Hammond took his first step toward the door, Alex squeezed his eyes shut and summoned all of his will into a single word.

*::Stop!::*

Crystal's father stopped mid-stride.

Alex exhaled. He peeked around the door and saw Crystal's father frozen in time, his eyes locked on Alex but totally unresponsive.

Alex stared into Mr. Hammond's eyes. ::You don't see me.::

Mr. Hammond shook his head slowly.

::It's been a long day. We're all tired.::

"It's been a long day," Mr. Hammond droned. "We're all tired."

::You should get some sleep.::

Mr. Hammond turned to look at Crystal, his voice regaining its usual cadence. "You should get some sleep."

Crystal looked back and forth between her father and Alex, who stared at her, wide-eyed, and nodded.

"Oh! Right!" She yawned. "You're right, Daddy. I'm *really* tired."

Mr. Hammond held up the helmet. "We'll discuss *this* little development in the morning, young lady."

Crystal nodded enthusiastically. Her enthusiasm quickly faded when her father turned and walked toward the door with the helmet still clutched in his hand.

"All right," Mr. Hammond said, shutting the door. "Goodnight, sweetheart."

"Night, Daddy!"

As Mr. Hammond's footsteps retreated down the stairs, Alex slapped his forehead and groaned.

"What?" asked Crystal. "What's wrong?"

"The helmet!" Alex whispered. "I forgot to make him drop the helmet!"

He reached for the doorknob.

"Where are you going?"

"To get it back," Alex explained.

Crystal grabbed his hand. "Don't worry, we'll get it back. We just have to wait until he goes to sleep. My dad snores so loud you could land an airplane on the front lawn and he'd never hear it."

Alex sat down on the bed and sighed. "So what do we do in the meantime?"

Crystal's lips curled into a sly smile. "I have an idea."

"What?"

She sat down on the bed next to Alex and planted a long kiss on his lips. Alex returned the kiss, his mouth working against hers as his hand wandered up her side. Crystal placed a hand against his chest and pushed him down onto the bed. Alex's eyes grew wide as saucers as Crystal slowly unbuttoned her pajama top.

"Crys," he whispered. "Are you sure?"

Crystal smiled and nodded as she allowed the satin top to slide off her shoulders and down her arms. Alex felt his ears getting warm as he stared at his girlfriend's body. She leaned down and kissed him again.

"Wait," Alex said, breaking the kiss. "What if your dad hears us?"

Crystal grinned and shook her head. "Stop talking, then!"

She had a point. "Oh, what the hell," he said, pulling her in for another kiss.

Crystal giggled and reached over to turn off the bedside lamp, plunging the room into darkness.

*"Alex!"* she gasped. "You're so bad!"

Alex chuckled.

# TWENTY-NINE

*October 22nd*

THE NEXT MORNING, THE HEROES WERE BEGINNING TO FEEL THE effects of the previous day's exertions, both in the line of duty and recreational. Moe, Lamont, Robert, and Quintin all sat around the kitchen table picking at their breakfasts while Rene stood at the counter and poured himself a heaping bowl of cereal.

The Cajun turned to take his place at the table and said, "Anyone get the license number of the thing that hit us yesterday?"

"Yeah," Lamont groaned. "Mongolian vanity plates, 'KHAGHAN1'."

Rene grimaced as he poured milk generously over his cereal, his head pounding from the high quantity of Phaedojian moonshine he'd consumed at the party.

Moe downed his third glass of water. "I've never been this thirsty in my life, and that's saying something."

"That's nothing," Rene mumbled, milk dribbling down his unshaven chin as he took his first bite. "I'm feeling scars I forgot I had."

Quintin caught Rene's eye and ran his middle finger down the length of the fresh scar on his cheek.

Rene pointed his spoon at the teen. "You're not too old for me to take you over my knee, boy."

"Simmer down, you two." Robert stood to refill his coffee cup.

There were two coffee makers on the counter; the carafe on the right bore a piece of masking tape that read *"REPLODIANS!!!"* The coffee inside the decanter bubbled in a rolling boil. Robert reached for this one before stopping himself and grabbing the other carafe.

Lamont set down his own coffee and looked around the table. "Where's Sam?"

"Don't know," said Quintin, rubbing his temples with his thumbs. "Don't care."

Robert pulled out a chair and sat. "I saw him leave the party early last night."

"Great!" Moe slammed his fist down onto the table, causing the dishes to rattle loudly. "Just great."

"Ow!" Quintin groaned. "Please don't do that again."

"We need to go find that little weasel." Moe shoved his chair out. "Or has everyone forgotten what happened the last time we turned our backs on him?"

The kitchen door slid open with a soft pneumatic hiss, and Sam walked into the room, his dirty Horde-issued coveralls replaced with khaki cargo shorts, white sneakers, a blue T-shirt, and a pair of dark sunglasses. He whistled as he poured himself a cup of boiling brew. Quintin plugged his ears with his index fingers to drown him out.

"What's the matter with you guys?" Sam said cheerfully, finally noticing the pained expressions on his teammates' faces. "Didn't *everybody* make it with a beautiful redhead last night?"

Quintin turned and stared at the Replodian.

"Oh, not you," Sam said, patting the youth on the back. "No offense, kid, but you're not exactly my brand."

Rene's spoon clattered on the table and fell onto the floor.

"What's the matter with you, Frenchy?" said Sam. "Somebody piss in your corn flakes?"

The Cajun shoved away from the table and stalked toward the door, pausing only a moment to stare vehemently into Sam's eyes before exiting the room. As the door sealed behind him, the muffled sound of his voice calling angrily through the corridors could be heard, "Cheryl!"

"What was that about?" Sam leaned against the counter. "Was it something I said?"

Robert leaned back in his chair and sighed. "Rene and Cherry used to be an item."

"*Awk*-ward," Sam sipped his coffee.

"You've just made an enemy for life," said Robert.

"Hey," said Sam. "Don't pin this on me, pal. *She* came on to *me!*"

"Well, gee," said Moe. "Who could possibly blame her, right?"

Sam made a crude gesture at his brother, disguised not so subtly as a nose pick.

"Well, Mr. Science Officer," said Lamont as he stood and collected his jacket from the back of his chair, "you'd better figure out a way to make nice with Boudreaux."

"Oh, yeah?" said Sam defiantly. "And why is that?"

"Because he's your mechanic," Lamont said as the kitchen door closed behind him.

Sam's shoulders slumped. "Great."

Moe stood to follow Lamont and slapped his brother on the shoulder. "It'll work out. Now saddle up, we've got to get to the hospital."

"What the hell for?" Sam called as Moe disappeared through the door.

---

THE STEADY BEEPING OF THE E.K.G. AT HIS BEDSIDE SLOWLY BROUGHT Sheriff Challis to a cloudy state of semi-consciousness. The morphine —though blessedly numbing the pain in his legs to a dull ache—had been giving him strange dreams. Ever since his admission, whenever he closed his eyes he would see strange people in gleaming suits of armor. And robots. Oh, God, those damned killer robots, especially the one that killed poor Tim Barker and would have killed him, too, if that blond man carrying the duffel bag hadn't shown up when he did.

The more he thought about it, nothing about the day before seemed to add up, but that was probably the drugs. Just thinking about the robots made his legs throb. He reached for the miracle button that would send more into his bloodstream.

"Sheriff Challis," said a voice from the corner of the room. "I'd appreciate it if you could remain alert while we speak with you."

Challis struggled to lift his head off the pillow. "Who's there?"

A black man wearing a leather jacket stepped up to the side of the bed. He held a syringe full of translucent blue liquid in his hand.

"What's that?" asked the sheriff, suddenly very worried.

"Something for the pain." The man added the blue liquid to the sheriff's I.V. "But without the nasty side-effects of morphine, like addiction."

Slowly, the pain subsided and the sheriff's vision came into focus as the mysterious drug took effect. The stranger's hazy features resolved into a familiar face.

"You," he said. "I remember you. You were the one who... tried to save my legs."

"My name is Lamont," the man said. "And I'm sorry there was nothing more I could do for you yesterday. Things got a little hectic. I had no choice but to leave you."

The sheriff shook his head. "You saved my life. The paramedics told me so. I owe you my life."

Lamont nodded. "Well, let's talk about that, shall we?"

Another voice laughed from the foot of the bed. The sheriff raised the bed for a better look. There, sitting in a chair underneath the television and reading an outdated issue of *Popular Mechanics*, was the very same blond man who had saved him from the robot the day before. The way he was laughing, one would assume he was reading the funny pages as opposed to a scientific journal.

"I believe you've already met my brother Sam," said Lamont.

The sheriff nodded. "Yes, thank you. Thank you, both."

"Aww, shucks," said Sam, tossing the magazine aside. "Twernt nuthin', Shuruff."

"Sheriff Challis," said Lamont, bringing the lawman's attention away from his wisecracking brother. "We have a serious problem."

"Problem?"

Lamont nodded. "I believe you saw something yesterday that could put our lives, as well as the safety of those close to us, in serious jeopardy."

"I don't understand."

Sam placed a large canvas duffel bag on the bedside table. The Replodian unzipped the bag and pulled out a scuffed silver helmet.

Lamont took the helmet and held it out where the lawman could clearly see it. "You recognize this, don't you, Sheriff?"

The sheriff's mouth suddenly became very dry and he desperately tried to swallow.

"If our identities were to get out, we'd have every three-lettered government agency in the world knocking down our doors," Lamont said. "Do you understand our dilemma?"

The sheriff nodded. "I won't tell anybody. You have my word."

Lamont smiled. "I appreciate that, but you can stop being afraid of us now."

"I'm not afraid."

"Please!" Sam rolled his eyes. "Fifty bucks says you're messing your sheets right now."

"Shut up, Sam," said Lamont. "Sheriff, I don't want you to get the wrong impression. We're not here to scare you into keeping quiet."

"Then why *are* you here?"

"We're here to *buy* your silence," said Lamont.

"I don't understand."

Lamont pulled the clipboard bearing the sheriff's chart off the hook at the foot of the bed and flipped through it. "It says here that you're scheduled for amputation tomorrow at 10:30 AM. Mid-thigh."

Challis nodded. "The doctors say I'll be in a wheelchair the rest of my life."

"There are no alternatives?"

"Extensive reconstructive surgery," Challis said. "Pins. Plates. Artificial knees. But the doctors doubt that even with physical therapy I'll ever walk again. They said it'll just be easier and cheaper to amputate."

"They're probably right," Lamont said. "Which brings me back to the reason why we're here."

The sheriff looked into the Replodian's eyes, searching for any indication of what could possibly come from this visit. What could they offer him? Money? What did that matter? He would rather have his career. He would rather have his damn legs. But then Lamont said something that stopped the sheriff's thoughts cold.

"How would you like to walk again?" asked Lamont.

"I'm sorry?"

Lamont looked over his shoulder at his brother. "Sam?"

Sam reached into the bag and pulled out a gleaming, metallic skeletal leg and foot. He passed it to Lamont, exchanging it for the helmet.

Lamont held up the leg. "Sheriff, with these cybernetic implants my brother has developed, and my medical knowledge, I promise that you will not only walk again, but run, jump, and kneel with absolutely no joint pain. You can keep your job. You can have your life back. All we ask in return is your silence, and your cooperation with our organization."

Challis reached for the leg, expecting it to disappear like a mirage. "How is this possible?"

"You've seen our technology," said Sam, "and you've seen our enemy's technology up close and personal. The piece you're looking at is only a crude model I made in the car on the way here. With a little more time and better materials, I can build you a pair of legs better than the ones God gave you. This is only a fraction of what we're capable of."

"And it's a small price to pay for your silence," Lamont said. "What's more, this county gets to keep a public official who's served the people bravely and honestly for over twenty years. What do you say? Do we have a deal?"

"But the operation—"

"Cancel it," Lamont said. "Do *not* give your consent. Tell them you want the reconstructive surgery and the physical therapy. Then, when a reasonable amount of time has passed, we will contact you and make arrangements to replace your organic leg bones with the cybernetic prosthetics. But you *must* do the therapy. It must appear that you are making progress in your recovery on your own or the ruse will never work. Do we have a deal, Sheriff?"

The sheriff stared at the mechanical limb for a moment. "I don't suppose you could make me a few inches taller?"

"Don't push it," said Sam.

Lamont smiled and shook his head. "People might notice."

Challis nodded. "Yes. We have a deal."

"Excellent." Lamont passed him the limb for examination. "Care to have a closer look?"

The sheriff took the prosthetic leg tentatively and looked at the door. "What if somebody comes in?"

"Don't worry," said Lamont with a knowing smile. "One of our top agents is guarding the door, making sure we're not disturbed."

---

"So tell me," said Moe, smiling as he leaned against the doorframe. "What's a nice girl like you doing in a dirty mind like mine?"

The nurse giggled and rolled her eyes, clutching her clipboard to her chest, "Seriously, sir—"

"Moe."

"Moe," said the nurse. "I really need to get back to my rounds and check on the sheriff."

Moe peered around the clipboard and read the I.D. badge clipped onto her scrub top, "Falkirk, D. So what does the 'D' stand for?"

"Please, Moe."

"Denise?" guessed Moe. "Deborah? Dana? Am I close?"

"No, but I'm close to getting written up if I don't check on the sheriff."

"Danielle?" he continued. "Deidra? Delilah?"

"Donna." She sighed and brushed a stray strand of brown hair behind her ear. "My name is Donna."

"Donna," said Moe with an approving smile. "I like it."

"I'm glad," said Donna, reaching past him for the doorknob. "Now, if you don't mind—"

Moe shifted his position, blocking the doorknob, "So tell me, Donna, what time do you get off work?"

She took a step back, flabbergasted. "I, uh... I don't think that's—"

"You have a boyfriend," said Moe, looking dejected.

Donna sighed. "I—"

Moe grinned. "I could take him."

She raised an eyebrow. "Could you now?"

"Sure. I know ten different martial arts."

"Really?" asked Donna, feigning interest. "Which ones?"

Moe ticked them off on his fingers. "Kung Fu, Tang Soo Do, Ninjutsu, Capoeira, Hapkido, Krav Maga, Goju Ryu, Silat, Kendo, and Kempo."

Donna nodded. "Not bad. But can you whistle?"

Moe twirled his finger in the air. "Turn around for me."

Donna sighed and lowered her clipboard, making a three-hundred-and-sixty-degree turn, giving him a good view of her entire body. Moe nodded slowly and wolf whistled approvingly, which sent her into loud fits of laughter until her face turned bright red.

Moe waited until her laughter subsided and shrugged. "I guess I can."

She smiled and sighed. "*If* I give you my number, will you let me finish my rounds, Moe?"

"That sounds fair."

She jotted her phone number down on a pink sticky note and stuck it to his shirt. "Now, I'm going to go check on my other patients, and if you're still in front of that door when I come back in five minutes I'm going to rip that paper up. Are we clear, Moe?"

"Clear."

"Promise?"

Moe looked at the phone number and held up two fingers. "Scout's honor."

"All right. I'm off at four," she said. "Call me."

"Yes, ma'am."

As she walked down the hall, he began to whistle "Donna" by Ritchie Valens. She turned to glare at him, her eyes narrowed and her lips curled into a wry smile. He grinned back at her and waved.

"What are you doing?" said a voice behind him.

Moe shouted and almost fell back into the open doorway.

Sam stepped past him into the hall. "Some sentry you are. I tell you to guard the door and I come out to find you humping some nurse's leg."

"Hey! I kept her out of the room, didn't I?"

"He did," said Lamont, stepping into the hallway and slinging the duffel bag over his shoulder. "You've got to give him that."

"And..." Moe snapped the pink sticky note between his hands. "I got her number."

Sam raised an eyebrow and peered down the hall, taking a long appraising look at Donna's backside. "*Hell-o*, nurse! Not bad, little sister. I'm actually impressed. And here I thought I was going to have to *build* you a girlfriend."

"Come on, you two," said Lamont. "We still have a lot to do today."

As they stepped out into the cool morning air and walked across the parking lot toward Mrs. Walker's car, they were nearly run over by an ambulance screaming into the parking lot toward the emergency room entrance with its lights flashing and siren blaring. The back doors of the ambulance opened, and the paramedics removed the gurney. Strapped to the cart was a national guardsman, his combat fatigues and face covered in blood.

A nurse met the paramedics halfway to the door. "What happened?"

"Gunshot wound to the head," said one of the medics. "Self-inflicted."

"He was investigating the crash site with two others in his unit," the other medic chimed in breathlessly. "The others heard three shots.

When they got there, the other two were dead, but somehow this guy was still alive and talking. He keeps saying the same thing over and over."

The nurse slammed her fist into the door control and let the gurney through. "They *all* shot themselves?"

"Yes!" the soldier on the cart cried out. "To serve my Khan! To serve my Khan! Anything to serve my Kha—"

The doors slid shut, sealing off the soldier's ravings. Moe looked at Sam, and the brothers shuddered in unison.

Lamont broke into a sprint, heading toward Mrs. Walker's car. "We have to report back to HQ immediately. Alex has to know what's happened."

"What does this mean?" asked Moe.

"Two things, little sister," said Sam. "One: you're going to have to cancel your house call with the nurse—"

"Great," Moe muttered under his breath.

"And two," Sam continued, jerking the passenger side door open. "Temujin didn't die in that crash like we thought."

"How could *anybody* survive that?" asked Moe.

Lamont started the car and put it into gear. "That's what I'd like to find out."

# THIRTY

*Temple of the Golden Horde*
*Gobi Desert, Mongolia*
*October 28th*

Captain Sükh stood on the loading dock of the temple's train house and waited anxiously, one hand resting on the pommel of his sword and the other with a thumb hooked over his belt. The message had come in the previous evening that his scouts had located the master and General Chuluun hiding in an abandoned farmhouse a few miles west of the *Ragnarok* crash site, and they were being transported back to the temple. This news was bittersweet for the captain; he feared the Khan's wrath for his failure to destroy the alien and allowing him to escape.

The train whistle brought his thoughts back to the present, and he stood at attention as the train slowed to a stop in front of him. He swallowed hard as a boxcar door slid open and there, standing in the doorway with a bearskin cloak draped over his body and the injured General Chuluun leaning against him for support, stood Lord Temujin. A bloody bandage covered the left side of Chuluun's face.

Sükh promptly dropped to one knee. "My Khan, words cannot express what I am feeling at this moment."

"Nor I, Captain," Temujin said venomously.

"I am so relieved to see you alive and well," said Sükh.

"No thanks to you, *Captain*," said the Khan, spitting the last word out as if it were a foul taste in his mouth.

"My Khan?" Sükh met his master's hateful gaze with pleading eyes.

Without warning, Temujin thrust his free hand into the air and Sükh screamed as he felt himself being lifted off the ground violently. The Khan curled his fingers, and Sükh clawed at his own throat, futilely trying to pry away the invisible fingers crushing his larynx.

"I grow weary of your incompetence, Sükh," Temujin said. He took a small step forward, his progress hindered by the weight of the general supported on his shoulder. "Your orders were simple: Destroy the alien. Yet there he was at the school, fighting alongside my enemies."

"My Khan," Sükh gasped. "The TDC—"

"Yes..." Temujin pulled the struggling Captain closer with a twitch of his wrist. "The TDC. Not the pathetic band of children playing soldier we were led to believe, eh, Captain? The battle was won. Alexander was in my grasp, but then—"

Temujin tightened his fingers, and Sükh's eyes bulged from their sockets as he gasped for air.

"Then," Temujin continued, "the alien, Samrai, appeared and ruined everything. He destroyed my weapons, crashed my *Ragnarok*, killed a hundred of my best men, and now my sarcophagus—my greatest treasure—is lost."

"Please," Sükh wheezed, "give me one more chance, my Khan."

"Save your pleas for the gods," Temujin said. "Their capacity for generosity far surpasses my own."

Sükh managed one last plea for forgiveness. "Please, my Khan, I can get the coffin back."

Temujin loosened his grip on Sükh's neck, but did not release him from the hold suspending him in the air. "Speak quickly."

"We intercepted a transmission... from the American Air Force...

just before you arrived," Sükh said, pausing to take a large, sweet breath of frigid air. "They have recovered the sarcophagus from the crash site... and are taking it to Wright-Patterson Air Force Base."

Slowly, and reluctantly, Temujin lowered Sükh to the ground onto his knees, allowing the captain to suck in large breaths of air. The Khan covered the distance between them in a few labored steps and gazed down at the man with utter contempt.

"You have one chance to redeem yourself, Sükh," Temujin said. "Succeed, and all will be forgiven. Fail me again, and you will beg me for death, but I cannot promise I will grant it."

"Yes, my Khan." Sükh rose to his feet and reached for the wounded general. "Here. Let me relieve you of your burden."

The Khan kicked Sükh back onto his knees.

"Do not touch him, you miserable cur," Temujin snarled. "General Chuluun has served me faithfully, which is more than can be said for you. When I was a boy, fasting in the wilderness, he alone came to my aid when I was accosted by wolves. He carried me home on his back for two days while I slept and bled upon his shoulders. I am *honored* to return the favor.

"Your filthy hands will not touch him. You are not worthy. He is not now, nor will he *ever* be a burden to me. Do you understand?"

"Yes, my Khan!" Sükh pressed his forehead against the cold ground at his master's feet. "Forgive me!"

"Make preparations to move the temple to a new, secure location," Temujin ordered. "I will not have Alexander's forces attacking us on our own ground, since you allowed the one person with that knowledge to escape."

"Yes, my Khan," said Sükh.

And with that, his master strode out of the train house and into the temple, his blood-soaked bearskin cloak flowing behind him.

Sükh's fingers curled into a tight fist. "It shall be done."

# EPILOGUE

*East Van Buren High School*
*Farmington, Iowa*

ALEX SURVEYED THE DEVASTATION LITTERING THE SCHOOL PARKING LOT from his perch on the edge of the roof. All the wrecked remnants of the Death Walkers were gone, collected by the military when they swept the area after the attack. Their discarded weapons were gone, too. The idea of the government possessing the same technology as his team worried him.

Quintin tapped his arm and passed him a paper cup with a straw sticking from the top. Alex accepted it and took a long sip; the thick chocolate shake soothed his raw, aching throat as he swallowed.

Quintin pointed across the lot. "There's your car."

Alex nodded. He'd already spotted it underneath the twisted wreckage of one of the police cruisers. He didn't know if it could be salvaged or not; it looked pretty bad. He pointed about twenty feet to the right at a tangled mass of metal.

"There's Pop's truck."

Quintin grimaced, remembering his painful arrival to the battle in the back of the truck. "Is he..." he struggled to find the correct word, "pissed?"

Alex snorted. "There isn't a word in English *or* Phaedojian to sum up how my dad feels right now, Quint."

"So... *really* pissed?"

"Oh, yeah." Alex laughed. "*Super* pissed."

Alex passed the cup back to Quintin and continued surveying the damage in silence. He picked up a broken piece of brick beside him and chucked it at the nearest wrecked car. It sailed through the broken windshield and landed in the back seat.

"Are you scared?" Alex asked.

Quintin placed the cup down between them. "No."

"I am," said Alex gravely. "You saw what he did this time. What will he do next? Who else is he going to kill just to get to me?"

"He's not going to get the chance," said Quintin. "We know where to find him now. We'll bring the fight to him."

Alex nodded. He already knew all of this, of course, but he still couldn't shake the feeling that it wasn't going to be that easy.

A distant hum vibrated the air around them, and the twins looked up to see the *Saber* hovering in the distance. The engines' hum grew in intensity and then suddenly became silent. Then, in a brilliant flash of light, the ship streaked through the air toward the upper atmosphere. They watched the craft for a moment until it disappeared above the clouds.

"What's that about?" asked Quintin.

Alex just smiled and took another sip of chocolate shake. "Just a little unfinished business, Quint."

---

*Office of Naval Administration*
*Federation of Allied Systems, Planet Phaedaj*

ADMIRAL OHRB STALKED DOWN THE CORRIDOR TOWARD HIS OFFICE. AN urgent communiqué had been delivered to him, interrupting some much-needed private time with his mistress. The message read that the Glynfarian ambassador was waiting in his office and refused to leave until he spoke to the admiral.

Ohrb had had quite enough of the little runt's constant meddling and snooping around his office. This was the last straw. He planned to throw the feeble old bastard out the nearest airlock; inter-planetary relations be damned.

The door to his outer office slid open to receive him, and the admiral barged through the room, not paying his secretary any heed as he stormed toward the door to his inner office. The door opened with a hiss, and Ohrb stepped inside to find the ambassador, Jiri, standing beside his desk, leaning on his walking stick. The admiral was about to give the ambassador an earful when he noticed his chair was swiveled around with its back to him. Pale fingers tapped the armrest.

"Whoever you are, you've got about three clicks to get out of that chair before I wring your neck," the admiral huffed.

The chair turned and the admiral found himself looking at a pale creature with strange yellow fur on top of its head and two forward-facing blue eyes in the center of its face. The alien held a plasma pistol in its five-fingered hand.

"Hello, Admiral," Sam said with a friendly smile. "Let's have a little chat, shall we?"

To be continued in

# FIVE STORIES UP
## A TALE of the TEMUJIN SAGA

a short story which sets the stage for

# WAR MACHINES
## BOOK II of the TEMUJIN SAGA

# ABOUT THE AUTHOR

Photograph by Jim C. Hines

Adam J. Whitlatch is the author of *The Weller, The Weller - Fear of the Dark, War of the Worlds: Goliath, Birthright, War Machines,* and *Vengeance For My Valentine,* as well as dozens of short stories and poems spanning the science fiction, fantasy, and horror genres. Adam lives in southeast Iowa with his wife and children.

**www.adamjwhitlatch.com**